MR. CONSEQUENCE

Ed Benedyk

Bird Brain Publishing

Bird Brain Publishing
Evansville, Indiana

Paperback

ISBN-10: 1937668851

ISBN-13: 978-1-937668-85-3

This is a work of fiction. Names, characters and incidents depicted in this book are products of the author's imagination or are used fictitiously. Any resemblance to actual events, locales, organizations, or persons, living or dead, is entirely coincidental and beyond the intent of the author or the publisher.

Bird Brain Publishing is an imprint of Bird Brain Productions.

Published in the United States by Bird Brain Publishing, a division of Bird Brain Productions, LLC, Evansville, Indiana. www.birdbrainpublishing.com

Cover Art by Whitney Arvin

Author photo courtesy of *Timeless Images*, Evansville Indiana

MR. CONSEQUENCE

Evansville, Indiana

Bad Guys—Be Afraid

Be Very Afraid

Dedication

I dedicate this book to my wife, children, family and friends who consistently urged and supported me to follow my dream. Especially my brother Matthew, whose example of never giving up was a constant encouragement.

PROLOGUE

Chicago 1969

"I'm in love," Mary Elizabeth dreamily decided, as visions of Robert Redford kissing her danced in her head and heart.

It was a dismal, frigid, winter day. Chicago was earning its nickname *Windy City*, as a north wind tormented the residents by blowing its cool to the tune of a -25 degree wind chill. Mary Elizabeth was wearing her new purple fake fur hooded suede jacket. She saved and sacrificed a month's pay from her after–school job as a clerk at Briskie's Hardware for the coat. Her little brother's comment that afternoon, "Oh, Mar-Beth, you look so pretty," made the sacrifice worth every penny. It was the perfect complement to the mauve corduroy bell-bottom jeans she wore. Her mom, after seeing the jacket, nicely matched it with the jeans for her birthday last week. While clad in her new stylish outfit, she was unconcerned over a wind chill that ruthlessly nose-dived the temperature. Thoughts of the dashing actor that she had just seen in *Butch Cassidy and the Sundance Kid* provided ample warmth.

Mary Elizabeth, or Mary Beth, as her classmates at St. Barbara High School called her, had traveled to South Ashland Avenue from her Pilsen home to meet her best friend, Cathy. They spent Saturday afternoon shopping at Goldblatts Department Store. Afterwards, they walked the few blocks over to the Peoples Theatre to enjoy a movie. She and Cathy watched and fantasized over the latest screen hunk, Robert Redford. His mesmerizing performance as the Sundance Kid would get the hormones running amok in any female, and he captured and enraptured Mary Beth's heart.

It was approaching 10:00 p.m. when she exited the Ashland bus. Her pace was as brisk as the wind as she headed to her South Wolcott home. Because of the brutal weather, streets and alleys were empty, as the masses huddled in the warm cocoons of their homes – or the neighborhood bar. There was a bar on every block and each prospered despite their proximity to one another. Few families had cars, so a quick walk for a quick nip was good; so were the nickel and dime beers.

In one of the seedier bars, *The Black Cat*, three of the latest members of the Satan's Dudes gang, Ramon, Aldo, and Luis gathered in the back room to watch some porn. This deranged group of society's losers liked to prove their manhood by acting viciously and without any connection to a conscience. They were dressed in the acknowledged uniform of the gang: black tee-shirts, black leather cabrettas, baggy grays, engineer boots-(aka-shit kickers), with each head topped off with a black and white checkered porkpie hat.

"Nice tits," sneered Ramon as a grainy porn film filled the screen.

"She could use a shave," giggled Luis, "it looks like she has a shag rug between her legs."

"Hell, with tits like that, I wouldn't mind a little rug burn at all," countered a drooling Ramon.

"Holy shit," Aldo yelled as the big bosomed star proceeded to take on three studs simultaneously, "she is really fucking talented. Damn, these lucky guys get paid to get laid, I gotta check out that career."

"First you need a bigger dick, man," Luis laughed.

"Both of you shut up and let me watch this," Ramon growled before taking a long pull from a bottle of Seagram's 7.

Their testosterone levels were on high alert when they left *The Black Cat*. They hustled into a dirt-covered van with almost impossible to see in or out of tinted windows.

Luis said, "I'm hungry. Let's stop at McDonald's. That new *Big Mac* burger is fucking great."

Aldo asked, "What the fuck is a *Big Mac?*"

"Two all-beef patties, special sauce, lettuce, cheese, pickles, onions, on a sesame seed bun," Luis slowly recited, having memorized the sign that proclaimed the new burger.

"Sounds expensive," Aldo complained.

"It is, almost a half of buck, but man, are they worth it," Luis said.

Pooling their money, they headed to McDonalds. After wolfing down two *Big Macs* apiece, they belched and left the Golden Arches laughing. Getting back in the van, they headed toward the gang's hideout in Pilsen. At the wheel, Luis drove through the alleys to avoid cops.

They knew from experience that Chicago's Finest had no problem beating on suspected gang members. The fact that the van had recently been purchased from a friend in a chop shop made the alley detour even more judicious.

Mary Beth pulled her hood tightly over her ears as she hurriedly chose an alley shortcut. The freezing wind had finally conquered the Redford warmth. *I can't wait to get home and sit by the space heater*, she eagerly thought while tightly yanking the hood around her frozen face. The dirt-covered van with the grossly tinted windows entered the alley from the other end. Mary Beth's head was bowed in an effort to stave off the stiff wind. She abruptly looked up as the van's noisy muffler loudly farted its approach.

CHAPTER ONE

Present day Chicago

Petras Alekas continued the tradition of offering fine cuts of meat as well as the home-made succulent Lithuanian sausages that when tucked in a bacon roll resulted in *Baltic Nirvana*, which also happened to be the name of his store. His father, Andreas, started the business in the 1950's in Marquette Park's Lithuanian neighborhood. It was an immediate success with the *Lugans*—(a nickname for Lithuanians that would cause a fight when uttered by any rival nationality, but amongst each other was a term of endearment).

Not surprisingly, this section of Marquette Park was dubbed *Little Lithuania*. The residents bragged it had more *Lugans* in the neighborhood than any city in the world, other than Vilnius, the capital of Lithuania. The shop was very successful. The prices were reasonable and the quality impeccable; two traits heartily endorsed by *Lugans*: cheap and good.

This proud settlement to generations of Lithuanians was about to come to a crashing end. Seeking to pounce on Marquette Park's sheltered ethnic homes were a group of disreputable real estate reps. They viewed the streets of Little Lithuania as the shining gold lined streets of Eldorado due to the impending civil rights legislation of the 60's.

They creepily hatched a scheme they dubbed the Black Scare. They pounded the pavement knocking on doors and holding "emergency" neighborhood meetings warning the residents that very soon black families would be moving into the neighborhood bringing their slovenly ways and criminal atrocities along with them. They warned that dramatically plummeting home values would be the result.

Since these shysters claimed that they were very concerned about their good neighbors, they offered to buy the houses at what they claimed would be a fair price so that the current residents would not have to worry about losing money once the blacks moved in. What they did not say was their definition of fair price was one that they intended to flip at 100-200% to the black families they were already actively courting.

These slime-balls became millionaires overnight, as the majority of the families in the neighborhood took the bait; hook, line, and sinker. The thought of losing money on their homes was bad enough, but the thought of a black family living next door was even worse! The exodus began.

Andreas, realizing that his base of customers was leaving, did the same. The Bridgeport neighborhood, all white at the time, was where most *Lugans* escaped to. Although its main population was Irish, there was still a substantial base of Eastern Europeans established there, and the Marquette Park refugees were welcomed with open arms.

Petras's four siblings had no desire to pursue a butcher's career. So Petras, being the only one in the Alekas clan that enjoyed working in the family business, eschewed a college education and became his father's partner after graduating from De LaSalle High School in 1975. He became sole owner in 1990 when Andreas sold his stake to Petras so that he and his wife Rebecah could become Florida snowbirds.

That is how Petras ended up owning this thriving Archer Avenue store, located on the borderline of Bridgeport.

CHAPTER TWO

Chicago 1969

Luis stared with demonic eyes as Mary Beth drew closer. "Whoa, check out that sweet pussy, let's pick her up and show her a good time," Luis slurred the words as his fellow Dudes loudly grunted their approval. With the van rapidly approaching, Mary-Beth moved to the side of a garage so the van could pass. Luis, the driver, stopped the van parallel to her while Aldo exited from the passenger door. This placed Mary Beth in a corner with no escape; the door of the van barricaded her on the left while two very large city garbage cans on the right completed the trap.

Aldo stepped out saying, "Hey girl, we're lost, can you help us."

Ramon then scurried out the back of the van, grabbed her ankles while Aldo covered her mouth. They quickly tossed her in the back of the van. "Go, Go, Go" screamed Ramon. Luis crushed the pedal and the black van lunged out of the alley.

As he hustled to his seat, Aldo asked, "Where we going?"

"I know a great place in Harrison Park where no one can see us, or the van," an excited Luis replied.

"That sounds boss!" yelled Aldo.

"It may be cold, but we're gonna to make it real hot in here for you, bitch; gonna make you nice and warm," Ramon exclaimed with a maniacal giggle.

Mary Beth shivered violently as she considered the vile objectives of her abduction. Her hands, mouth, and feet were bound by duct tape, thoroughly suppressing any hopes of escape. Within a few minutes, the van was hidden behind the graffiti decorated outdoor toilets of Harrison Park.

"Perfect," said Luis, "ain't nobody gonna be pissing here in this weather. The park is emptier than my wallet."

"Hey Aldo," Ramon piped up, "turn on the radio, so we can get some mood music going for the cunt!" Aldo hit the radio button and Jim Morrison was beseeching his girl to "Touch Me Babe."

"Hey bitch, you hear that, you are going to touch all of us tonight," Ramon bellowed, "and we will be touching you."

"Hey, grab her purse and that Goldblatts bag and see what she got there," Luis yelled, thinking about his empty wallet.

Ramon rummaged the purse and pulled out her wallet, and tossed the contents on the floor.

"Shit, only three dollars," Aldo groused. He dumped the contents from the Goldblatts bag and out plopped the two new brassieres she had purchased.

Aldo threw the bag at Luis and cackled, "No money, but here is some new underwear for you, Luis."

"Fuck you, asshole," said Luis.

"Well, lookie, lookie," hissed Ramon as he began retrieving some of the wallet's scattered items. "We got ourselves a Mary Elizabeth here, and look at the pretty picture we got."

Ramon passed the picture around after pulling it and her student ID from the wallet. It showed Mary Elizabeth and a young boy posing with a woman under a sign that welcomed one and all to the Damen Avenue Free Fair.

"Is this your mama and your brother? Nod your head if it is," demanded Luis.

Fearfully, she nodded yes.

A wicked smile broke over Luis' face as he gave Mary Elizabeth the rules for the night. "Here's the deal, bitch, we gonna cut you loose and you gonna strip real sexy for us, then we gonna take you to places you never been—there will be NO screaming and NO going to the cops, you know why?—because if you scream I cut your tongue out, if you go to the PO-lice then we visit your mama and baby brother and cut them to pieces while you watch, and we will tell them before they die it's all because of you!!"

Ramon piped in, "do you think we are kidding Miss Mary Elizabeth! Do you know who we are? We are Satan's Dudes, we OWN this neighborhood, so we can do what we want, UNDERSTAND! AND, if you play along, the reward you get is you get to LIVE, do you UNDERSTAND!"

Realizing the horror that awaited her and the brutal attack promised on her mother and brother if she did not comply, she knew that there were no options, so she reluctantly nodded yes.

"Let the good times roll," shouted Luis.

As he pulled the duct tape loose, the skin on her hands, mouth and feet became painfully raw. Trembling from cold and fear, Mary Elizabeth fumbled awkwardly attempting to remove her clothes. Luis slinked closer with his switchblade swinging menacingly. Remembering the cruel warning, she hurriedly complied and a few moments later was naked; horror and shame overwhelming her. She immediately positioned her arms and hands attempting to cover her womanhood. It was a futile attempt.

"Hey, Louie, you got that Vaseline you use on your hair with you?" Ramon queried, as he desperately tried to get out of his tight jeans that now housed an enormous hard-on.

"Yeah, it is in the glove compartment, why?"

"You remember that movie we saw tonight where the puta took on three at once. Let's grease up our girlie here and have a repeat performance."

"Great idea," chimed the other two as they too stood naked and hard in front of Mary Elizabeth.

She recoiled at this display and her wide eyes went vacant as she slumped to the floor.

"I got dibs on the front door," drooled Luis.

"I got back door," Ramon quickly moaned.

"And I got that that pretty mouth to suck me dry," Aldo snickered.

The vile assault began. The Satan Dudes lived up to their reputation for cruelty as Mary Beth was subjected to painful thrusts.

Sounds of "YEAH BABY—AHH, AHH, AHH – OOH, OOH, OOH" filled the van as they proceeded to mimic the scenes from the porn film.

As the vicious attack evolved, Mary Elizabeth was consumed with unbearable pain and humiliation. The human mind has a one-way door that exists for those seeking numbness and escape. Once entered, there is no return. Tragically, numbness and escape mate with oblivion once there.

As Aldo approached, pressing his cock dripping with pre-come to her lips, Mary Elizabeth passed through that door.

Meanwhile, a few blocks away, the little boy asked his fretting widowed mama, "when is Mar-Beth coming home? She needs to read me my bedtime story."

Desperately trying to deny a mother's intuition, she answered, "I'm sure she will be back any minute now."

But the minutes became hours, as the resisting three year old eventually succumbed to a troubled sleep.

CHAPTER THREE

Chicago 1975

Mary Elizabeth was only alive that fateful night due to the regularity of JC, Mr. Karr's German shepherd. No matter when he was fed, each night, every night, JC's bowels required evacuation at precisely 11:45 p.m. It was on one of JC's jaunts through the alley to do his duty six years earlier, when the dog's frantic barking and subsequent race behind a garbage can, alerted Mr. Karr to the crumpled body of Mary Elizabeth.

She was unconscious, dressed in tattered clothes with her coat blanketed over her. Finding a pulse, he scooped her in his arms and rushed back to the house and called both an ambulance and the police.

"What kind of animals could do this to a child?" asked Mr. Karr's wife Penny, noticing the bloody underwear smeared with semen as she attended to Mary Elizabeth.

"I don't know, but what I DO know is that these animals should be SHOT!"

"NO, you're wrong, they should be cut into little pieces with a dull knife." After savagely cursing the unknown bastards, he added, "and I would pour the salt on the wounds, pounds of it."

Mary Elizabeth's mother, Sophie, had spent the last frantic hour calling all her daughter's friends, but to no avail; the answer was always the same: "I haven't seen her today." It was the call to Cindy that scared her the most when Cindy related that Mary Beth had gotten on the Ashland bus at about 9:30 p.m. after they left the movies.

At half past midnight, Sophie was putting on her coat, determined to search for her daughter despite the sub-zero temperatures, when there was a knock at the door. In her rush to the door, she slammed into the coffee table and her beloved collection of Hummel figurines that were proudly displayed on top of the table's shiny cherry wood fell to the hardwood floor and shattered. An event that normally would bring her to tears was totally ignored as she continued the anxious rush to the door.

She frantically pulled the door open. Mike, the neighborhood cop, and his partner were standing on the enclosed front porch. The anguished look on the policemen's faces spoke volumes before either one could get a word out. Mike started with "I'm very sorry…" He got no further before a tormented cry burst from the depths of Sophie's soul as she swayed and fainted. Mike quickly responded and caught her in his arms. "Man, there are times that this job really sucks," Mike's partner lamented as they gently carried Sophie to the couch.

As the years passed, Sophie fell into a not surprisingly robotic routine caring for her daughter. Mary Elizabeth had taken on a zombie-like persona, staring into space without ever again speaking another word. Numerous physicians and psychiatrists were stymied in their attempts to reverse her mental state.

Her baby brother refused to give up. He lovingly helped with feeding her and with whatever Sophie asked him to help with, regardless of the task, no matter how gross it was. Every moment he was with Mary Elizabeth, he talked to her non-stop; telling her about his day, what her friends were up to, how much he loved and missed her. A blank stare was always the result. He cried often.

One night, an inner voice entrenched itself in the catatonic mind of Mary Elizabeth. She listlessly arose from her bed and shuffled over to the pantry door. Behind the Ovaltine and Silvercup bread, Sophie kept a three month supply of sleeping pills, occasionally administered to Mary Elizabeth when a sleeping aide was called for. Somehow she was aware that these pills would make her sleep, and with the inner voice urging her on, she now longed to sleep forever. She reached behind the pantry's staples, took the three bottles of pills, then retraced her steps and dropped them on her pillow. She opened the first bottle dumping the contents on her blanket and starting to swallow the pills, one at a time. She was half way through the third bottle when her head drooped downward, and her body rigidly fell to the mattress.

The first paramedic on the scene filed it in as a suicide. However, after researching Mary Elizabeth's medical file, a sympathetic coroner, knowing the harsh burial rules regarding suicide in the Catholic faith, re-filed the death as an accidental overdose. "Whoever raped her years ago, murdered her today. Those bastards are the ones who should be in coffins, not her!" These were his thoughts as he cursed the injustice that fate threw at this precious girl.

The neighbors turned out in droves and packed the funeral home every day and night of the wake. Hundreds of mass envelopes and wall to wall flowers were the gifts presented to Sophie and her son along with heartfelt words and embraces.

The funeral director did an excellent job displaying Mary Elizabeth, prompting the mourners to comment "she looks like an angel, so she must now be in heaven."

Hearing these words made her devoted brother bristle. Being in heaven was not enough, he wanted more! He peered at his now peaceful looking sister, and reached in, tightly holding her hand. With a determined voice and tears flowing down his cheeks, he vowed, "I promise you Mar-Beth, someday I WILL find a way to make the bad guys PAY!"

"By God, I hope you do, little one," thought one of the relatives standing nearby.

They most certainly would PAY, as this young boy always kept his promises.

CHAPTER FOUR

Present Day Chicago

He clicked the end button on his untraceable GO phone he had bought at Wal-Mart, using cash, of course, and did a fist pump. His exuberance resulted from the conversation he had just completed. This was the final piece of the puzzle that would launch the justice of *Mr. Consequence*, the prophetic code name he assumed as he formulated the team that would *make the bad guys PAY*, fulfilling the promise he made years before to his sister. Its completion was now assured.

First, the plan required years of thought and preparation. Once conceived, he realized team members were essential. Working alone would not be feasible. Knowing what and who he was searching for in a team and having the proper resources available made the quest easier, but definitely not easy. All the members would have to be responsible members of the community. The roles that they would be taking on would require that they be Teflon-clothed to suspicion. The common thread among them would be an unresolved personal reason embracing the notion that justice must supersede law when called for.

It took ten long years to bring the final conception of the plan to its fruition, but it was worth the wait. *Mr. Consequence*, or *Mr. C*, as he now liked to refer to himself, had the disciplined patience to realize that a plan seeking justice would be fruitless if he or any members of the team found themselves rotting away in a jail cell. The agonizing problem he had faced was how to complete and finish the cycle of retribution, without endangering the lives of the team members.

The cell phone call he had just completed was the solution to this final hurdle. *The Don* was the skilled stroke of the brush that completed the masterpiece. The team was now complete.

Each member had similar GO phones and code names to be used to ensure that the secrecy of the mission would not be compromised by the inadvertent escape of their real names. *The Don* would be joining *Surgeon, Eyes, Ears, Biceps, Abs, Actress*, and, of course, *Mr. Consequence*.

It was time to get to work and he relished the task ahead.

"Now the promise begins, Mar-Beth. He would always know her by this beloved childhood nickname. "It begins."

CHAPTER FIVE

Surgeon

Jack Baxter's family moved to Chicago in 1960 when he was ten years old. His father, Eugene, an esteemed thoracic surgeon, had long pined for the big city offerings since he vacationed in Chi-town quite often. He heartily agreed with Sinatra. It was *His Kind of Town!* He rejoiced when Presbyterian St. Luke called to offer him a position on its staff. He couldn't leave his hometown of Sturtevant, Wisconsin fast enough.

He had commuted to Racine and served as the head of Wheaton Franciscan's cardiothoracic team for over twelve years. Eugene was a lifelong resident of Sturtevant because he was a son that truly loved his parents. They had sacrificed much to send him to medical school on a shaky income derived from cabbage and potato farming. When they took ill, only a few years apart, the farm was sold and Jack felt an obligation as both of them refused to leave the only town they had ever known. Being an only child added to the pressure, so he reluctantly agreed to remain in what he considered a town without a future in sight, building a home for his parents next to his.

Nature eventually took its course, and Eugene's parents died within a few months of each other in 1959. Two weeks after the funeral, résumés were produced like rabbits as James applied to numerous hospitals in the *big cities*. He passionately sought the elusive brass ring as he rode his carousel of dreams. The offer from Presbyterian St. Luke was so wonderful that James toasted the news with a bottle of Dom Perignon an hour after the offer was made. He even allowed his son, little Jack, a glass.

Jack's education consisted of strict Catholic schools due to Eugene's belief that Chicago public schools were beyond hope. Jack excelled, especially in the sciences. After graduating as valedictorian from St. Ignatius High School, he was determined to follow in his dad's footsteps and become a surgeon. Surprisingly, he turned down a scholarship from Harvard so that he could remain in Chicago. He said it was a city he had grown to love. What he didn't say was it also happened to be the home of his lover.

He enrolled at University of Chicago's Pritzker School of Medicine. He proudly declared, "U of C was far superior to any of those overrated Eastern schools anyway."

His interests in the areas of surgery were so varied that he sometimes changed his mind on a weekly basis. This indecision was due in a large part to his abilities, which were considerable. He was confident enough to realize he would be among the best at whatever specialty he chose. Finally, he opted to become a specialist in brain surgery. He jokingly told his parents, "Dad may be the heart of the family, but I'm the brains."

He became one of the most successful surgeons ever to have graduated from the University of Chicago. Recognizing his brilliance, in 1981, the University Med Center offered the head of department position to him. At the young age of thirty-one, he was a *wunderkind*, and the powers to be at the university had no intention of letting a rival snare him from their grasp. The day before his thirty-second birthday, the Board of Trustees unanimously appointed him as the youngest head of brain surgery in the country. This decision was indeed a "no brainer."

Upon receiving the news, Jack sped to his apartment in Hyde Park, a penthouse apartment in a multi-complex overlooking Lake Michigan on Lake Shore Drive. He carried a bottle of Dom in HIS hands now, excitingly looking forward to sharing the news with his live-in lover. Opening the door with a rush, he yelled, "sweetheart, I'm home, and do I have some news for you!"

Busy in the kitchen baking Chicken Vesuvio, Jack's favorite dish, Gary closed the oven door and in seconds had crossed the room to the door and enveloped Jack in a passionate hug and kiss. As Jack relayed the news, Gary coyly suggested, "Since the champagne needs chilling, and the Vesuvio needs another two hours, I say we celebrate early." He then took Jack's hand and both of them started to undress each other, kissing and touching, as Gary led Jack to the master bedroom with its massive sleigh bed and Art Deco drawings on each wall.

After their amorous desires were placated, they were ravenous. The delectable dinner that followed, along with multiple glasses of Dom, made the evening truly special. "Jack, this news is one hell of a birthday present for you. It makes my present I'm giving you seem small by comparison." Jack reached for and rubbed Gary's erection playfully. "Presents from you can never be small." He followed that statement with a passionate kiss. Confirmations of their love and happiness continued as they later lay naked in bed holding each other tightly, culminating in a restful sleep.

Like most gay couples in the late 70's and early 80's, Jack and Gary were careful and understood the personal and business ramifications about outing, and although upset over the obstacles a gay lifestyle represented, they were pragmatic and careful about remaining in the closet.

In public, they never exposed their true feelings for each other, although resentment did fester whenever they passed a hetero couple either holding hands or stopping abruptly to tenderly kiss or hug.

Both lovers' families suspected the direction of Jack and Gary's sexual predilections, but like many families facing news they did not like, chose the path of silence, as if not speaking of it would make it go away. They did, however, stop asking if their sons had found a Mrs. Right.

On June 5th, 1981, a report by the United States Disease Control Center had a doomsday effect for gays everywhere. A new virus was discovered and scientists attributed its spread to homosexual activity. The deadly virus was named Acquired Immune Deficiency Syndrome, or AIDS for short.

It was so widely believed to be a homosexual issue that it initially was named Gay-Related Immune Deficiency, aka GRID. As with any new viral discovery, little was known as to how contagious it was, or what caused it to spread. What they did know was that it was a killer.

Consequently, the gay community's efforts to gain society's understanding in condoning gay rights were severely derailed by the panic that ensued regarding this new weapon in death's arsenal. Gay bashing became a widely popular form of activity.

Months after the promotion, Jack's new position was on the fast track, both professionally and financially. Seeking a more domestic arrangement, Gary resigned his manager's position at IBM and became a stay at home software programmer and consultant. Since he was also a gourmet cook as well as a fastidious homemaker, this worked out to be a most appreciated situation for both of them.

Being an above average doc, Jack fully understood the benefits of exercise. So much so, that regardless of the elements, he would pedal his scarlet red 1981 Schwinn Voyageur 11.8 to the Med Center, which was a mere one mile from the apartment.

On a Saturday in December, Jack was assigned the night shift, and he was in the process of retrieving his beloved Schwinn from the spare room to begin the journey to the Med Center. Gary was taking a leak. Jack shouted, "Bye, I'm going," to the closed bathroom door. Pushing the bike to the elevator, he entered and hit the ground floor button.

Exiting the john, Gary immediately noticed that Jack had forgotten the scrumptious Poor Boy that Gary had assembled containing all of Jack's favorites; prosciutto, provolone, sopressata, and capicola. Gary grabbed the lunch bag and rushed to the balcony that overlooked the parking lot that Jack would cross as a shortcut to Garfield Blvd. He arrived just as the ground floor elevator opened and Jack had just jumped on the bike and was slowly pedaling away. "Jack, wait, you forgot your lunch. I'll bring it to you."

It was a typical frosty and dark night. A blustery Northeast wind produced the often mentioned *lake effect,* which is why many locals, not wanting to freeze their asses off, avoided brisk walks on Lake Shore Drive in winter, creating the illusion of a ghost town. On nights like this, Jack rarely saw another human on his ride to work. Gary approached Jack admonishing him and holding up the lunch bag, "I went to all this trouble for you and you leave without this gourmet delight!"

Jack, furtively glanced around to make sure they were alone and unwatched. He then simultaneously grabbed the bag and Gary's crotch, rubbing him seductively while French kissing him. Gary immediately turned rock hard as Jack purred in his ear, "I'll make it up to you with a different kind of gourmet delight later."

"Promises, promises," snapped Gary, albeit with a huge grin on his blushing face as they parted.

"Mother-fucker, come look at this, quick!" Kenny moved quickly to the darkened kitchen to see what his brother Jimbo was pointing to from the window over the sink. The window offered a "scenic" view of the parking lot from their ground floor apartment. The two brothers were spending an evening together eating pizza and drinking beer, a lot of beer. *The King*, Richard Petty, was the main attraction that played on the VCR. Playing was that year's Daytona 500. They knew exactly when to cheer. This was their tenth viewing of Richard's victory at Daytona. Jimbo clumsily weaved into the kitchen for refills. As he carried the beers from the fridge to the bottle opener attached to the wall near the sink's window, he shockingly witnessed the heated actions between Jack and Gary.

The brothers housed no leanings to the left as both were proud rednecks from Alabama who had relocated to Chicago in search of better jobs. They worked in construction and as a result, their muscles were well toned and used often, mostly in bar fights when some patrons did not have the foresight to share their redneck philosophies. They proclaimed these philosophies to be undeniable; ship the niggers back to Africa, in the good old U S of A – speak *ENGLISH*—not *SPANISH*, and of course Fags need to stay far, far away from *real* men.

"Holy shit, 3 F's are out there," Ken blurted using the acronym they coined for homosexuals—*Fucking Faggot Fairies*—as they watched the entire amorous exchange take place.

"Fuck, I think they live upstairs, these fuckers are the ones spreading that new AIDS shit all over the place," Jimbo moaned.

"Maybe we can convince them to move so they won't have a chance to spread it in this neighborhood," Ken ominously continued. "Hurry up and grab your ski-mask and gloves, and let's see what apartment he goes back to."

Jimbo punched the pause button on the VCR as they stealthily opened the door while making sure the lights were off. They waited until Gary entered the elevator and the doors shut. They hastily positioned themselves behind a massive maple tree which allowed them a view of the apartments without being seen. Gary exited the elevator at the top floor and prompted by the chilling wind, jogged quickly to apartment 501. He swiftly entered, closing the door behind him.

"Let's go. It's 501, make sure you wear your gloves and the ski-mask," Ken advised. Jimbo was already doing just that.

The knock occurred moments after the lunch bag incident. Gary nonchalantly opened the door, assuming that it was Jack, forgetting something else, like his keys. "You would forget your head if it wasn't screwed on," he exclaimed. "Oh my God, *who* are you!"

Ken and Jimbo roughly pushed him to the floor slamming the door. "Please don't hurt me, take what you want from here."

"Fuck you, you stinking cock-sucking fag," Ken railed while he continuously kicked him in the groin and stomach. "We want you and the other fairy out of our hood so you won't be killing the neighbors with your AIDS shit."

Jimbo sneered as he approached Gary with this warning, "Just so you know you're gonna have to move, we're gonna give you some incentive. Your head looks like a fucking football, and I'm going for the field goal," Jimbo added. He then mimicked a placekicker's stance and delivered a crushing kick to the head, rendering Gary unconscious.

Over the next few minutes, the brothers continued their onslaught, kicking Gary's head and body viciously. Jimbo delivered a final kick to the head as he laughingly exclaimed, "Hey, I had to go for the extra point."

Ken found some magic markers and began writing over the walls, **Three-F's—Fucking Faggot Fairies—not wanted here—Take your AIDS and LEAVE TOWN**, and **Faggots that stay—DIE**. He repeated these phrases throughout the walls of the apartment, then turned to Jimbo, "OK, let's go, *The King* still has lots of laps to go."

Weeks later, life was still a blur for Jack. He had arrived home that fateful morning fully expecting a satisfying breakfast of Gary's imaginative gastronomic creations. His shock was devastating. He went two days with no sleep as he climbed into the ambulance with Gary and insisted on advising the brain surgeon who valiantly but fruitlessly attempted to relieve the swelling of the brain during a marathon six hour surgical effort. Jack painfully realized that Gary's PVS (Persistent Vegetative State) was irreversible. This was the start of a downward spiral for Jack.

The attack's viciousness and the fact that it involved homosexuals, normally a taboo subject, made it the lead story on TV and the papers. The police had no suspects and not surprisingly, showed little concern in apprehending the culprits. Chicago cops at that time considered homosexual crimes a small step above similar minority incidents occurring in the inner city. The common thought amongst too many of the officers was that if blacks and homos were getting beaten and battered—no big deal.

Upon returning back to work a few weeks after the assault on Gary, Jack was sipping his morning coffee when Julie, the CEO's secretary, buzzed him on the intercom. "Mr. Carter wishes to see you immediately." Jack bounced up and headed to the CEO's office.

"Send him in," Mr. Carter's voice echoed through the speaker as Jack waited, sitting anxiously by Julie's massive mahogany desk in Carter's lavish office lobby. As he responded to the summons, Jack eerily scrutinized the walls of the lobby, which held the portraits of past University's CEO's. He spookily felt their eyes were seeking him out with admonishment as their goal.

Carter dressed as if he was a cover model for GQ. He had held the position of CEO for over a decade. During that time he acquired the most necessary skill required of the position: fund-raising.

As Jack entered the office, nary a trace of the usual smile of welcome could be seen on Carter's countenance. Jack was waved to sit in a nearby chair next to an even larger mahogany desk as Carter continued to stand.

"Jack, you know how much you have been valued here at our esteemed Medical Center?" The *have been valued* part instead of *are valued* concerned Jack immediately. "But, as you know this new homosexual AIDS thing is scaring many, many people, and the fact that your unfortunate situation has been publicized over and over, along with the fact that you are a homosexual department head at our hospital has many patients concerned for their safety here. In addition Jack, as you well know, without funding from the private sector, many of our necessary and state of the art programs would undergo reduced staffing, if not complete extinction. You can understand why benefactors may not choose to have their companies' names attached to us due to the current AIDS concern."

Before Jack could utter a word, the hammer came down.

"Jack, it is with great regret that in the Medical Center's best interests that your position with us is terminated immediately. You know that I carry no judgment towards a person's sexual orientation, so this is not personal, it is simply business."

"Is there anything I can do to defend my position?" Jack pleaded.

"NO," was said tersely as Carter went to the door and opened it while saying, "best wishes on your future. Good day."

He received a rather large unexpected severance check, hush money he supposed, and quickly found employment at County Hospital whose location was in the bowels of Chicago. With its large population of indigent patients, Cook County Hospital was not quite as concerned with Jack's baggage as Carter was. Most gifted surgeons considered County Hospital a bad joke and avoided it like the plague. Its board of directors wasted no time in hiring Jack.

The severance pay and the financial package County Hospital offered allowed Jack to place Gary in a caring nursing home. Jack was a daily visitor.

The visits at times were both hopeful and depressing as one of the symptoms of PVS is that the patient unknowingly offers a physical response to sounds or touches. At times Jack would optimistically react to these responses, but then his professional knowledge quickly negated the optimism. He fully understood what was really happening.

Jack kept his “marriage vows” intact as he painfully cared for his soul mate who lingered for twenty-five years before finally succumbing to death. Gary’s passing rekindled the fiery anger Jack had carried with him since the attack.

“Damn, Gary, I wish that there was some way to get revenge over the lowlife that did this,” his mind raged.

CHAPTER SIX

Present day Chicago

Mr. C was nursing a beer Friday night at O'Hara's bar, not an uncommon thing in Chicago, a bar with an Irish name. What was uncommon was the bartender, Coleen.

Coleen had long lustrous locks of fire red hair and emerald eyes topping off an hour glass-like body that produced dreams of wild imaginative sex from any of the male patrons. Astonishingly, she would brazenly let any and all know she was unabashedly a confirmed lesbian. Telling people wasn't necessary. Her t-shirt said it all: *A Muff Diver and Proud of It!!*

This was a non-issue for the owner and patrons at O'Hara's due to her infectious exuberant personality, good looks, and a grand sense of humor. The regulars would often tease her, and chose that night to mock homosexual marriage legislation.

Normally she would counter these remarks with witty banter; not this night. "Let me tell you something about marriage vows," she uncharacteristically stormed. "Just how many husbands you know, present company included, would keep their marriage vows for over twenty-five years if their wives were in an accident that turned them into vegetables for the rest of their lives?" She paused to get their reaction. "Hell, I've seen guys that would break the vow in a minute whenever a girl with a tight ass and big tits saunters up to the bar and displays a *minor* interest."

The bar became silent during her tirade, "You all know that I march in the Gay Pride parade each year. It was today. I met a doctor, and not just any doctor, he happens to head the brain surgery department at Cook County."

She then tearfully described the tragic happenings in the lives of Jack and Gary. "True love is true love, keeping your vows in sickness is the real clincher. It doesn't matter what's between each other's legs," Coleen finished, wiping mascara from beneath her teary eyes. Guiltily, the patrons that had teased her now offered words of comfort. Deep down, they truly cared about her.

Mr. C smiled to himself. He had found his surgeon.

CHAPTER SEVEN

Chicago 1968

Eyes and Ears

Greg Simmons was one year older than his brother John. Neighbors would joke with their father Hank over the stark differences in hair color between the boys. Greg's head was carpeted with a thick scarlet rug and John's blond hair was so bright it was pushing platinum. The creative minds in the neighborhood nicknamed the boys "Red" and "Whitey."

More than once, Hank would hear neighbors pointing out that the milkman had red hair, insinuating Greg was the milkman's prodigy. A strong marriage coupled with a strong sense of humor allowed Hank to laugh along as he exclaimed, "If he wants to milk my cow, the least he could do is deliver free milk." That would set off a chain of guffaws amongst the neighbors.

In 1968 it was a common practice for men to bring their tin pails and paychecks to the local tavern of choice on Friday nights. The bartender would cash the paycheck and the pails would be filled with tap beer to be taken home and enjoyed while watching certain TV shows that were revolutionary to the period by being broadcast in color. The favorite was *Bonanza.* Another popular choice for entertainment in the neighborhood would be plopping a lawn chair on the front porch and visiting with the passers-by, and if feeling generous that day, sharing a glass of draft from the pail.

This was foundry worker Hank's Friday night routine. He walked the four block trip every payday at 7:00 p.m. It turned out to be too routine.

One of the regulars at the bar was Frankie, a slovenly dressed, often unemployed loser whose body mirrored his apparel. He was simply and accurately called "Fat Frankie." Not having enough cash at times to pay the $20.00 weekly rent for a basement apartment *under the sidewalk* in Pilsen did not keep him away from the *Purple Pleasure Bar* on Friday nights. His love of beer and the free hot dogs Mary the owner served every payday evening was too tempting to resist. An even dozen wieners was his usual intake for those evenings.

It was the first Friday in January of 1968. Frankie's New Year's greeting that day was another pink slip to add to his collection. He was outraged. He believed it was no big deal showing up late to work a few times a week. His latest boss disagreed.

Hank walked in precisely at 7:15 p.m. "Fill it up, Mary," passing the pail and his check over. He grabbed a hot dog and ordered a boilermaker before leaving for home, another habit of his.

"Wow," exclaimed Mary as she looked at the check Hank had handed her.

"We got an order for a rush job and the overtime is flowing," Hank smiled. "It should keep flowing until the completion date, so the next two weeks I'll be having a gravy train."

Fat Frankie's eyes grew wide as he watched Mary count the substantial sum of $332.00 and hand over the bills to Hank.

After Hank left, Frankie guzzled down his beer and wolfed his last dog. He rushed over to his friend Paulie's house. Paulie was 135 pounds soaking wet. No one could possibly mistake him for the 325 pound Frankie.

Frankie banged repeatedly at Paulie's door. It finally opened, revealing a bleary-eyed man dressed in a food-splattered t-shirt and equally stained sweat pants. He was well into his weekend drinking binge. "Let me in, I have got a way to score us a lot of money," Frankie boasted. He sailed by Paulie and sat on the love seat whose springs cried out in agony as Frankie squeezed in his enormous ass. "Next Friday is going to be a nice payday for us!"

"Whatchu mean man," Paulie groggily asked while draining his can of Buckhorn, a beer so cheap that its aka was *Moose Piss*.

Frankie spent the next few minutes delivering his plan to deprive Hank of his weekly pay next Friday. Paulie grinned drunkenly as he imagined the numerous cases of Buckhorn beer that his share would buy.

The following Friday, Paulie hid behind the telephone pole just outside of the alley entrance where Hank would be passing at approximately 7:25 p.m. He was thin enough to go undetected by any possible pedestrians. He then relieved his bulging bladder against the pole while cursing himself for drinking a six-pack minutes before leaving for his hidey hole.

In his left hand was the ski mask he would wear to hide his identity. His right held a two foot long crow bar he had stolen from an Ace hardware store by hiding it in his baggy pants' leg.

The plan was to cut through the backyard opposite the telephone pole and quickly go through the gangway leading to the next block the moment Hank passed by. The result would place Paulie directly behind Hank.

Hank soon approached walking slowly while carefully balancing his tin of beer. Paulie, now wearing the ski-mask, was counting on the five degree temperature and 23 mile an hour north-east wind to provide an empty street. The plan was to come up behind Hank as he entered the next alley opening, rush forward, and deliver a crushing blow to the head with the crow bar. Hopefully it would render Hank unconscious, allowing Paulie to push the body into the alley, grab the payday dollars, and quickly leave the scene.

Unfortunately for Hank, the streets were indeed empty.

He never saw it coming. The crushing blow was immediate lights out for Hank. Paulie pushed the limp body into the alley while grabbing for the tin pail in hopes of getting a slug or two. After draining the tin, he rifled through Hank's pockets, copped the cash, and was about to take off when he heard Hank moan. Not wanting to be seen, he swung the crowbar again, this time missing the head and striking the thoracic region of the spine.

This blow did more than put Hank back into a deep sleep, it caused a spinal cord injury destroying the T1 through T5 parts of the spine. Hank's extremities below the waist would be forever paralyzed.

Because Hank never saw Paulie, Frankie made his rent and Paulie bought enough Buckhorn to last two months.

Hank's popularity in the neighborhood could be seen and smelled by a visit to his hospital room. Every imaginable flower protruded from dozens of vases. Initially, well-wishing visitors flocked to his room with those flower filled vases, magazines, candy, and other homemade goodies.

Soon after, Hank's tragic attack wasn't completely forgotten by the neighbors, but it did eventually get a significant push to the side as human nature kicked in. The neighbors returned to dealing with their more important personal life concerns such as mortgage payments, bills, vacation plans, what's for dinner, or simply raising the kids.

The disability check helped, but not enough. Estelle, Hank's wife, was forced to take a third shift job cleaning offices and toilets downtown at the National Bank Office building. This allowed her to be home during the day to feed, dress, and clean Hank while Greg and John became the guardians after coming home from school during Estelle's third shift.

The moment Estelle left, Hank would cajole the boys to bring him some booze: whiskey, wine, beer; it didn't matter. Either of the boys would be directed by Hank to walk over to the tavern and have one of Hank's friends do a *run* to the liquor store. The spinal cord injury took away his manhood, reasoned Hank, so the least he should be allowed was to get blitzed every night, which he did.

No longer was he the dad that took the kids to the park, played baseball and basketball with them, and afterwards treat them to a banana split at Lindy's Ice Cream Emporium. Instead, he completely shut them out, not wanting to talk to them other than to give orders; usually for the booze runs. The shutting out was his effort to forget those happy days as that memory placed him in a severe depression mode, made worse by the daily imbibing.

The lack of concern for his health, and the impairment sustained by his bladder caused by the injury, made a catheterization necessary. The catheterization led to urinary sepsis, a very serious bacterial infection that can lead to septic shock and death. With Hank, it did. The septic shock symptoms of chills, palpitations, lightheadedness, mental confusion, and skin rashes were ignored by Hank as he reasoned that they were a result of his daily binges. He never mentioned them to Estelle.

She dismissed the apparent skin rashes as a consequence of Hank's confinement to the wheelchair. The infection started with dysfunction of the renal organ, and rapidly rampaged through Hank's major organs and tissues to a stage called multiple organ dysfunction syndrome (MODS). Death was quick. Sadness and relief were equally represented by his death. Sadness over the wonderful father and husband Hank once was; relief over the end of the spiraling downward direction his life had taken since the attack.

Sophie, carrying her sleeping two-year-old son entered the funeral chapel with her daughter Mary Elizabeth. Sophie and Estelle were best friends since first grade at St. Adalbert's. Sophie's husband Ed was killed while working for Union Central in a railroad yard accident. Estelle was a blanket of comfort for Sophie for months after Ed's fatal accident and now Sophie planned to be that shawl for her dear friend.

Greg and John rushed over to hug Mary Elizabeth, both having a major crush on their all-time favorite baby sitter. Hugging her friend closely, Sophie said, "I'm so sorry Estelle, Hank was a good man."

Mary Beth quietly offered as she gave Estelle a warm embrace, "If you like, I can take the boys to the side room and make a supper plate for them." A sumptuous buffet that neighbors had prepared was arranged there.

"That would be wonderful Mary Beth. Boys, make sure you listen to Mary Beth," said Estelle.

"They always do, they're just like two angels," Mary Beth added while taking both of their hands.

With their plates filled, they looked to find seats on the crowded benches. Room for all three of them opened as Fat Frankie got up after gorging down two plates of piled high food.

Fat Frankie never bothered expressing sympathy to Estelle. He was there for the chow. He now was anxious to grab a beer at the *Purple Pleasure Bar.* His lack of remorse was glaring as he quickly mouthed, "Sorry about your dad, kids," while exiting the funeral home.

Years later, at Mary Elizabeth's funeral, Greg and John overheard her brother's words, "I promise you Mar-Beth, someday I *will* find a way to make the bad guys PAY!"

Hearing the young boy's words, Greg and John walked over and sympathetically laid their hands on each of the boy's shoulders.

Greg and John's anger over Hank's attack had also festered over time, mirroring the same intense rage over their father's death as their friend's did over his sister's death. They understood his thirst for revenge.

CHAPTER EIGHT

Present day Chicago

Petras Alekas smiled broadly as he took the Easter orders for his meats. Advance orders of Lithuanian sausage were pushing two ton's worth and ham orders were approaching seven hundred. He grimaced at the advanced work that would be required to deliver all the orders on time, but after calculating the profit, the grimace quickly transformed into a grin.

Ray-Ray and Jo-Jo, a couple of ruthless ex-cons, were cruising down Archer in their black late model Camaro when they noticed a huge crowd streaming in and out of a strange store named *Baltic Nirvana.* The two roommates had just left their Brighton Park apartment and were cruising down Archer on a mission to buy some weed from their supplier in Chinatown.

"Park when you see a spot, dude," Ray-Ray suddenly spouted, "Let's see what the big crowd is all about." Archer was packed, so Jo-Jo pulled into a Burger King parking lot a block away.

Jo-Jo, the better con man of the two, struck up a conversation with a burly man wearing a White Sox cap and jacket. "Go Sox!" he exclaimed as he sided up next to the patron. The man smiled back and said, "Pitching looks real good so far in spring training, I hope it carries over to the regular season."

"Me too," Jo-Jo responded as he clenched his hand offering the Sox fan a fist bump. "I'm new to the neighborhood, why is this place so crowded today?"

"You must be new around here. *Baltic Nirvana* has the best sausages and hams in the city. With Easter coming up in two weeks, you have to place your order in advance to make sure you have sausages and ham for the Easter dinner table."

"What sausage tastes best?" asked Jo-Jo.

Sox fan's reply was quick, "the Lithuanian sausage is pure heaven!"

"Thanks, then that is what I will get too. I appreciate your information, catch you around and GO SOX!" Jo-Jo blurted as he walked back to Ray-Ray.

As they headed back to Burger King, Jo-Jo noticed an interesting sign in *Baltic's* window, no checks, no credit cards, *CASH ONLY.*

A sinister seed immediately was planted in Jo-Jo's brain, as he whispered to Ray-Ray, "I think we will be into some easy money real soon."

"I like easy money," smirked Ray-Ray. They entered Burger King, ordered some Whoppers and sat in a far corner booth and began to formulate the plan on obtaining easy money.

CHAPTER NINE

Chicago 1978

Both Greg and John had experienced severe cases of puppy-love over Mary Elizabeth. Her death had been a devastating blow. They knew how much Mary Elizabeth loved her little brother. Not wanting to lose their memories of her, they decided to honor her by taking her little brother under their wing.

The three of them became inseparable. One day Greg and John invited Mary Beth's brother to their house.

Greg said, "Let's go upstairs and play in the attic."

John then winked at his brother and said, "That's a great idea." As usual, Mary Elizabeth's little brother followed them willingly.

Once they entered the attic, Greg led them to a far corner and motioned for them to sit down. John then produced a single blade razor and some string.

Taking the razor from his brother, Greg spoke. "Today we make it official. The promise you made to Mary Elizabeth is now our promise also. Today we become brothers. Blood brothers."

Greg solemnly started the ritual cutting each of their fingers until a trickle of blood appeared. John then bound the bleeding fingers with the string. Greg closed the ceremony with the words: "We promise you, Mary Elizabeth, someday we will make the BAD GUYS PAY!"

Decades later, the two brothers developed an extremely successful security company with state of the art surveillance equipment.

When *Mr. C* approached them with his plan to fulfill their long-ago pledge, they enthusiastically agreed.

After hugs and strong handshakes, *Mr. C* took his leave, thrilled that he now had his *Eyes and Ears.*

CHAPTER TEN

Biceps and Abs

The plan to develop affordable housing for low income families may have been a noble idea, but there are good ideas and bad ones. The Robert Taylor high-rise homes turned out to be a very bad one. They were built in 1962 and initially claimed some famous African-Americans as their residents such as Kirby Puckett and Mr. T.

The homes' resident reputations soon transformed from famous to infamous. The reasons for its future infamy should have been obvious to the planners. This cluster of high-rise homes stretched on State St. from South 39th (Pershing Rd.) to South 54th Street in neighborhoods that were rarely visited after dusk. Hell, even daytime was deemed treacherous by those wise enough to value their life and limbs. The many gangs on these streets; the Black Kings, the Sharks, the Black Disciples, Vicelords, Black P. Stone Nation, and Mickey Cobras slowly but surely took over the 28 high-rises that comprised the Robert Taylor homes. Viciously ruled turf-like fiefdoms were the result.

Trapped within the mayhem of the Robert Taylor homes was a solid Christian family of five: Dennis Johnson, his wife Bertha, their teenage daughter Tabitha, and ten-year-old twin boys, Max and Mike. It was 1975. Twelve years earlier they had received the key to their new Taylor home apartment.

The thrill of entering the new building with newly painted walls in the hallway and easy to ride elevators soon became history. Within three years, they now ventured past walls spray painted with gang slogans and urine soaked stairwells. A stair climb was now necessary as the elevators no longer functioned. Their still well-kept apartment now had three bolt locks on the door.

Dennis was a night janitor at the Crane Company plant on South Kedzie and Bertha cooked reception dinners on Saturdays at a nearby tavern and wedding hall. This worked well as the children always had a parent around, in case there was a dangerous situation lurking, which there usually was.

Amazingly, surrounded by every vice imaginable, the family's faith and love for each other overcame their foul circumstances. On Sundays, as they gathered around the kitchen table, the reading of bible passages and sincere laughter resonated throughout the day. Each family member was immensely contented. Albeit, Bertha's excellent fried chicken and mashed potatoes may have added to the contentment.

After graduating in 1976 from DuSable High School, Tabitha was looking forward to attending the University of Illinois at Chicago Circle (UICC). The sprawling 300+ acre campus was located a short "Blue Line L" ride away for Tabitha, making it convenient jaunt. An offered scholarship made it affordable for the family.

Tabitha's desire to help others made her uncertain about career choices. She whittled it down to two choices: a career as a nurse or a social worker. She decided to attend the Career Exploration Day that was being offered at UICC next Friday morning to help her make a decision.

The first booth she visited that Friday was the Jane Addams College of Social Work booth. It was manned by numerous student volunteers. A very handsome young man caught her eye. He saw her looking his way. He readily smiled and approached her.

"Hi, my name is Alex Timmons, welcome to the Circle."

"Thank you. My name is Tabitha Johnson. Nice to meet you."

"Do you have an interest in social work?"

"Yes I do. But I also am considering nursing. That's why I am here today, hoping to make a final choice."

Alex offered, "How about I give you a guided tour of the Jane Addams College and fill you in on the types of career choices it can offer for your future?"

She was giddy over the invitation, especially since it was being offered by a very good looking guy.

"That is very kind of you to offer. Are you sure it won't be too much trouble?" He laughed, "Heck no. In fact it would be a pleasure. I can sure use a diversion. I've been at this booth for three hours. Plus, giving a guided tour to a pretty girl is no sacrifice on my part. In fact, I'll even take you to lunch afterward at the cafeteria. My treat." She smiled at his remark and said, "You are a very nice guy. Lead the way." They began the tour.

Alex was a very competent guide. It became obvious that social work was extremely important to him as he pointed out numerous career benefits to Tabitha, both monetary and self-fulfilling.

"Well, that wraps up the tour, Alex said. " Are you ready for lunch?"

"Yes. I hardly ate anything for breakfast, I was so nervous this morning. I'm starving," Tabitha answered.

"Let's get us a couple of Chika-burgers," he said, grabbing her hand while leading her to the cafeteria.

"I never heard of burgers made from chicken," she said.

Alex laughed loudly at her words. "It is a regular beef burger. It isn't chicken. It is spelled C-H-I-K-A. It is the nickname for our athletic teams. Its origin is from the Chickasaw Indian Tribe."

"Oh, I feel so stupid not knowing that. I don't follow sports too much. Sorry," she apologized.

"No need to be sorry. Let's order some now," he said as they reached the cafeteria's counter.

Once their bellies were filled with Chika-burgers, Alex passionately expressed the importance of social work and its urgent need to the communities of Chicago.

She thoughtfully asked, "You are very convincing, but what impact can one person like me have?"

He very seriously answered, "What impact can one little-bitty person have? Ask Mohatma Gandhi, ask Martin Luther King. There is a saying that goes: If you think you can, you CAN. If you think you can't, you're RIGHT. The choice is yours."

Tabitha never bothered visiting the Nursing Career booth. Her conversation with Alex was the clincher. The fact that he asked her for a date a week from Saturday was an added benefit.

She now was absolutely certain that she could make a difference in the world, especially in the Robert Taylor homes. She so wanted to improve life there. The reasons were plentiful as throughout the years Tabitha formed many close friendships with her neighbors. This allowed her to discover that the strong Christian close-knit family she was fortunate to be a part of was the exception and not the rule.

The people Tabitha came to know and love, eventually faced many curves in the road of life. STD's during and even prior to puberty, prostitution involving mothers, daughters, and sons, drug and alcohol abuse, gang wars, and both petty and vicious crimes were a few of the battles that were daily fare at the Taylor homes. Tabitha was convinced that a degree in social work would provide the knowledge and the assist she would need to help rid the Taylor homes of these depravities.

Tabitha was a responsible young lady and wanted to help with the family finances so she got a summer job at Church's Chicken. It was a convenient short three block walk from her home.

One of the benefits of working the last shift was the plastic bag clutched in her right hand filled with leftover chicken. It may not have compared to Bertha's, but as her father put it, "This is some of the best chicken you can get. IT'S FREE!!"

Various types of garbage littered the alleys in Tabitha's neighborhood; broken bottles, rusted cans and rusted anything that was metal, dog and people poop, old newspapers, and overflowing trash cans that hosted larvae parties in the sweltering heat.

On the Fourth of July, Tabitha worked the night shift and closed the store at 11:00 p.m. A different type of garbage hovered that night in the alley that

Tabitha was approaching, just a scant block from home; a heroin addict was holding a gun as he threatened to shoot his supplier for a fix.

Tabitha heard a shout of "FUCK OFF" as she entered the sixteen foot distance between buildings that contained the alley space. She kept her head down trying to ignore them when she heard the junkie reply, "FUCK YOU!" She was just four feet away from safely passing the alleyway when she heard the "pop-pop" that was all too familiar to ghetto residents.

The junkie had shakily fired his pistol at the dealer, wildly missing his intended target. One of the stray bullets found a home in the heart of Tabitha—four feet more and she would have been out of the bullet's range and be alive to complete her life's dream. Instead, death was instantaneous as she slumped to the ground, her blood gushing over the fried chicken that lay under her. There would be no justice served as the two gutter rats, seeing Tabitha fall, took off immediately. The junkie dumped the never to be found pistol down a street sewer.

Rev. Daggert presided over the funeral. He was the pastor at Calvary Baptist Church, the spiritual home for Dennis and Bertha for two decades. The parishioners all knew and loved the special girl Tabitha. She was involved in numerous programs for the youth as well as the elderly in the parish.

The overflowing crowd concluded with their *Amens* as the final strands of "What a Friend We Have in Jesus" hung in the air.

"We have lost a true angel, in Tabitha,'' the reverend stated as he began the funeral sermon. "An angel that Jesus took to be with Him, and there are very few of us that can truly understand why. This ANGEL would have made a difference in the future of our race, our culture, our neighbors, our neighborhood, a GOOD difference, a WONDERFUL difference, a NEEDED difference," he roared as hearty *Amens* leaped out seeking to confirm his words.

"So WHY, we ask, WHY Jesus, did you take her, why take our angel from us? Those of you who met with Tabitha regularly know how much she hoped to eliminate the problems we face on a daily basis so that we all could be proud of our race, proud of our neighbors and neighborhood, PROUD to be CHRISTIAN men and women."

The *Amens* were deafening as he continued, "SO—this is the WHY of her death, Jesus knows that this noble mission Tabitha embarked on needed an ARMY of soldiers, an ARMY to combat gangs, an ARMY to combat drug use, an ARMY to clean up our neighborhood and our SOULS, so the REMINDER to enlist in this ARMY can be summed up by this: DO NOT LET HER DEATH BE IN VAIN!!!"

"That's RIGHT," joined the *Amens* in response.

"We need to start today, just as Jesus cast out the moneychangers from the temple we need to cast out the criminals, drug dealers, gangs and the reasons for using and needing them, DO NOT LET HER DEATH BE IN VAIN!!! We need to seek and encourage others to build a Christian home that houses a father and mother watching over their children like brother Dennis and sister Bertha did with Tabitha, and does with Max and Mike, DO NOT LET HER DEATH BE IN VAIN!!! We can make a difference, a GOOD difference just like Tabitha wanted to do, DO NOT LET HER DEATH BE IN VAIN!!! Are you with me?"

"YES" was the frenzied response.

"I said, ARE YOU WITH ME!" the response was the same but louder. "I said, ARE YOU WITH ME – DO NOT LET HER DEATH BE IN VAIN!!!" It did not seem possible but the response's decibel level rose even more. "Thank you my brothers and sisters, but more importantly, our ANGEL Tabitha thanks you," he said as he ended the sermon in a low reverential whisper, "do not let her death be in vain."

The casket was being wheeled to the back vestibule where the final goodbyes could be made. Six of her former teachers from DuSable served as her pallbearers. They carefully steered the casket. They did so slowly, their vision blurred from salty tears.

Rev. Daggert led the trailing procession of mourners holding the hands of Max and Mike, with Dennis supporting Bertha a few steps behind.

As they walked, Max asked the Reverend, "Why doesn't God kill the person that killed Tabitha. The bible says-an Eye for an Eye."

"In that sermon Jesus also says to forgive our enemy and when struck on the cheek, simply turn the other cheek," the Reverend responded.

Max and Mike were not sure they agreed, but remained silent. As the casket arrived at the vestibule destination, the boys touched the casket and tearfully said goodbye to their sister. Then Dennis and Bertha approached. The crowd hushed to show respect to the mother and father saying their goodbyes.

The silence was suddenly shattered as a wailing "NOOOO!" escaped from Bertha's throat as she fainted and plummeted to the ground. A doctor in the parish rushed forward and administered to her. If Rev. Daggert could have seen the look in the eyes of Max and Mike as they knelt close to their mother, he would have realized that there would be *NO CHEEK TURNING* in their future.

Body-building became their passion as Max and Mike vowed that in the future, no one was going to push them around. The passion was fueled by the unrequited anger over their sister's unsolved killing. By their eighteenth birthday their bodies were rock hard and powerful. Deciding to place their physical attributes to good use, they joined the U.S. Army Rangers. Showing immense skill and courage, medals soon covered their shirts.

After a successful *DESERT STORM* campaign, they were being treated to a farewell dinner by their sincerely grateful lieutenant. "I knew you guys were going to be great once I heard you were from Chicago," the lieutenant, a

Chicago native, toasted as the number of beers consumed quickly moved to double digits.

Lips, overly oiled by the brewskies, soon became loose as Max and Mike shared the gruesome details of Tabitha's death with the lieutenant and related their anger that the fucker was never caught, and how that really, really, pissed them off.

Listening quietly and with intense interest, the lieutenant asked them if they would like to fulfill their sister's unfulfilled vocational vision by making Chicago's future bad guys pay the price. Their animated response was a loud "FUCKING-A!"

The lieutenant told them about a venture he was preparing for the future. It was their turn to now listen intently, and when he finished his narration, Max and Mike, with huge grins, reached out and shook the officer's hand enthusiastically and said, "We're in!"

Hearing the commitment in their voices, he then continued, "Good. One day I will be in touch. Now I would like to tell you about my sister, her name was Mary Elizabeth."

The brothers left the Army and returned to Chicago and became successful entrepreneurs. They soon had strength and conditioning *Max to the Mike* franchises throughout the city and suburbs. It was approximately two decades later when their former lieutenant walked in on them. Max and Mike recognized him immediately. After hugs and handshakes, they went to their office and closed the door.

"It's time," the lieutenant simply said.

"ABOUT time," Max and Mike smiled as they all clasped hands in a solidarity shake. *Mr. C* now had his *Biceps and Abs.*

CHAPTER ELEVEN

Actress

Chicago 1980

The little girl drank her imaginary tea from the tiny porcelain Strawberry Shortcake tea cup while chatting with her tea party guests; Raggedy Ann, Barbie, and a now silent Chatty Cathy, whose ring was pulled too many times over the years rendering her speechless.

Her pretend party was one of her several escapes from reality. They ranged from tea parties with her dolls to being a loving mother to them. The reason she needed these diversions could be explained by the long sleeve blouse buttoned to the neck that was being worn by her mother. Despite the 90 degree temperature and high humidity in an apartment with no air conditioning, the blouse was never unbuttoned or the sleeves rolled up. She wore similar blouses daily. It was a great way to hide the bruises.

At work, Jose Lopez was considered to be a demanding but fair supervisor at Michael Reese hospital. He was a jack of all trades, so supervising the maintenance crew seemed a perfect fit to Jose. He often bragged about being king of his castle at home to his mostly male crew. He did have four women on the team to whom he assigned the sole responsibility of cleaning toilets.

What he did not mention in bragging about his *monarchy* at home was that he also had appointed himself judge and warden, embracing swift and violent action when the situation demanded it. Situations that received the brutal retributions usually required that he consume a quart of Tequila prior to dispatching his version of justice.

As a child, he had watched his father beat his mother repeatedly over her transgressions. The number of transgressions increased in direct proportion to the amount of tequila he consumed. Not wearing the right clothes, not cooking dinner the right way, watching the wrong television show, were a few of the transgressions committed by his wife Maria that required punishment.

The transgressions that merited the most severe beatings were not spreading her legs fast enough when he wanted to fuck her or when her blow jobs failed to get him hard. He never blamed the tequila.

Jose's father taught him it was a man's duty to keep a wife in line. He taught him that beatings as well as the tequila were necessary components in this process. Unfortunately for his wife Maria, Jose turned out to be an excellent student and learned his lessons well. Thus, the long sleeve blouses.

Rejecting escape or retaliation, Maria endured the beatings due to an old school warped belief in a culture that emphasized a wife was expected to be quietly submissive and the husband was expected to be independent and dominant. Throw in the facts that she emphatically embraced the martyr's role, harbored self-esteem lower than a snake's belly, had a delusional belief that Jose would soon change, and harbored an extreme maternal fear that leaving Jose would place her little Rosanna and her teen-aged son Renaldo in grave danger. These foolhardy beliefs caused her to endure Jose's sadistic assaults.

The lessons that Jose embraced from his father regarding spouse control were not received well by his son Renaldo. In fact, he despised his father for hurting his mother. So much so, that killing his father would bring out the same pang of conscience in him as swatting a fly.

Unfortunately for Jose, Renaldo's body at age 16 was growing at the same vicious pace of his obsession to end Maria's suffering. As he sprouted to 6'2'' and 195 pounds, his confidence came along for the ride. He no longer feared the menacing tequila-laced threats of violence tossed at him by Jose.

Jose started noticing the indifferent disposition now displayed by his son. It angered him, but he also sensed his son would no longer be indifferent to his mother's beatings and just stand by and watch. He saw the fire of hate in Renaldo's eyes, and realized the boy wanted to hurt him bad, mucho bad. Wisely, he now conveniently punished the transgressions only when Renaldo was not at home.

This worked fine as Maria continued to make good use of the long sleeved blouses, and Jose was able to play man of the house without watching his back.

He would now his drink tequila shots at the bar across the street from his house. He would take the corner seat so he could not be seen but he could see his front porch. It was the front porch that Renaldo would walk down as he hurried on to his part-time job at Paradise Tacos. This was Jose's signal to go home and check for transgressions by Maria.

One day, with Renaldo gone, Jose shuffled home from the bar. A major transgression immediately angered him as he swung open the front door. Jose swore as he removed his shoes. He cursed the fact that his slippers were not placed near the doormat as he had ordered. Maria would be forced to pay for this incompetent error. "Maria, get your ass in here NOW," Jose growled, conveniently forgetting that he had placed the slippers in the laundry bin before leaving for work.

She had been eating and drinking imaginary cupcakes and tea with her daughter Rosanna in the dining room, along with the other doll guests as they celebrated Chatty Cathy's birthday.

The violence in Jose's voice caused Maria to jump and run, scattering the dolls and cups to the floor and more importantly, she forgot to send Rosanna to a locked room to protect her from seeing her father's release of anger.

The feral sound emanating from his throat was so menacing, that Rosanna shivered as she gazed at the scene from her hiding place under the table. In a locked room, she could play her escape games to avoid thinking about the brutal beatings. Now there was no benevolent locked door to shelter her.

Tears streamed down her cheeks as the beating commenced. "I work on my feet all fucking day, and all I expect from you is to make sure I can cushion my feet the moment I walk in," he bellowed. "Come here, Bitch, I am going to make sure you DO NOT forget my slippers again!" The moment Jose's hand was raised to strike Maria, Renaldo rushed in to retrieve a forgotten wallet.

Seeing the attack on his mother pushed him over the edge as he attacked Jose screaming, "I will KILL YOU, I will KILL YOU." He drove Jose to the ground. His hardened muscles, fueled by rage, produced sledgehammer fists that Renaldo used to pummel Jose relentlessly. Maria screeched, "Stop, please stop, Renaldo." Renaldo paid no attention and continued his assault. It was when he shifted to the other side of Jose to do more damage that he finally noticed Rosanna.

His bloody knuckles braked on their way to the face of his father, and instead reached out to hold the little sister he loved. She barreled towards him and leaped in his arms, surprising him not by her action but by her words, "Thank you Renaldo, now he will stop hitting mama."

Her face was bright with admiration and a smile that went on forever. "I'm sorry you had to see this," Renaldo whispered in her ear.

"I'm not," she excitedly replied. "You are my hero, just like The Incredible Hulk. He makes the bad people stop doing bad things, no matter what anyone thinks or says, even the police." Rosanna was a big fan of the TV show and never missed an episode. "And that is how it should be, if you didn't stop him, mama would have been hurt bad."

Renaldo flushed at the words and said, "You're right, Rosie, sometimes you just must do it, rather than wait for it to stop."

She enthusiastically offered, "When I grow up, I'll help you and The Hulk make bad people get what they deserve!"

Afterwards, Jose groaned loudly as he attempted to stand up. Screams replaced the groans a few minutes later as Maria applied the iodine and alcohol to his injuries.

When she fixed him up as best she could, she courageously announced, "it ends here—NO MORE." Holding Renaldo's hand tightly, she continued, "Seeing my son beat his father was terrible, but necessary. However, I do not want to see it again. If it becomes necessary for him to do so, then I want you to know that you will never see any of us again, we will pack up and leave you, never to return."

Jose responded as he meekly gazed at a glaring Renaldo, "I promise. No more."

"That is a promise you better keep," warned Renaldo.

"Yeah," echoed Rosanna.

He did. From that point on, whether out of fear or want, Jose stopped the daily Tequila ritual, and came straight home. Once there, he embarked on a journey to win his family's love and trust back. This was a trip long overdue.

Jose found that the most shocking element of his transformation was that he enjoyed this new life much more than his life as *Master of His Castle*. His father had been wrong, he deduced, as Maria served him another one of his favorite meals while planting a kiss on his lips.

Rosanna learned a valuable lesson that day too. When bad actions are dealt with using force, the bad actions stop. She not only learned it, she took it to heart. Years later, the make believe sessions she acted out behind closed doors sheltering her from watching her mother's beatings resulted in an acting career.

While performing in a Christmas Nativity dramatization as the Virgin Mary, she was noticed by Tony Cortez, a director at Steppenwolf Theatre. Tony, who was visiting his grandmother in the old neighborhood, was thoroughly impressed by Rosanna's portrayal. He invited her to grab a cup of coffee with him and he offered her a role in his upcoming spring play. This was her dream come true, so her answer was a resounding "Yes!" accompanied by a ferocious hug.

Her ability to lose herself in a role was enhanced by her amazing ability to transform her looks through make-up and body posture. This ability allowed her to play both young and old parts so well that her fellow performers at Steppenwolf nicknamed her the female Lon Chaney –The Man of a Thousand Faces.

Both Hollywood and Broadway took notice of her skills and she soon became one of the most sought after actresses on screen and stage. Producers found themselves in a very long waiting line to sign her. Her enormous talent was matched by her sweet and polite personality, resulting in producers and directors drooling over the opportunity to work with her.

Renaldo remained her hero. Without consequences that would squash horrid behavior, she felt bad behavior would not only continue, but would worsen. Proof of this opinion shattered her heart while she was performing on Broadway.

After a brilliant Saturday night performance that garnered three curtain calls, she texted the audience reaction to Renaldo. This was their custom after each performance. He then would text back his congratulations as sympathy for a poor performance was a rarity. There was no response. She waited an hour and called his cell. His recorded message was the result. She was about to try again when an incoming call signal erupted. Rosanna happily punched in the call after seeing her mother's name pop up. The happiness was short lived.

A sobbing Maria explained the atrocious tragedy that occurred that evening.

Renaldo's fiancé, Justine, a very successful real estate broker, had just surpassed ten million in sales that day and she and Renaldo celebrated with giant steaks at Morton's. They had left Morton's with both steak and champagne lingering on their taste buds. The couple's original plan for romance afterward was sidetracked by a last minute request for a showing at 7:00 a.m. the next morning.

The new president of Chicago Bank, Adam Coultis, was relocating from New York and had been working with Justine on a home purchase. He was hard to please. She had shown him thirty-six homes in five days, and he had thirty-six reasons not to buy, along with an attitude that was as irritating as his accent. His return flight to New York was booked for 12:00 p.m. on Sunday.

As they were leaving Morton's, she received a call from Adam. He said he found the house he wants. He saw it in a magazine on the Real Estate display at a Dominick's grocery store. Since the list price was $1.6 million, Justine called the owner and was able to schedule the 7:00 a.m. showing so it would not conflict with Adam's flight. However it did conflict with her romantic plans for the evening. Understanding Justine's need to get to bed early, instead of joining her in bed, Renaldo reluctantly walked her to her car.

They had driven in separate cars because Justine had been on a sales call. Arriving at her snazzy BMW, Renaldo kissed her and bid her good-bye and good luck.

Due to lack of street parking near Morton's, Renaldo decided to park few blocks away at a two level parking lot. He climbed the stairs to the 2nd level where he had parked his SUV.

"That's weird," he thought. All three of the bulbs illuminating the area had gone dark, leaving the lot as murky as a London fog. As his hand reached for his car door, another hand came out of the shadows holding a Glock 22.

"I want your money! Get on the FUCKING ground now or I blow your brains out," Glock man ordered.

Renaldo bent his knees as if to comply, then instead, sprang up and charged. That was a mistake. The multiple shots that Glock man discharged all caught Renaldo in the face. He slumped dead to the ground, his face resembling a platter of steak tartare.

Glock man, aka Jajuan Jones, rifled through Renaldo's pockets grabbing the valuables. Killing the lights on the 2nd level was Jajuan's way of hiding and getting the advantage over his victim. It also gave Richie Morales, an off-duty police officer the advantage over Jajuan.

Richie had just parked his new Harley in an open space across from the parking lot. He was headed to the latest hot spot, The Martini Palace, a few blocks away. He had just locked his cycle when he heard the unmistakable triple tap of a Glock. He whipped out his cell phone and speed dialed 911.

"This is Officer Morales, I am off duty and am by the parking garage at 1400 North State Street. Shots have been fired inside the garage, send back-up. I am now proceeding to the scene."

He immediately drew his 45 caliber SIG-Sauer P-220 and carefully zeroed in on the 2nd floor of the parking garage. Jajuan was removing Renaldo's wrist watch with the Glock resting in front of him in full view when he heard, "POLICE! LET ME SEE YOUR HANDS NOW! GET THEM UP!" The darkness had allowed Richie access while remaining out of sight. Jajuan's IQ was never on the high side and once again he decided to prove it.

Richie was in *the stance,* with both hands on the 45 when Jajuan rushed to grab the Glock. He was way too late. Richie rapidly fired the Sig-Sauer and Jajuan's body jerked spasmodically in the throes of a death dance.

Richie approached, kicked the Glock aside, and speed dialed 911. "This is officer Morales. I called for back-up a few minutes ago when I heard shots coming from parking garage at 1400 North State Street. The offender tried to shoot me as I approached. I fired and took him out. The apparent victim and offender appear to be dead. Send ambulance and my supervisor." He reported the exact location and gave the operator other requested information and waited for assistance.

Rosanna and Maria were led to the morgue of Northwestern Memorial Hospital by Michelle, a twenty year veteran from homicide. She tried to comfort them, but comfort was not allowed in the same room with the rage that was boiling up in both women.

When they discovered Jajuan was previously arrested four times for armed robbery and five assault charges and was recently released after spending only five days in jail for violating parole, Rosanna's temper was on fire. "Once again the law has failed us!!" A Channel Nine cameraman was taping as Rosanna continued to fume to the crowd that had gathered. Each onlooker wanted to get a close look at the celebrity.

"My brother was a good man, killed by a man who had already been arrested NINE different times for violent crimes," she ranted. "These animals commit crimes over and over and are responsible for most of the vile acts in our city. When will someone make sure that real justice is served and these vermin are punished appropriately? The legal system is a joke, and the criminals are the ones laughing at it. When will we learn that until something happens to this garbage that really scares them (thoughts of Renaldo's beating of her father rushed to her mind) MORE innocents will fall prey to this vicious violence." She then collapsed in Maria's embrace and was led away.

"Amen," a suddenly interested man proclaimed to his TV screen.

"Good evening, this is Jason Wells reporting from the Northwestern Memorial Hospital where Chicago's own, Rosanna Lopez, the famous actress, arrived here this evening to face the gruesome task of seeing the bullet riddled face of her murdered brother, Renaldo. Renaldo was shot in an armed robbery attempt by Jajuan Jones, a previously convicted armed robbery felon that was recently released from prison. Off duty patrolman, Richie Morales, hearing gunfire, arrived at the State Street parking garage too late to save Renaldo. Jones was stripping the pockets of Renaldo when Morales arrived. Jones then attempted to shoot Morales. The officer fired immediately and Jones was killed. Here is a clip of Rosanna taken at the hospital as she exited the morgue housing her brother's body." The gut wrenching tirade by Rosanna was shown.

"With me now is Chicago Police spokesman Mark Torres. Mark, do you have any comments on this horrible event?"

"Well Jason, unfortunately Ms. Lopez was right when she stated most violent crimes such as armed robbery, rape, murder, spouse and child abuse, etc. are committed by repeat offenders. Our statistics show that it represents 70+% of these crimes."

"No shit, Sherlock," an interested *Mr. C* exclaimed to the glowing HDTV screen.

"I want to assure the public that we will continue the battle of keeping our city streets safe. The Mayor and the Superintendent will be meeting at City Hall tomorrow and will be seeking answers to this issue," Torres promised.

"What BULLSHIT," *Mr. C* mouthed. His thoughts then turned to a possible recruit for the *Actress* he was pursuing for the role in his upcoming drama. Yes, he concluded, this one is a distinct possibility.

CHAPTER TWELVE

Present day Chicago

As the sunlight streamed through windows that framed a majestic mural of Lake Michigan, Mitch leaned over and reached for the warm body of Natalie in hopes of rekindling the heat from last night's escapades. The pleasure he had anticipated evaporated as he found himself alone in bed. However, a different pleasure greeted him as the smell of fresh coffee and sizzling bacon filled his nostrils. This substitute pleasure was intensified by the fact that he was not doing the cooking.

Detective Mitch Mrozek was a 14-year veteran of the Chicago Police Department. He was admired greatly for his abilities on the streets, and in the bedroom.

There were many reasons that contributed to his charm. He looked like a young George Clooney, but with black wavy hair, not gray. Women like that. His baby blue eyes twinkled seductively. Women like that. He could make a girl laugh with his Jay Leno-like wit. Women like that. His hand-holding was as if a girl's hand was bundled in warm velvet, but exceptionally strong when giving a muscle relaxing massage. Women like that. He was such a good conversationalist that one of his dates said it was like chatting with one of her best girlfriends. Women like that. Regardless of a crowd, he would make a girl feel like she was the only person in the room worth being with. Women like that. The real clincher was he was a first class listener that paid attention to every word spoken by his date. Women *love* that! All that and a finely-toned hard body whose muscular butt beautifully filled out a pair of jeans made him the perfect catch to be hauled in from the sea of love. Unfortunately he insisted on catch and release.

In his mid-forties, Mitch had never married, claiming the job left no room for a wife. It was pretty evident he was a committed officer. As a beat cop, numerous citations proclaimed his talents and since his promotion to detective, his case close rate was top notch.

He also had a number of notches in the bedroom. He realized that the job might not allow a wife, but he was human enough to understand the need for sex and the comfort that tagged along with it.

His innate ability to charm women resulted in numerous affairs with a bevy of beautiful females. That, coupled with intense pride in his Polish heritage, earned him the nicknames of *Don Juanski* and *Casanovaczek* at the station. The members of the squad peppered him daily with these two monikers. The ribbing he got from both happily married and not so happily married officers was loud and constant, with envy covertly providing the fuel.

He cherished his various lovers and treated them royally and with respect. He and his paramours always established the boundaries of commitment in each affair. He always promised a monogamous relationship while it lasted, but marriage was not to be in the equation.

He was honorable enough not to pursue any woman who had any hesitations about this arrangement, regardless of how attracted and interested he might be. His considerable sexual skills were matched by his magnetic personality, so much so, that all of his exes not only considered him a great former lover, but also a great friend. Those that eventually married did not hesitate to invite Mitch to their weddings.

Natalie was a raven-haired thirty-something with Medusa-like curls that snaked around an angelic face that was countered by lips painted a smoldering devilish red. Her face could be seen every weekday morning as she was a reporter and co-host for the cable show, *Time to Wake Up, Chicago.*

Two weeks earlier, each sitting alone at neighboring tables while taking in Second City's latest revue, she and Mitch snuck glances at each other. Both liked what they saw; on stage—and at their neighboring tables.

As usual, the revue was hilarious and the two of them happened to belly laugh at the same times. This prompted Mitch to remark to her, "You have a great sense of humor!"

"Back atcha handsome," she countered while producing a definite come hither smile.

They exchanged first names and when the last skit finished, Mitch suggested going for drinks at the Underground Wonder Bar.

"I absolutely love that place," she exclaimed.

"I take that as a yes," Mitch chuckled.

"Oh, yeah." She quickly slipped her arms into her stylish Jones of New York jacket and then slipped her arm into his. Mitch had walked to Second City, so they hopped into Natalie's candy apple red Infinity G37.

"Nice wheels," Mitch commented.

"The car, or my legs," she challenged as her skirt inched higher.

"Both."

"Right answer," she deadpanned before emitting an engaging laugh.

Once there, the soulful music led to soulful conversation that culminated in Natalie's offer to continue the evening at her place. Mitch gallantly agreed. The rest of the night was indeed soulful.

They had been getting together a couple of times a week for dinner and would always saunter over to Natalie's condo in Lincoln Park for "dessert." She insisted that they go to her condo due to Natalie's need to rise early for her cable gig.

Today was a Saturday. They both had the next day off, so after a stuffed pizza dinner at Lou Malnati's, Mitch offered his pad for the evening's delights. They climbed into Mitch's non-descript Impala and headed over to his place.

Natalie was exposed to a number of surprises once arriving there, some sexual, some not.

The first was the building Mitch pulled up to. It was a gargantuan tower on East Erie where a valet quickly arrived at Mitch's vehicle before it even stopped. Natalie was greeted with a "Good evening, Miss," as the valet opened her door and offered a pristine white gloved hand.

"Evening, Sam," Mitch smiled, as the valet responded with a "Good evening Mr. Mrozek," before moving into the driver's seat to park the Impala.

The next surprise was the militarily dressed doorman standing back straight. He opened the door for them echoing the valet's "Good evening, Mr. Mrozek."

"The same to you, Scott."

Her eyes grew as large as Lou Malnati's pizzas when they entered an elevator that was dripping with shimmering Italian Marble from ceiling to floor. She was dumbfounded as she watched Mitch hit the Penthouse button for the ride to his place. Mitch smiled languidly at her apparent confusion.

She gasped at the chic surroundings as Mitch ushered her into the penthouse. This unexpected environment hatched a multiple birth of questions in Natalie's head. It also produced a very lustful glow throughout her body.

"Mitch," she blurted inquisitively.

Immediately interrupting the direction of her inquiries, he murmured,

"How about we save the questions for morning."

He then reached behind her back and expertly unzipped her dress. His subtle action released a firestorm in her belly and she felt the wet need between her legs overwhelming her.

"Let's do just that," she whispered in his ear while she proceeded to lick and nibble it.

Both were very glad they postponed the inquisition as the multiple climaxes they shared reduced the firestorm to a flicker.

"Time to get up Chicago," she parodied, yelling from the kitchen. Mitch hastily pulled on a pair of Chicago Bear gym shorts and covered his unruly hair with a Cubs hat and hurried to the kitchen as the aromas permeating the air beckoned him.

Thick bacon, rye toast slathered in butter, a mushroom-cheddar-chive omelet, and fried potatoes with onions were artfully laid on a plate before him. A large cup of coffee next to the plate was spewing a palate pleasing scent. "Thank you, thank you," he gratefully exclaimed as he planted a hard kiss on her lips.

"You're welcome, you're welcome," she replied, with an equally hard kiss of her own. Breaking the kiss, they converged greedily to the table as their appetites were ravished after running in their evening sex marathon.

For the next few minutes, the conversation between them consisted of "crunch," "chew," "gobble," "slurp," and multiple "YUMS."

"Thanks Natalie, that was superb!"

With a mischievous smile, she said, "Don't feel too bad, but I did it as much for me as for you. I woke up famished!"

"Hopefully a contented famished," Mitch offered, as he mimicked Groucho Marx's moving eyebrows with an accompanying wide grin on his face.

"Fishing for a complement are we?"

"Wouldn't mind one," his eyebrows *Marxing* again.

"OK-OK, having sex with you is like rockets, fireworks, sirens, and me—all going off at once. How's that for a complement," she challenged with a smirk.

"Not the best I've gotten, but I guess it will have to do."

He immediately started laughing as he dodged the punch she threw at his arm. Both continued to giggle as they wrestled to the ground attempting a tickling contest. When the tickles transformed into caresses, their bodies eagerly sought a different form of play.

Suddenly, Natalie placed her feet on his chest and pushed, hard. Mitch's face was a mask of confusion as he simply grunted, "Huh?"

"Let's cool off for now, handsome, you promised to have a Q & A this morning."

"I did, didn't I? I'll meet you in the den. Bring a couple cups of coffee and we can talk there."

"Yes master." Natalie gave him an exaggerated bow and fetched the coffee. She handed Mitch a cup as she plopped into a very cushy emerald green futon facing Mitch as he leaned back on a black leather Lazy-boy that displayed the Chicago Bears logo.

"You may fire when ready, Gridley," Mitch beckoned.

"What the hell is a Gridley," exclaimed Natalie.

"It was a famous quote from Commodore Dewey to his captain. It has since become jargon for *Let's Get On With It*. And I thought you were a reporter."

"I am Mitch, on current events," she countered.

"OK, I am ready to fire—here goes question number one: Are you filthy rich or are you a cop on the take?"

"Definite no to both," was his immediate response.

"Then explain how we spent an unbelievable evening making love in an unbelievable penthouse condo that must be worth $3 million?"

"First of all, it was an unbelievable night of lovemaking because you were with me," he slyly grinned. "Now sit back my dear and listen, and I will tell you a story," Mitch said as he sipped his coffee. "Have you ever heard of Angel Construction?"

"Of course," she replied, "Matt Kuraszek owns it. His company is one of the largest construction conglomerates in the country. He is famous for malls, business parks, and luxury condos, not just in Chicago, but nation-wide. I know, because I have interviewed him for my show a few times, most recently on his latest venture on the mall in DeKalb. His vision on that place was right on, as he explained how Chicagoans once considered Northern Illinois University a far-away college campus, famous for its cornfields. However, years ago, with the expansion of toll roads, he foresaw Northern transitioning to a *commuter* college for Chicagoans, and he conveniently swept up prime real estate that now houses numerous lucrative office parks and the new mall, all of which HE built. Quite the entrepreneur."

"Glad to hear you talk so nice about my uncle and godfather."

"What! If he is your uncle, why the hell are you working a dangerous beat on the streets, when you could be working for him?"

"Okay, it goes like this," he sighed. "He and my mother, his sister, were Polish immigrants from the town of Częstochowa, the one famous for the Black Madonna painting. They didn't have much money but they both were rich in a common Polish trait, pride. They were wealthy with it, but my dad exceeded them. He was the King Croesus of Pride in comparison. Wanting to succeed in his adopted country became an obsession for Uncle Matt, forgoing any family of his own; he never married and probably never will. He worked construction, saved his money and started his own company; the rest is history. He named the company after his mother, Angeline, and to this day I would bet he cares more about what he accomplished that he does over his bank account."

As she carefully refilled his cup, he continued, "My father on the other hand, applied his pride to his family, keeping us happy and cared for gave him the same thrill as Uncle Matt's company gave him. Uncle Matt tried desperately to hire my dad and me, but my dad considered that to be charity, and refused the repeated attempts until Uncle Matt finally gave up. I inherited that same proud stubborn streak and was intent on making it on my own, doing what I wanted. Yes, it can be a dangerous gig, but it is what I do, and I do it well I might add. So yeah, I am proud of my accomplishments, and am content with my career choice. You may not agree, but for me it is very important that I do what I do and do it well."

Trying to get a handle on this surprising story, Natalie inquired, "Okay, but if you have all this pride why did you accept this condo?"

Mitch chuckled, "I didn't at first when it was offered to me, but Uncle Matt is not only a successful businessman. He is also extremely crafty. One day he asked to meet me for lunch and said he needed a favor from me. As we chomped on a massive plate of sauerkraut pierogis at his favorite Polish restaurant, he pleaded, 'Mitch, I need your help desperately. I still have too many vacancies in that luxury condo complex on East Erie, and you can really help me a lot.' How? was my puzzled reply. He answered, 'People today are extremely concerned with security and safety and I would like to be able to reassure them by not only demonstrating the state of the art security systems in the building but that one of the complex's tenants is a highly decorated Chicago Police Detective. It would be similar to the comfort subdivision owners feel when one of their neighbors is an officer who keeps his squad car parked in the driveway, representing a beacon that repels any would-be criminals that may stray into the neighborhood. Please, will you do this for me?' I may consider it, I conceded, but I insist on paying rent."

"'Great,' my uncle enthused, 'I'll have my lawyer draw up a rental agreement that will be a fair price for both of us. I'll have it by tomorrow. Let's meet back here for dinner to finalize it. Tomorrow's special is smoked butt and potato pancakes and I love that stuff,' he said, obviously not wanting to waste any time hooking me in. That *fair price* turned out to be one hundred dollars a month," Mitch sarcastically proclaimed.

Natalie burst out laughing while challenging, "I thought you had this intense Polish Pride thing."

"Natalie, I said I was proud; I did not say I was stupid," he challenged back.

"I felt that since he had worked so hard on the sales job he laid on me, and that he and I are the only remaining living relatives, not to mention that I'm his namesake, I couldn't find it in me to say no."

Gazing around the rooms and taking in all the luxuries, with tongue in cheek. Natalie commented, "Yeah—it must have been a real sacrifice for you. Wait a minute, you said you're his namesake, but your name is Mitch not Matt."

He launched a loud laugh explaining, "Now that one is a real Polish Joke! Uncle Matt was baptized Mitchell, but for whatever reason, everyone, including his parents, always called him Matt. So, I was named Matt after him but, ironically, everyone, including my parents, always called me Mitch. Go figure." Sighing, Mitch concluded, "Okay, story time is over, we're both off today, what do you want to do today?"

"Does this place have a pool and a boutique?"

"Hey, for a hundred dollars a month, of course it does," he quipped.

"Well," she suggested, "first you can buy me a bathing suit at the boutique, then we'll take a relaxing swim, and then my vote would be to have Lou's deliver a large loaded pizza along with a couple Italian beef sandwiches for our fuel for the day. Then I vote that the rest of the day, and night, we can visit each of your gorgeous rooms and see if we can find some creative ways to indulge ourselves in each of them," she purred with that coy smile of hers.

"Like I said before, I may be proud, but I am not stupid. I heartily endorse that plan."

He then moved to her, opening her robe so that her breasts escaped, the excited rose budded nipples pointing upward in feverish anticipation. "In fact, here's my seal of approval," he exclaimed as his mouth and tongue proceeded to cover the jutted red floral patterns on the tips of her breasts.

A loud and primal "Yes," was her response. This response was mutually echoed throughout the rest of a very pleasant day and night, as the rooms of the condo unabashedly witnessed numerous inspired scenes of creativity.

CHAPTER THIRTEEN

Jo-Jo sipped an Old Style as he explained the plan of action to Ray-Ray for the tenth time.

"Jesus, Jo-Jo, I got it already, I have had it with this planning bullshit," Ray-Ray complained while taking a long pull from a bottle of Sauza tequila.

"Hey, my proper planning has kept us out of jail many, many times, hasn't it?" Glumly Ray-Ray nodded, calculating that he and Jo-Jo should be spending just about the rest of their lives in jail had they been convicted of all the shit that they had pulled.

So far the count was seven rapes. Six were partnered with armed robbery. They were only in their mid-twenties. The thought of having to spend the rest of his life in prison was *scary, very scary*. Getting their victims to *Monkey Up* (Hear no Evil, See no Evil, Speak no Evil) had been the key to their freedom. In addition to casing the target for money or sex, Jo-Jo had come up with the idea to get an accurate count of all family members. The younger, the better; children worked the best. Ski-masks only went so far in avoiding arrest.

In each of their previous crimes, the victims were warned to *Monkey Up* or their loved ones would be targeted for vicious revenge. Even if Jo-Jo and Ray-Ray were arrested, and could not personally make good on their threats, there was an abundance of willing participants in neighborhood gangs to do whatever dirty deed they required for the right amount of money. That fact was always emphasized to their victims.

Part of all their plans included tailing targets to their homes and checking out the family members. Jo-Jo would then show the victims photographs of family and homes that he had taken, identifying the loved ones and their homes. The warnings were always chilling and cruel: promises to gang rape a young sister or daughter, break arms, legs, and heads of children, parents, or grandparents, or simply setting fire to the homes displayed in the pictures. The extra time this took in planning was well worth it. Only one of the seven crime victims had been brave enough to press charges.

After being raped and robbed by the two, Connie, a beauty shop owner, had noticed an unusual tattoo, a jalapeno pepper, on Ray-Ray's neck as they exited the salon. She notified the police, and the two were arrested soon after. However, when Connie arrived home one night, she found her grandmother, the person who raised her, tied and taped to a chair naked from the waist up with ugly purple welts on her back from the whipping that was administered. The chair she was sitting on had a pool of urine dripping down its legs. On the table next to her was a sheet of paper with the words, *Time to monkey up*.

Connie recanted her testimony the next day. The police did end up arresting them on five of the remaining crimes due to the similar MOs. But with overcrowded courts and only circumstantial evidence and no witnesses willing to come forward due to *Monkeying Up*, they were released each time after spending only a few days in holding cells. Prosecutors were more interested in slam dunks. The arresting officers were understandably upset, but such is life in the big city.

The day that Jo-Jo announced his *easy money* idea to Ray-Ray, they finished their Whopper sandwiches and went back to check out the lay of the land.

The sign in *Baltic Nirvana's* window stated that the store closed at 6:00 p.m. At 5:50 p.m. Ray-Ray parked at the end of the alley to watch the back. Jo-Jo was watching the front as he slowly walked on the other side of the street. At 6:05 p.m., all of the employees were gone, leaving through the front door that was then locked by Petras from the inside. Jo-Jo joined Ray-Ray in the Camaro. At 6:30 p.m., the rear entrance of *Baltic Nirvana* opened. They were confused at first by Petras just standing by the door holding it open. This confusion led to excited howls as Nina, Petras's beautiful nineteen-year-old daughter, exited and walked to the car while Petras then locked the rear door and placed a lock and chain on it.

"It's gonna be *money* and *honey* when we hit this joint," Ray-Ray drooled.

"Yeah, Baby," agreed Jo-Jo.

For the last seven months, undecided over what to major in at college, Nina decided to work at *Baltic Nirvana* until a decision could be made. Her younger sister, Julka, told her she could be a fashion model because she had an awesome body with a face to match. Little Julka did not exaggerate, not at all.

Before heading home for dinner, Petras had a custom of stopping by St. Joseph's church on his way home from work to light a candle in memory of his grandparents, Zan and Rebecca.

Jo-Jo, following in the Camero pulled into the church parking lot and waited a minute after Petras went in and then entered the vestibule. He could not believe his luck. Nestled on the vestibule table was a parish directory.

Remembering Petras's last name stenciled prominently on *Baltic Nirvana's* front door he hurriedly paged to Alekas. Not only was the name and address there for him, but a bonus to boot. Staring at him was a photo of the entire Alekas clan: Petras, his wife Teresa, Nina, Julka, and Thaddeus. Jo-Jo excitedly noticed that Julka and Thaddeus were easily ten or under. He quickly grabbed his cell phone and took a picture of the group along with the address. He closed the book and exited the church with a maniacal hyena's grin.

"Why you so fucking happy?" Jo-Jo's answer was to hold the cell picture in front of Ray-Ray's face.

Ray-Ray grinned wildly and said, "No need to follow him home now, let's go smoke some dope and down some shots!"

"That works for me." The Camaro streaked away.

The following days, the punks were at the store each day checking out the routines. The key was the closing routine. The employees always left at 6:05 p.m. and Petras and Nina always followed at 6:30 p.m. Both knew this would work in their favor. Tuesday morning revealed the bonanza. They were wondering how Petras took the money out of the store, as they never saw the canvas bag that most shopkeepers used to take their daily deposits with them. At 10:00 a.m. the Brinks truck pulled up.

As robbery veterans, they knew that this was very good news for them. "That means the motherfucker must keep the money in the store, probably in a safe somewhere," Jo-Jo deduced.

"And the cocksucker must make a hell of a lot of money to be willing to pay Brinks," Ray-Ray added.

"Hey, remember what that dude in the Sox hat said," Ray-Ray rattled on.

"He said Easter Weekend the place will be swamped with customers. That means lots and lots of cash, and Brinks don't come till Tuesday."

"That means we make our withdrawal on Saturday night," Jo-Jo said.

The next day they both entered the store feigning to be customers. They slowly covered the entire layout, pretending to check various foodstuffs in order to find their real interest: *where was the safe?*

Nina was leaving the back office near the same aisle that Jo-Jo was perusing a jar of sauerkraut. His peripheral vision rewarded him with not only a look at Nina's luscious ass as she locked the door behind her, but also the sizable safe located in the back of the room. He wasn't sure what caused his ensuing hard-on, Nina's ass or the safe. Probably both.

Grinning, Jo-Jo went to the cashier and paid for the sauerkraut, which he dropped in the first garbage can he passed.

"Let's get some planning materials," Ray-Ray laughed as he pulled into the liquor store for some beer and tequila.

"Fucking-A," Jo-Jo agreed, adding, "*Baltic Nirvana* is going down!!"

CHAPTER FOURTEEN

Energized by fond thoughts of Natalie and their Kama Sutra week-end, Mitch entered the station curious who the captain would assign as his new partner today. Larry, a twenty-five year vet had decided to call it a day and retired last week. He was an avid fisherman and with spring coming, he decided he would rather chase and catch elusive walleyes much more than scumbags. Mitch understood, but would dearly miss the guy. More than a partner, he had been Mitch's mentor and was a key component in the successes Mitch had enjoyed both on the streets and in a john boat.

Wearing the carpet down around Mitch's desk was the squad's resident amazon, thirty-six year old Diane Ryan, a twelve year vet. She was blond with a five-foot nine inch frame that housed a playmate of the month body and a face that could rival Helen of Troy. Yep, it too could launch a thousand ships, maybe more.

She had come to Mitch's attention a few years ago, and not because of her looks. She, like Mitch, was driven to be the best cop she could be. They had met in a martial arts class, a department sponsored effort to encourage top physical condition in its officers. Mitch, always in great shape, wanted to improve his fighting skills. Mitch assumed she was doing the same. What Mitch did not know that this was simply a refresher for Diane. Five years earlier she had qualified as a black belt.

He was shocked and shook when she painfully took him down in a mock attack exercise. "That was lucky," he groused as he tried to lift his bruised left butt cheek off the mat.

"Probably," she deadpanned, "let's try again."

By the fifth takedown and both of his cheeks now bearing bruises, it dawned on Mitch that luck was not involved. Diane was sometimes referred to as Di-Di by her male counterparts in their conversations about her. It was coined to belittle her abilities. This was necessary as the male officers' pride was further offended as she consistently turned anyone down asking for a date. However, the risk was too great to use that nickname in any conversation she was a part of. When she was present, they wisely stayed with Diane or Officer Ryan.

She was similar to Mitch in that she too believed that she was married to the job, thus remaining single. This commitment to the law placed her in the line of fire many times. She had no intention of stressing out a spouse because of this. But that didn't mean she was a nun, far from it. Being a healthy mature woman, she relished the comfort and release great sex and orgasms provided. In her mind, sex was a natural hunger that from time to time needed to be fed.

Because she refused to date co-workers, it was assumed by those rejected that any sexual escapades she might have, were lesbian in nature. Nope, she was straight, but she adamantly kept her private affairs just that. Private.

"You're late, partner," she said.

Looking at his watch, Mitch said, "I'm right on time, it's twelve noon. Hey, did you just say partner?"

A Cheshire cat smile inched across Diane's face as she explained, "I always work Lombardi time, to be on time means fifteen minutes early, if you get here on time, it means you're late…and, yes, I said partner."

A very surprised Mitch was mutely processing this information when Captain Krol barked loudly, "Mrozek and Ryan, in my office now."

They hurried into the captain's office, each grabbing a cup of coffee from the captain's credenza. The captain's pot always housed hot and freshly made Gevalia, not the cheap insipid shit the peons drank. The pot was always the first thing officers zeroed in on when invited to the captain's office.

Mitch and Diane sat down on both sides of the captain's spacious desk."You two are now partners, but judging by the facial expressions back at Mrozek's desk, it looks like I'm giving you old news. Let me say that I think that you two will prove to be the best team we have in the department. Both of you have the dedication and complementary skills that will produce exemplary results."

I should have worn my boots, thought Mitch as he listened. Diane's thoughts were that the captain should consider politics, his BS was that good.

"Yes sir, I look forward to this new challenge," Mitch responded with the reply he knew the captain wanted.

"As do I, sir," Diane added.

"Glad to hear it. Take today to get acquainted and compare detective strategies. Tomorrow will be soon enough to hit the streets on open cases. Preparing yourselves as partners today takes precedence over anything else, understood?"

"Yes sir," they said in unison.

"Remember the words of the great football coach, Tom Landry. If you are prepared, you will be confident, and you will do the job. So go get prepared!"

* * * * *

"Hey Mitch, before we discuss strategies, I want to discuss something privately first," Diane said as she pointed to an empty private office.

"Sure."

Once inside, she quietly closed the door. "Ok, here is the deal. I know all about your reputation, *Mr. Don Juanski*, so I wanted to be up-front on one very important issue: my dating rules. I have heard the rumors about my so-called gay tendencies when it comes to dating. I want to assure you, it is all bullshit! I enjoy a roll in the hay with the right guy as any normal, healthy, hetero woman would. But, I do not shit where I eat. So here is a fair warning, do not try to hit on me, if you do, I will kick you in the balls so hard you will be chewing them. I know you know I can. Are we clear on this?"

"Crystal," Mitch responded quickly.

In an abrupt change of tone and body language, Diane offered with a smile, "I had an early breakfast, how about we compare notes over lunch?"

"Sounds like a plan, where do want to eat?"

"Anywhere that has one of my five main food groups," Diane offered.

Expecting tofu, alfalfa sprouts, edamame, veggies, and greens as the prime suspects in the five groupings, Mitch groaned, "Which are?"

"One, Vienna hot dogs in poppy seed buns, two, Italian beef with hot giardiniera, three, thin crust pizza, four, sausage, Polish or Italian, and five, fresh cut French fries, especially if you know somewhere where they are breaking the law by frying them in beef fat," she said laughing at the shocked look on Mitch's face.

Mitch thankfully said, "I'm pretty sure I can accommodate those food groups very, very well indeed… partner."

Diane smirked, "I take it you approve of my food groups."

He smiled, "as Roger Ebert would say, two thumbs up."

They were smiling and joking on their way out, both thinking that they might just be the great team the captain expected after all.

CHAPTER FIFTEEN

It was Easter Saturday, 5:30 p.m. Jo-Jo and Ray-Ray were ready. Ray-Ray had an aluminum baseball bat hidden under his coat. Jo-Jo packed a .357 Colt King Cobra. He liked the Cobra because of its intimidating size. He often would jokingly say, "Size Does Matter," as he held the gun in one hand and grabbed his crotch with the other. The Camaro had been parked on Archer, one block from *Batltic Nirvana* since 4:00 p.m.

"Let's do it," Jo-Jo ordered as he pulled away from the curb and parked next to Petras's Jeep Cherokee in the alley. Both anxiously awaited the rich pay day while having lascivious thoughts about Nina's hot snatch.

It was closing time and the employees were leaving through the front door. A front door that Petras smilingly held open for them as each had their arms wrapped around gigantic smoked hams that Petras and Nina had generously provided for their Easter tables.

After locking up, they gathered the receipts for the day. Today, they needed four money bags, Petras happily noted, as the sales had exceeded even his high expectations. The money was transferred to the 11.8 cubic foot AMSEC safe in the back office. Its 90 minute fire protection and its heavily reinforced steel construction for better burglary protection meant it was costly, but Petras wanted the best in security, and was happy to pay the price. He also liked the lifetime no cost warranty against break-ins, especially the no cost part. He spun the traditional dial combination lock, grabbed the handle to make sure it was locked, and said to Nina, "a very good day indeed!"

Jo-Jo and Ray-Ray first gave the alley a once over to make sure that they were alone. Thinking that unconventional masks were really cool after seeing *The Town* starring Ben Affleck, they covered their faces with Iron Fist Vampire ski-masks then lurched out of the Camaro.

Ray-Ray gripped the bat and Jo-Jo gripped the gun as they positioned themselves on the right side of the door so they would be hidden as Petras opened it. They heard the lock turn and waited for Petras to exit. His back was exposed as he held the door for Nina. Ray-Ray jumped out while delivering a crushing blow to Petras's head. Before Nina could scream, Jo-Jo rushed past the falling Petras, grabbed Nina's hair and positioned the Cobra directly under her chin.

"Don't say a fucking word," Ray-Ray cautioned to Nina while Jo-Jo pushed the unconscious Petras through the door, quickly locking it.

"Tape him up quick," Ray-Ray ordered, tossing Jo-Jo a roll of duct tape. When Jo-Jo finished taping the lifeless Petras, Ray-Ray took it from there.

"Listen up, NINAAAA," he mockingly drew out her name. "First, open the safe."

"And if I refuse," she defiantly countered.

"Oh, we got us a bitch with balls, let's just see how big your balls are," Ray-Ray said as he pulled out his cell phone and flashed the picture of her family, then the picture of her home. "Recognize them?" he tauntingly asked a now shocked Nina. "You have five minutes to get it open, if not, bad things will happen at this pretty house on Throop Street, very bad things."

"You're bluffing. If I don't open the safe, you can't either. I doubt that you would kill us and get nothing in return, except going to jail for murder," she hopefully stalled. "I think you are about to change your mind."

Ray-Ray then dialed the bogus number that was part of the plan. He waited a few seconds and then spoke to a dial tone, "We're here, are you in front of the 3030 South Throop Street house," he paused as if getting an answer. "Good, as we planned, wait five minutes for my call, if I don't call back, you and monster man go in there and beat the shit out of the boy and old lady, and fuck the hell out of the little girl, her name is Julka."

Again pretending he was getting a response he said, "*Sure*...you want to do the old lady too? Go right ahead, just make sure everyone in the family gets to watch," he said laughing to the dial tone. "Okay, check your watch now, five minutes starts now," he said while clicking off the phone. "Your move, bitch," he said as he purposefully looked at his watch.

The call worked as planned. Nina frantically rushed to the safe and worked the combination. She panicked as the first attempt failed and heard Ray-Ray say "three minutes left." Taking a deep breath she worked the lock slowly and deliberately and a click echoed through the silenced room. She then tossed the money bags out of the safe pleading, "Please, make your call now!"

Ray-Ray smiled as he speed dialed the dial tone again. He convincingly bellowed, "Do not enter the house, we are A-OK here. But, stay in place just a little while longer and I'll call you back."

Grabbing the money sacks, he placed them on the table and peered inside them. "We are fucking rich," he gloated to Jo-Jo. "Now comes the fun part, take off your clothes NINAAAAA!"

"No, please," Nina fearfully pleaded. "You have the money, just go!"

"But Nina, we always like some honey with our money," Jo-Jo said while he began to unbuckle his pants.

"Look Nina," warned Ray-Ray bringing his cell phone out again, "you want me to make that call? This time you have 30 seconds to start stripping, starting now." He grimly glared at his watch. "But I'm a virgin, please don't do this," she begged.

"Hey Jo-Jo, did you hear that, we got us a cherry!"

Jo-Jo hooted in response, "Not a problem, we LOVE to go cherry picking, Nina!"

"Ten seconds left," Ray-Ray declared, lifting the Samsung Infuse 4G phone from his shirt pocket. "I'll do it, but first call them and tell them to leave my family alone," she bravely countered. Ray-Ray again speed dialed the non-existent number saying, "Yep, me again, you and monster man can leave now, we are all good on this end." Continuing the sham he said, "Yeah, both of you will still get paid what we promised."

Grinning, he closed the phone and ordered Nina, "I did my part, now you do yours."

Before disrobing she glanced at her father and it was a small relief to her that he remained unconscious, as she knew the shock of watching this atrocity might kill him. Resigned to her fate, the brave girl mentally braced herself to be strong not just for survival, but revenge.

Ray-Ray handed the Samsung to Jo-Jo with a wink. After ordering the now naked Nina to lay on the floor and spread her legs, he unzipped and released his erection. "Beg me to fuck you," he taunted as his hand swung his cock towards her. Her widened eyes expressed her shock at these words.

"You heard me, I want you to say 'Please fuck me. Or, I can still make a phone call," he sneered.

"Please…fuck me," Nina tearfully whispered.

"Louder," he demanded. A screaming "Please fuck me," was her panicked response.

"Did you get it?" Ray-Ray asked Jo-Jo.

"Yep, check it out," Jo-Jo said passing the phone over. The Samsung Infuse 4G phone not only takes a very nice picture but its audio recording is first rate as well. Ray-Ray laughed as Nina's face screamed "Please fuck me," on the phone's screen.

"Since you asked so nice, here I come." He violently plunged his erect penis into her dry vagina. Blood soon seeped down her thighs signaling the destruction of the hymen.

Jo-Jo dropped his pants and placed his engorged cock next to her lips, "Now beg to suck my dick, Nina!"

Wanting to bring a fast end to this nightmare, she robotically responded, "Let me suck your dick."

"Good girl, if you suck it real nice I promise not to come in your mouth."

She immediately cringed at that disgusting thought. Nina closed her eyes and placed her mouth upon Jo-Jo. The darkness created by the closed eyes helped her mind ease into a dark bleak emptiness where pain and despair abated. This small escape from reality shattered as a stream of warm semen filled her mouth. Gagging and spitting, she choked out the words, "You promised not to do it in my mouth!"

"I lied," Jo-Jo smirked as he buckled up his pants.

"My turn," Ray-Ray panted as he moved his penis from her vagina to her breasts, splaying ejaculate over her breasts. She retched. They pushed her in the bathroom, threw her clothes at her and said, "Now clean up and get dressed."

As she tried to close the door, Ray-Ray's foot aborted the attempt. "Door stays open," he said, admonishing her again to "hurry up!"

They laughed as she tried to wipe herself clean with a wet wash cloth. "We're in a hurry, so stop playing with yourself," Jo-Jo taunted her with cruel laughter.

After she finished dressing, Ray-Ray pushed her down next to her father while Jo-Jo duct-taped her wrists and legs and placed a gag on her mouth.

As they grabbed the money bags, they stooped over Nina and relayed this threat. "If by some unbelievable chance we get arrested, you better *Monkey Up.* That means you must *Hear no Evil, See no Evil, Speak no Evil*. Remember, we know where to find Teresa, Nina, Julka, and Thaddeus. For their health and yours, if we do get caught, you don't testify against us. Do you understand, bitch?"

She nodded yes, knowing to do otherwise would be suicide.

As they slithered out, Ray-Ray said, "Man, that sex was good! It's so much nicer when they beg for it."

Jo-Jo laughed and gave Ray-Ray a high five. Copious tears streamed from Nina's eyes.

When the door slammed shut, Nina vowed revenge and visualized numerous forms of torture and death. She hoped that the very stupid mistake they made would be the nail for their coffins. She had a name: Jo-Jo.

CHAPTER SIXTEEN

Actress

Rosanna loved her fans but she loved her privacy more. She used her well-honed skills of disguise when she ventured out for simple personal tasks or pleasures so she could avoid the over-zealous crowds that descended on celebrities like jackals on a carcass. The always vigilant and unscrupulous paparazzi were another reason for her going out incognito.

Fame and money did not change Rosanna's desire to be close to family. She lovingly purchased a home for her mother in the Little Village neighborhood. Little Village, or La Villitav, as her mother fondly called it, was the lifelong residence for Maria Lopez, now a widow. This is where her friends made their homes and she resolutely refused to leave this familiar enclave.

Rosanna finally gave up trying to convince Maria to move into some fancy digs in an upscale area. Instead, she bought the house next door to her mother on the South 2500 block of Albany. This was a mistake. Her doorbell rang constantly as the middle class neighbors all wanted to meet the famous Rosanna. Simple tasks like going for groceries or buying shoes would attract fans like metal to a magnet. The neighbors' eyes were always glued to her front door, so even disguises did not ensure her privacy.

Desiring some solitude, she moved to the Palmolive Building. With low end condos there starting at 2 million, the Palmolive's security delivered on the solitude. More importantly, her wealthy neighbors living there thought they were pretty famous themselves. They refused to demean themselves by flocking around some movie star as if they were middle-class groupies. Their arrogance was a delight to Rosanna.

One of her pleasures that bordered on necessity was her workouts in the gym. Three days a week she embraced her routine of running four miles on the elliptical machine, then lifting weights. Her arms gripped the dumbbells to work her triceps, shoulders, biceps and back. Her legs pumped iron to tone her glutes, calves, hamstrings, and quads. She ended with each session with 100 crunches to keep her abs firm.

She was a member at the *Mike to the Max* athletic club a few shorts blocks from her Walton Street condo on the Magnificent Mile. Three years earlier Rosanna had asked one of the owners to help her with a conditioning plan. The goal was to maintain a fine tuned supple body. This was essential for her character transformations. Max Johnson, who co-owned ten *Mike to the Max* franchises with his brother Mike, drew up the exercise plan and walked her through the first couple of weeks until she had a handle on the regimen. His expertise and his willingness to keep her identity a secret led to a strong friendship.

Keeping with a fitness goal, *Mike to the Max* gyms all contained a fruit and smoothie bar that also supplied numerous nutrients and healthy lunches. After her workouts, Rosanna would order the salad of the day along with a tall glass of juice as well as a smoothie. Max would be waiting for her in the corner booth as they relished their friendly conversations as well as the workouts.

Today, their moods were somber. "I'm so sorry about your brother, Rosanna. I really have missed you the last few months, but I understood your need to grieve."

"Thanks Max, It's been really hard on me and mom. Renaldo was my hero as well as my brother. It never should have happened, the scum that killed him should never have been allowed back on the streets." At this point, Max, acting on a recent discussion with Mr. C regarding Rosanna, decisively decided that Rosanna was another link to their mission. So he forged ahead with the previously discussed proposition.

"We share a tragic similarity," Max started.

"What do you mean?" she asked.

"My sister was also my hero," Max stated in a soft voice. A passionate fury replaced the soft voice. "Her name was Tabitha." He then described his loving sister and her brutal killing. "The cops said it was either a gang dispute or a drug deal gone bad. I guarantee you it was another scumbag that was arrested before and released to do more bad stuff just like the punk that killed your brother."

He paused awaiting her response. It was immediate. "Damn it, what kind of idiots do we have in our courts that allow this shit to happen?" Rosanna boldly uttered pleading for an answer. "Max, Renaldo may be dead but I still harbor an insane thirst for revenge. How the hell can we allow these criminals to go free when we know most vicious crimes are committed by these goddamned repeat offenders? There's got to be a better way."

Max passed a napkin. She wiped the tears away harshly. "I feel the same," he said as he gently squeezed her hand. Cautiously he offered, "I may know of a way." He carefully waited for her response.

"Please tell me how, I would really like to know. I need to know how."

"Here is an idea a friend of mine put together. I'm taking a chance here telling you, but I know I can trust you."

"You can." He then shared the vision of *Mr. C.*

"How would I fit in?"

Max then explained *Mr. C's* need for an *Actress* and the *roles* she would be playing. After a moment of contemplation, through a sultry smile she announced, "I want in!"

After a handshake and a hug, the *Actress* was secured.

CHAPTER SEVENTEEN

The Don

"I'm sorry Tony, but the results indicate an inoperable status."

"How long do I have left?"

"Well, depending on your progress in a drug program," Dr. Stein began.

"No drugs! How much time do I have? Give it to me straight."

"Eighteen months on the far end, 12 months on the short end."

"Good, now I can finally join Carmela," thought Tony.

Tony Dagonatti, aka Don de Dago was the longtime Outfit capo of the South Side 26th Street crew, now retired. He ruthlessly worked his way up in Chicago's Outfit due to his exceptional IQ and disregard for the idiots that were dumb enough to seek out juice loans and then gamble or piss the money away on drugs. His collection tactics from juice loans, *Street Tax* (protection for businesses), and gambling losses were legendary and highly respected by his bosses and the *idiots.* He partnered impressive physiological verbal tactics with an inbred ruthlessness, achieving unprecedented success. His promotion to capo moved quickly.

He anxiously planned a retirement filled with trips, sightseeing, fine dining; the works. The joy of being close to Carmela was the catalyst. Unfortunately, instead of exciting trips with the love of his life, the only traveling they did after retiring was to the oncologist.

In their teens, Tony and his buddies, Nick and Gino, decided to try out the new Italian Festival sponsored by Saint Michael's parish. The combination of carnival rides, great food, and lots of girls to ogle, made the trip to Roosevelt and Cicero an easy choice.

While waiting in line for the *Tilt-A-Whirl*, Tony heard melodious laughter from one of the spinning cars. He searched it out and when the car twirled and exposed its passengers, he was in love. The proverbial thunderbolt hit him hard. Carmela's auburn curls glowed like precious amber as they enveloped a face any artist would love to paint, and adore. She was dressed like any other bobby-soxer of the era. That face, however, quickly set her far apart from the crowd. Tony saw his angel.

As his friends rushed forward to nab a car on the ride, Tony snuck over to the ride's exit gate. As Nick clamored into a choice ride, he exclaimed, "Where the fuck is Tony?"

"Excuse me miss, may I ask a favor of you?"

As Carmela was exiting the ride she looked up at the tall muscular Tony. "What kind of favor?"

"I want to try some of the gelato, but I am not sure which is best. I need someone to help me taste test them. My treat!"

Her eyes demurely surveyed him. She liked what she saw. "Sure, I'm game."

The smitten Tony wasted no time in winning the hand of Carmela. The attention and tenderness he showered on Carmela during their courtship effectively hid the Mr. Hyde side of his Dr. Jekyll. She was a devout Catholic and remained a virgin until their wedding night. Tony, on the other hand, had committed his future to the Outfit. His Uncle Vito, an Outfit soldier, recognized early that Tony was as smart as he was tough. Nobody in Little Italy messed with Tony. He relayed these facts to his boss and the recruitment began.

At his graduation party from Loyola with an accounting degree, Vito simply asked, "Are you ready to join us?"

"Yes, but only after the honeymoon."

"No problem, you and Carmela have a great time in Acapulco, I'll see you next month at the wedding."

Hopelessly in love, they doted on each other. Their frequent love making was passionate and filled with affection. They dreamed of raising a large family, but fate soon reared its ugly head on this dream. After two miscarriages, both painful and dangerous, her doctor recommended sterilization. Tony agreed immediately. "I love you too much, I can't bear the thought of living without you, we must do this," were the words he spoke to a sobbing Carmela.

After the operation, Tony continued to be a knight in shining armor to her. Her happiness was paramount to him, nothing else mattered.

Carmela was not a stupid person. She realized the massive income that was generated by Tony's *accounting firm* was extreme. "Please, let's not talk business, let me worry about it," was always his brusque response to her suspicious inquiries. Her love for him would end the inquiries. However, she feared for his immortal soul.

Carmela's jaundice and fatigue began a few weeks after Tony retired. During those weeks they gleefully planned their future together. As the symptoms escalated, a fateful visit to Dr. Stein revealed pancreatic cancer, advanced stage.

Carmela bravely suffered the excruciating back pain the disease forced upon her. The additional pain brought on by the simple task of eating resulted in a massive weight loss robbing her beauty and leaving behind a skeletal ghost. Never did she complain, she accepted her suffering as God's will and focused on the perpetual life that the next world offered.

Tony soon realized that all the money and power he had acquired were useless in saving Carmela. He became her shadow and servant, wanting to fulfill any desire she might have.

She had one. A big one.

"Tony, I'm not long for this world."

"Carmela, please don't talk like that, you still have a long time."

"Wishing it so will not make it so," She smiled, pausing before continuing, "Tony, before I meet with Jesus, I want you to do something very special for me."

Uncharacteristically, Tony wept. "Anything. Anything you want."

"Tony my love, I want to spend eternity with you in heaven. Christ Jesus receives all who accept Him and sincerely repent of their sins." As Tony squeezed her hand she continued, "I know about the bad things you have done. Because I love you, I prayed for you every day of my life."

Tony tried to weakly protest, "But—"

Carmela's fingers immediately reached out and brushed his lips with her fingers as she aberrantly commanded, "Silenzio!"

Although surprised by the gesture, he nodded affirmatively. "You must promise me you will repent and give your life and soul to Jesus Christ. If you love me and want to be with me forever, you must promise me this!"

In a voice that left no doubt of its conviction, Tony answered, "I promise you Carmela, I will do this for you, I will do this for you."

A smile etched across her face and she said lovingly, "Do it for us." There was one last squeeze in her hand for Tony as her eyes suddenly grew wide and she exhaled the words, "I'm coming Jesus." Her hand went limp, her eyes closed, but her smile remained.

CHAPTER EIGHTEEN

Surgeon

One week after hearing about Jack Baxter's tragic tale from Coleen at O'Hara's, *Mr.C* realized this was the opportunity he had been waiting for. Jack possessed both the skills and a very good reason to become his *Surgeon*.

He visited Cook County Hospital and he was fortunate. Hanging on the wall in the reception area were photos of the heads of all the departments. He committed Jack's portrait to memory and stealthily used his cell phone to record the photo as a back-up.

The next day he called and asked about Jack's hours. He arrived thirty minutes before Jack's shift was ending and parked near the employees' lot. Exactly thirty-five minutes later Jack entered the lot and climbed in a metallic blue Porsche Panamera 4S. *The man has very good taste in cars*, thought *Mr. C* as he cautiously followed the Porsche after letting it get a good lead on him.

Jack headed north on Lake Shore Drive then turned west on Belmont and north again on Halsted. He pulled in front of *Sidetracks*, a popular gay bar and handed his keys to a valet.

Mr. C drove by and returned twenty minutes later. He cautiously donned a baseball hat and slid on his Oakley sunglasses while adjusting the fake beard he had taped on. He saw Jack sitting at a far corner table. Jack was alone reading the Sun-Times.

"Excuse me, are you Dr. Baxter?" he inquired.

"Yes. Who are you?"

"I'm here to make a very special offer to you. May I join you for a moment?" Jack's suspicious eyes gave *Mr. C* the once over, then he nodded yes.

"You must be the guy who followed me from Cook County," Jack announced.

Momentarily taken aback, *Mr. C* asked, "How did you know?"

"I dismissed it as paranoia at first, but then a man I have never met wants to talk to me wearing a poor imitation of a beard and tries to enhance the masquerade with sunglasses on a cloudy day and a cap pulled down to his ears. I have been called many vile names in my life, but no one has ever called me stupid."

He again sized up this newcomer. Then with a smile on his face, said, "I have a very good antenna when it comes to zeroing in on other gays. That antenna is indicating that you are as straight as they come. You did not come here to ask me for a date, so why are you here?"

Mr. C came right to the point with the single word, "Gary."

Pain and fury flashed in Jack's face as he demanded, "How do you know Gary?"

"I did not know him, but I am very familiar with the pain we share: *losing a loved one*." *Mr. C* related Coleen's diatribe from that night at O'Hara's bar. He then forcefully stated, "Gary death was murder. The murderers were never caught. Neither were the murderers who killed my sister." He then described the horrific attack on Mary Elizabeth. Wiping his eyes after relating the tragic story, he added, "These animals did not immediately kill them, but it was murder." He paused while he studied Jack's facial response. It was the one he was hoping for, so he continued. "Did you know that over 70% of violent crimes are committed by repeat offenders?"

"Hey, I work at Cook County and I have a front row seat in the gallery. So, yes, I am aware."

"What are the odds that those bastards who attacked Gary and my sister either had done it before or did it again?"

"Pretty damned high," Jack confirmed with his fist pounding the table.

"Right. Basically the legal system is broken and justice is being pushed to the side. How would you like to honor Gary by drastically reducing those odds in the future?"

A long silence followed.

"How?"

"Like you said, you're no dummy, so I'm sure what I am about to offer will be held in the strictest confidence. It isn't pretty but it will have a major effect on stopping those who plan to hurt the future Garys and Mary Elizabeths."

"You have my word. I am very interested in reducing these odds. You definitely have my attention and my confidentiality." *Mr. C.* then described his plan of delivering severe consequences to the bad guys. "I see where my role would be essential," Jack pondered. "You're right on. Without you, Doc, this won't succeed. With you, the bad guys will pay, big-time!"

A lifetime of anger spawned first by society's hatred toward gays and nurtured by justice being ignored by the Chicago police towards apprehending Gary's attackers simply because he was a homosexual, Jack's response was no surprise.

"I took an oath to cure people and save lives," Jack pronounced after a few minutes of rage-filled contemplation. "I have always been a huge advocate for preventive medicine. This qualifies as the ultimate in that regard. If you are indeed on the level, you have your *Surgeon*."

Mr. C grabbed Jack's hand and shook it warmly saying, "Mary Beth and I thank you. I am sure Gary would be proud of you too."

It's payback time Gary, Jack reasoned to himself.

The next hour was spent diagramming future missions and listing the necessary equipment.

Mr. C bid farewell and exuberantly headed to his car. *One more to go and the team is complete.*

CHAPTER NINETEEN

The Don

Tony was true to his word. The confessional was his first stop after Carmela's private funeral. He kept it private to avoid the media circus a public display would invite. He needed to buy a rosary as the penances handed down by the priest at St. Michael's required the purchase, as numerous decades of the rosary were required to cleanse his sins. Not wanting to shortchange his odds for forgiveness, he tripled the number.

Something still did not seem right to Tony. His fear of never being with Carmela again was exacerbated by Dr. Stein's diagnosis.

Wanting to have a serious discussion about his soul's redemption, he invited his sister Theresa, now a nun for the Sisters of Mercy, to dinner. She was his only remaining relative. She had taken the name Sister Mary Frances in honor of the brave Sister Frances Cabrini who had established the order in America in the 1800's. Sister Cabrini's efforts brought her to Chicago where the founding of Mercy Hospital was a result. Its location at 26th and Calumet in 1862 was considered to be too far out for Chicago residents. The Great Chicago Fire of 1879 changed that perception quickly. Its location sheltered it from the inferno and was able to assist more victims than other hospitals severely handicapped by the fire. Its location no longer was considered to be in the boonies. The Sisters of Mercy made assisting the ill and injured a priority, especially the poor.

Taking this mission to heart, Sister Frances took her highly advanced nursing skills and volunteered her time at a hospital that would best serve her ambition to minister to the poor, Cook County Hospital.

Because of its violent surroundings, numerous blunt trauma victims crowded the ER daily at Cook. Sister Frances focused her skills in that area. She and Jack Baxter soon formed a formidable team as well as a formidable friendship.

Over pasta Bolognese and sautéed sausage and peppers at Rico's, their favorite Italian restaurant since they were kids, Tony anxiously formulated how he would approach Theresa about Dr. Stein's conclusions about his future.

As the waiter served the cannoli and espresso, Tony said, "Terry, I need to tell you something important." Sister Frances listened intently as Tony addressed her by this affectionate nickname from childhood. She disdained the name Theresa in grammar school and insisted on being called Terry. When Tony wanted to bug her like all brothers do, he mockingly emphasized her name by calling her "THEEERRRREESAAAA." When he wanted to have a serious discussion with her, he always deferred to Terry.

"I have not been a very good person in this life. You and I have had many discussions over the years about my activities, and you urged me to change my ways. I should have listened, but I did not."

She joined her hands with his and said, "Go on."

"You and Carmela were gifts from God. I should have been more thankful and respectful of Him for bestowing the two upon me." He paused, then went on to share Carmela's last request and Dr. Stein's diagnosis.

Silent tears creased both sets of eyes and their hands tightened. "I want to make peace with God, I must have the chance to see Carmela again, hopefully for eternity. Will you help me?"

"You know I will, how?"

Tony gulped the remains of the espresso and said, "In my life I have accumulated substantial wealth. I tried to give some to you many times, but you insisted that you would not break your vow of poverty, so I will not attempt the same offer. Instead, I was hoping that you could direct me to a place that I could best benefit society in the eyes of God."

After some reflection, a thought came to her. "Tony, you know I am committed to administering to the poor and less fortunate. Cook County Hospital helps me achieve this, but, we desperately need more modern equipment to really help our patients there."

"Consider it done. Who should I see there?"

"Jack Baxter."

He made the appointment for the next morning with Jack. Sr. Frances had made Jack aware of the situation, and he was effusive with his excitement.

Warmly shaking her hand, he said, "This will be a real boon for us here at Cook, Thank you sister!" As she left his office another thought brought a smile to Jack's face as he contemplated, "This might also be a boon for *Mr. C.* too."

Tony's visit went just as his sister had described. Promises of new equipment were made and would be kept.

As the meeting was coming to an end, Jack offered to take Tony to lunch. Tony readily agreed once Jack suggested Rico's.

As they sipped a glass of Chianti Classico, Jack suggestively stated, "Tony, how would you really, really, like to help your fellow man?"

"I'm all ears, what's your proposition."

Jack asked Tony to honor confidentiality.

Tony simply stated, "You have my Omerta."

Jack then paraphrased the invite *Mr. C* had given him.

It soon became apparent that Tony's interest was piqued. "I agree, the laws of the courts are crap, but how can I make a difference and help stop the insanity?"

Jack then explained *Mr. C's* plan and the team that was assembled and its need for one critical member, someone like Tony.

"It sounds like a good plan, however, I am curious. I want to make amends so I may join my Carmela. What motivation does the team have?"

"I'll tell you mine and *Mr. C's*. I don't have details on the rest of the team's reasons, but I can assure you that they're similar to ours."

He then shared the tragic details about Gary and Mary Elizabeth.

When Jack finished, Tony commented," those are powerful motivations indeed." He then was silent a long time. He reasoned action might be more helpful for his soul than decades of the rosary. Did not Jesus grab the bull by the horns as he ousted the money lenders and traders from the temple? They had been cheating the poor and causing much hardship. Don't these criminals to whom Jack referred deserve the same type of action? He decided yes.

He reached out to shake Jack's hand, and resolutely stated, "We'd better start soon. I don't have much time. I'm in."

Moments after Tony hailed a cab, Jack took out his cell phone and speed dialed *Mr. C*. He relayed the recruitment of Tony. "What code name will you give him?"

Mr. C grinned. "*The Don,* of course."

CHAPTER TWENTY

Petras was still recovering from a basilar skull fracture compliments of Ray-Ray's bat. He was experiencing some paralysis and his motor skills were especially shaky, not a good thing for a butcher handling sharp knives all day.

After an arduous struggle to free herself from her bonds, Nina had immediately called 911. An ambulance arrived minutes later. On the ride to Mercy Hospital, she stayed with Petras in the back of the ambulance clutching his hand tightly. He stayed unconscious the entire time. He would groggily awaken twenty-two hours later.

Embarrassed, yet determined for revenge, Nina allowed a sexual assault nurse examiner (SANE), to compile the forensic rape kit. Fortunately she had not washed off all the semen. The nurse skillfully obtained a swab of it and carefully packaged it for DNA testing.

After three hours of poking and prodding, detectives Bill Wilhemus and Bob Higgins arrived.

"Are you feeling up to answering some questions?"

"Not really, but I will," she stammered. "I want those vermin caught.

Calmly, Bill reassured her, "believe me, we do too."

She then related the events as best she could, until it came to the sexual attack. "I have some more to say, but, would it be possible to say it to a female officer," she pleaded.

Both Bill and Bob were aware of the need for the rape kit, more importantly, both had teen-age daughters. Their response came in unison, "We understand. We will have someone here first thing tomorrow morning. Go ahead and get some rest if you can and we'll be back around 8:00am."

"But tomorrow is Easter. I don't want to take you away from your families.

Her honest concern for them caused Bill's eyes to tear up as he imagined his daughter Debbie in Nina's position.

"Young lady, you are more important to us than any holiday. Our families are used to it. It's part of the job, but thank you for caring."

As they were leaving, she yelled, "Wait!"

Bill and Bob rushed to her bedside, "What is it Nina?"

"I almost forgot. One of the robbers called his partner Jo-Jo."

"That's important. Very good, Nina," Bob said as he quickly wrote the name down. He then reached out to shake her hand good-bye and was furious when he recognized the slight recoil from her in an attempt to avoid his touch. Knowing the reason for her action, he slyly shifted his hand elsewhere.

As they walked down to their unmarked car, Bob said, "those god-damned bastards!"

Bill patted Bob's back and angrily replied, "I would love to have those cocksuckers in my gun-sights right now. It would not be hard to pull the trigger on those fuckers. Not hard at all."

"If this happened to my little Pammy, I guarantee you if I arrested them, no way they'd make it to the station. I definitely would ask Petras for some tips on butchering!"

In the car, Bill inquired, "Do you have anyone in mind to meet with Nina tomorrow?"

Bob paused only for a moment and said, "I was thinking Diane Ryan would be the best choice."

"Yeah, I agree. She's tough, experienced, and smart." Bill punched in the number to Diane's desk.

As the phone rang, Bob whispered, "Do *not* call her Di-Di."

That brought on Bill's first smile of the night as he mouthed, "No fucking way."

He relayed Nina's request and Diane readily agreed to the meeting.

"I'll meet you guys in the hospital lobby. You can brief me more there, but I would suggest I visit with her alone."

"Not a problem, Diane. Thanks for your help on this one. It's a bad one," Bill said.

As Diane hung up, she looked at her partner, and said, "Why in hell does God allow scum assholes to exist."

Understanding her anger, Mitch said, "I guess to give people like us some purpose in life."

"Well if that's the case, I would gladly give up some of my purpose if He wants to zap these assholes from the face of the earth."

Knowing it was time to listen and not speak, Mitch simply nodded.

CHAPTER TWENTY-ONE

Jo-Jo and Ray-Ray picked the wrong neighborhood to rob and rape. Very wrong. The mayor really, really, loved his mom. Her wish was his command. LaVerne Kelly loved shopping at *Baltic Nirvana*. She loved to talk. Occasional loneliness caused by her widowed status enhanced this need. Petras was a willing listener. He was honored that the mayor's mama, a lifetime Bridgeport resident, chose to frequent his establishment. Besides that, he truly liked her. She truly liked him. She was one of the Easter ham customers that fateful Saturday. Because it was da mayor's mom's neighborhood, the vicious attack was front page news. The Monday after Easter she called her son at City Hall.

"Joseph Chester Kelly, you must catch those monsters that attacked Petras and hurt poor Nina!"

"Yes, mom," Mayor Kelly answered to the shrieking voice blasting from his cell phone.

"Make it a priority, understand!"

"Yes, mom."

They then fell into familiar banter about her grandkids, but she did end the call with, "Don't forget, make sure to keep me posted."

"Yes, mom." The mayor, a dutiful son, immediately buzzed his secretary Eleanor. "Get the Superintendent on the phone now."

"Stash, what have you got so far on the *Baltic Nirvana* case," he inquired.

Stanley Kowalski, the hard-nosed superintendent replied, "Nothing yet. It's only been two days, but I have two of my best officers working on it."

"Stash, I want to be very plain on this, both victims are good friends of LaVerne's. I'm sure you know what that means."

"Boy, do I. I have a Polish mom. Irish moms have this in common with them: they are relentless."

"Exactly. So I would appreciate it if you increase the pressure so we can close this case quickly."

"I'll do my best."

Joe knew Stash's best was way above the average so he ended the call with a thank you.

CHAPTER TWENTY-TWO

The Don wasted no time in completing the task that *Mr. C* ordered via *The Surgeon.* Because of his health, no one questioned the transformation that took place in his River Forest home. It was not unusual for rich Baby Boomers in very bad health to have a hospital emergency room built as an addition to their homes.

Tony's massive ornate basement family room now boasted all the bells and whistles of a first class hospital room: medicine cabinets overflowed, a sterile area was assembled, proper hospital apparel, oxygen tanks, an anesthesiologist section, and, a surgeon's area. It had all the appropriate hardware to perform any type of surgery. The project started on a Monday. By Wednesday evening it was complete.

"Wow, this is really first class, I can't believe you got it done so quickly."

"Like I said, Dr. Baxter, I don't have much time to waste," was Tony's laconic reply.

"*Mr. C* wants us to communicate with each other if necessary only by using our code names." Jack then shared the assembled team's names, *Eyes, Ears, Abs, Biceps, Actress,* and of course *Surgeon.*

"What's mine?" asked Tony.

"*The Don.*"

A faint smile crossed Tony's face as he commented, "I like that one very much. It shows nice respect."

"Please don't be offended, but *Mr. C* wants the rest of the team to be anonymous to you and to some of the others as a way to protect them and to make your role work best. So you will not be meeting with them or learn their real names."

"I'm not offended, rather I'm impressed," Tony replied. "I would not have stayed alive in my business without being very cautious. I highly respect caution. In this case it is a smart thing to do."

Jack released a sigh of relief upon hearing this.

"What I do want to know is when do we get started?" Tony asked.

"I spoke with *Mr. C* yesterday and he has one in his sights as we speak."

Tony nodded and leaned forward and asked, "What and who?"

"That I do not know yet," Jack answered. "He told me the details will be on a need to know basis for the team members, but he assured me it will be worthwhile and the result will be available for us."

"Good, I will then wait for my need to know." Tony reached for the bottle of his beloved Grappa and poured two generous glasses. He handed one to Jack, and toasted "Salute, *Surgeon*."

Jack could not hold back his smile over the use of his code name by Tony. "Salute to you too, *Don*."

A solemn silence followed as both men considered the beginning of this journey for justice.

CHAPTER TWENTY-THREE

The black, non-descript van driven by *Ears* with *Eyes* riding shot-gun proceeded to pick up the passengers at the pre-arranged locations for the evening meeting. Once loaded, silence prevailed. As the van drove up to the abandoned warehouse in the now closed industrial section surrounded by railroad tracks on South Pulaski, the garage door silently opened and the van snuck in. Most Chicagoans were sleeping off Easter leftovers.

On Tuesday, two days after Easter, at precisely 1:00 a.m., *Mr. C's* team exited the van and approached the chairs that had been set up for the evening's discussion. A small lantern nestled on a small table a few feet in front of the chairs emitted a faint glow. From the shadows, a man with a ski mask moved to the table and placed his notes next to the lamp.

"Good morning, I am *Mr. Consequence*. We all know why we are here." He then pointed to the ski mask and said, "Some of you know my identity, others do not." He took a sip of water and continued, "I trust all of you, but I thought it would be prudent to keep my identity covert to those who do not. I do not want to put any of you at risk, your value to this operation is paramount and knowing my identity might cause an inadvertent slip up. In fact, to protect us all, everyone was given a code name. Our real names will not be used from this point on. Agreed?" All heads nodded. "Good. Before I share our first objective I thought it would be beneficial for all of us to share our experiences so we all understand the intensity of our individual commitments."

The next thirty minutes reinforced the zeal of each member as the heart-wrenching stories about their victimized loved ones brought on tears as well as clenched fists.

Lastly, when *Actress* finished recounting Renaldo's tragedy, *Mr. C* gravely stated, "Ok, ready to get started?"

Biceps' passionate response of "Fucking A," accurately summed up the team's readiness.

"Is the camera in place, *Eyes*?" *Mr. C* asked.

"Yep," he responded as he held up the tracking monitor he carried in the palm of his hand. "If anyone approaches within 1000 yards of this place, this baby will tell me pronto." *Mr. C* smiled and said, "I told you I like to be cautious."

He continued, "Here is our first mission. I assume you have all heard about the attack at the *Baltic Nirvana* butcher store?" Various signs of consent followed. "I am fairly certain that based on data I have reviewed, the attack on the owner Petras, and his daughter Nina, is pointing to a blatant act committed by repeat offenders." He took another sip of water then explained. "Recently,

Eyes and *Ears* were able to help me pinpoint a lead on the perps that did this. A number of businesses on Archer use their surveillance company. *Eyes* did a quick scan of their monitors at the time of the attack and he was able to get a partial plate number and a vehicle description of a car that was parked in the alley behind *Baltic Nirvana*. It shows two masked men leaving *Baltic's* back door and getting in the vehicle."

Ears then added, "Yesterday morning I immediately visited the two detectives on the case and shared the information." He grinned, "While I was at the station I placed a miniscule listening recorder under their desk. If they get a bead on who the punks are, we will know. In fact, I have already shared some important elements of the crime with *Mr. C*."

"Once we know who, what *is* the plan?" asked *Abs*.

"*This* is the plan," *Mr. C* solemnly stated. He recounted the aspects of the case that *Ears* had uncovered and then laid out the details. "The team members needed to carry it out will be *Abs*, *Biceps*, *Actress* and *Surgeon*. As you can see, *Surgeon* is the key player."

All eyes turned to *Surgeon* as *Biceps* asked, "Can you do this?"

Jack declared, "Not only can I do it, I'll enjoy it!"

Biceps responded with a fist bump and a strong hug.

"I hope to have it coordinated within a week," *Mr. C* said. "You all know how my sister died. Rapists murdered her. This attack on Nina is very close to my heart. Let's make our first mission a successful one."

No one spoke, no one needed to, as nodding heads and resolute faces guaranteed a successful operation. *Mr. C* then handed out Go phones to everyone with code names and phone numbers. "These phones should be untraceable for our use. Just make sure you only use code names. I will replace the phones every thirty days. That's it. We're done for now."

With headlights dimmed, the van drove off. Minutes later, a dark sedan exited as the driver pulled off his ski-mask. He was humming along with the CD which was blasting out the Rolling Stones' song *Satisfaction*.

CHAPTER TWENTY-FOUR

On Monday, Mitch had greeted his partner with, "How did the hospital visit on Sunday go?"

Diane ruefully shook her head before answering. "It sucked big time. That poor girl went through hell." She gave him the blow by blow of the searing scenario that Nina had endured.

"Do the BB's (the nickname the partners Bill and Bob had acquired) have any ideas yet?"

"Some. At least they have a name to scour the streets with. One of the perps is named Jo-Jo. I gave them the rundown on Nina's attack and right now they are checking the M.O. files now to see if they can get a hit. Thank God for computers!"

"Bill, I think I found something here," Bob exclaimed.

"What did you find?"

"Look at this."

Bill hunched over Bob's shoulder and looked at the screen Bob had highlighted.

"It was that *Monkey-Up* comment that Nina told us about," Bob said. "It looks like we have two real good suspects in our sights."

Bill read the names out loud, "Ramon Cortez and Jose Batista." Paging down, the report detailed their criminal past as well as their nicknames, Jo-Jo and Ray-Ray.

"A number of their victims refused to testify," Bob pointed out. "On two occasions, during their initial recorded testimony the victims had alluded to a warning to the same *Monkey-Up* threat that Nina described. That ultimately scared the shit out of them and they recanted, but I'm willing to bet my house that Nina won't cave in. She's one tough cookie."

"I agree," Bill replied. "Okay, look up car registrations on them and last known address."

Bob replied, "I'll also check known people and places they might hang out in," Bob replied.

"I'll print out any pictures I might find on them," Bill said, "and I'll go to the lab and compare them to the tape the surveillance guy dropped off, then we'll hit the streets, okay with you?"

"Copy that, partner."

Ears listened carefully as he meticulously noted the conversation between Bill and Bob. He then picked up his Go-phone and dialed. "*Mr. C*, we have a breakthrough on *Baltic Nirvana*," *Ears* reported.

"I'll stop by your office around 6:00 p.m. Is that okay with you?" asked *Mr. C.*

Ears smiled as he mimicked detective Higgins' response to detective Wilhemus: "Copy that, partner."

At 6:05 p.m. at his office, *Ears* went over the key points of the notes he had jotted down and then played the recording for *Mr. C*. As the tape ended, *Ears* asked, "What do you think? Did I do good?"

"Yes, indeed. This is a major breakthrough. I need to get the team on it ASAP." *Mr. C.* then coldly added, "I think this *Monkey-Up* thing might have real potential."

CHAPTER TWENTY-FIVE

On Wednesday, still dazed after a night of pot smoking and tequila shooters, Jo-Jo was violently being shaken awake. "Wake up now, Cabron!"

The person shaking him was Carlos, the owner of the three-flat in Brighton Park that currently housed about twenty renters, give or take a few. Rents were paid weekly in cash. How the cash was obtained was of no concern to Carlos as long as it eventually landed in his wallet. When Jo-Jo and Ray-Ray returned from the *Baltic Nirvana* that evening, with many bottles of tequila and enough pot to last a month, bragging that they had scored big, Carlos simply smiled and said, "The rent is due." When Jo-Jo peeled off the rent money from a huge wad of cash, Carlos added, "And rent will be going up soon."

Now, however, a major problem had cropped up for Carlos.

"God damn it Cabron. Wake up."

Jo-Jo groggily opened his eyes and said, "I'm up, I'm up."

Once Carlos had his attention he explained. "There's some bad shit going down with the cops about you and Ray-Ray. Two detectives were up and down the neighborhood a couple of hours ago asking about a Jo-Jo who drives a black Camaro."

Jo-Jo's reply reflected his IQ, "Oh Shit."

"You and Ray-Ray need to leave at once. It seems that big score of yours is about to blow up."

Carlos then offered a way out, for a price of course. "You can't take the Camaro, but don't worry, I moved it into my garage from the street once I got the word. I will make sure it disappears. I have a pick-up truck in good condition, you can have it for a reasonable price and then I suggest you get fucking far away from Chicago. Hell, head for Mexico. You can stay there a long time with the wad you got."

"How much is your reasonable price?" Carlos gave a figure.

Jo-Jo responded, "We'll give you an extra $200 if you forget we ever were here—make sure your tenants know to keep quiet too."

Carlos laughed, "The lack of green cards here will give them all amnesia, the police are not their choice for any conversation."

"Good, I'll wake Ray-Ray now and we'll be gone in an hour."

The pick-up left one hour and fifteen minutes later. The back compartment was crammed with duffel bags of clothes and cash.

"I just got a great idea," Jo-Jo shouted.

"Not so fucking loud, my head is still out of commission," Ray-Ray groggily answered with a cotton-coated tongue. "So what is this idea?"

"The cops are looking for a Jo-Jo and I just remembered why. That bitch Nina must have told them. Remember asshole, you called me by my name when we were there!"

"Ok-Ok, I'm sorry, so what is your idea?"

"We shave our heads and get new names. I know a guy on the Westside that can make us fake ID's. All the pictures that the cops have on file are us with long hair. We get the ID's with shaved heads and new names. I got a feeling we are going to need them since Nina blabbed to the cops so fast, I don't think she is going to *Monkey Up* for us. We need to get this done quick so no one will recognize us, plus it can get us across the border safely."

"Well, it sounds like a good idea, plus we got the money to get it done," Ray-Ray reasoned.

"OK then. I know a *No-Tell Motel* on the Westside near this dude's crib. It'll probably take two days at the most. Then we can head Mexico way," Jo-Jo explained as he headed to the motel.

Ray-Ray exited the lobby of the motel, walked back to the truck and said, "We're in room 164, it is in the back, so we can park out of sight."

Jo-Jo parked the truck directly behind 164. It was not only out of sight but the lot was deserted.

"Don't forget about that bag from Walmart," Ray-Ray said pointing to the bag in the rear compartment.

"Got it." Jo-Jo grabbed his cell and dialed. "Antonio, this is Jo-Jo, what is the name and number of your friend that gets you the fake ID's?"

"What's in it for me?"

"Just give me the fucking number and I'll leave fifty bucks with him to give to you, OK?"

"OK, fifty sounds good, here you go." Jo-Jo then dialed the number. "I need to talk to Smitty."

"Why."

"I'm a friend of Antonio's and need Smitty's skills. I'm willing to pay cash up front for a rush job."

There was a pause, then "How soon can you be at this address?" Smitty said as he recited the address.

"We're about fifteen minutes from there, how does an hour from now work?"

"You said, *we*, how many are you?"

"Two of us." Another pause, "OK, but I want five hundred up front or no deal."

"We'll bring the cash. How long will it take?"

"Once you get here, three hours later you will have them."

"Great, we'll be there in an hour. Just be looking for two bald guys at your door."

Jo-Jo then reached into the Walmart bag and took out the scissors and electric hair trimmer. "Let's get started, we need to get going in 30 minutes. There's a newspaper on the bed—spread it out so we can get rid of the hair easier."

Fifteen minutes later their heads were as smooth as cue balls.

Looking in the mirror, Ray-Ray said, "Fuck this shit. When we get to Mexico I'm growing it back."

Jo-Jo laughed until he looked in the mirror. "Fucking-A. We're definitely growing it back."

Antonio had few friends, but his best friend was money. He wondered, *Is this the Jo-Jo some grandma is looking for?* "What the fuck, I've got nothing to lose," he surmised while hitting speed dial to Hector, one of the street guys that *Abs* had anonymously recruited to spread the word about Jo-Jo and Ray-Ray.

"This is Hector."

"Antonio here. Is that bonus money being offered by grandma on finding those dudes legit?"

"Yes it is, she said she'd be willing to put up four hundred dollars for the information. She really loves her grandson," he added.

"Okay, give her my address and tell her I know where they will be at tonight. But, make sure she brings the cash or no deal."

"I'll get right on it."

Not only did they choose the wrong neighborhood to rob and rape, but they chose the wrong one to hide out and get new ID's. The Westside turf and its residents, law-abiding or otherwise, was well known to two very interested guys: *Abs and Biceps*.

CHAPTER TWENTY-SIX

The BB's were at a standstill as Jo-Jo and Ray-Ray no longer had the Camaro to trace and yesterday's visits to the previous addresses drew blanks as the landlords had no clue where they might be.

The last one angrily noted, "If you find those pricks, let me know. They still owe me two months' rent."

The BB's were back at the station, sipping cups of coffee. "Okay, Bill, today let's hit the known hangouts we have on them."

"What have you got so far Bob?" Bob then rattled off a half dozen places, mainly bars that he had compiled from their former arrests. *Ears* made sure he got them all.

"*Biceps*, this is *Ears* here, I have some info on our objective."

"Write it down and fax it to this number."

Ears jotted the number and within minutes *Biceps* and *Abs* carefully studied the fax and then shredded it.

Biceps said, "If the cops hit these places today and we get there first, it would be a little dangerous for our group. I'm guessing most of these places won't say shit to the cops. Let's wait until tomorrow and take some persuasion with us."

"What kind of persuasion?"

Biceps smiled as he gave his response. "Money."

"I already have some feelers out on the street regarding these guys in case they show up anywhere on the Westside, *Abs* said. "I picked very trustworthy guys to spread the word. I picked dudes that owe us big time for past favors. If they hear anything, I will hear about it. *Mr. C* was able to get the targets pictures and names of some associates. Based on the intel we have, the Westside is their main playground. The dudes I selected are discreetly passing around the hood that a bonus is involved by a grandma who is worried about her grandson and is willing to pay for information as to his whereabouts. Most of these assholes would sell out their grandmas for 10 bucks."

"Good cover," *Biceps* said, "I saw on NBC last night that the mayor is pushing hard on this case. We need to move fast if we want to beat the cops to these guys. I know three of the places *Ears* mentioned pretty well."

Just then *Abs'* Go phone vibrated in his pocket. He checked the caller ID. It was the son of a friend. The son had been an addict and *Abs* had stepped in to help his friend financially and spiritually to get the boy on the road to recovery. The boy had won the battle and now worked at the Westside *Max to the Mike*. He was clean now for three years and worshiped *Abs*. Even though he no longer did drugs, he still remembered his former street contacts. His name was Hector. Abs listened.

"Thanks, Hector." After the call from Hector, he immediately called *Actress.* "Remember the scenario we discussed?"

"Of course I do," she replied.

"Well we have got to move fast—how soon can you be ready."

"About 45 minutes. Will that work?"

"It should. We'll be calling back before we leave."

Thirty minutes later, *Biceps* anxiously suggested, "Call *Actress* and see if she is ready."

Abs picked up the phone and dialed. "*Actress*, this is *Abs*, are you ready to roll as we planned?"

"Just putting on the finishing touches now. Pick me up at the CTA stop on Roosevelt and Kedzie in 15 minutes."

"We're on our way." Pocketing the phone, he said, "Let's roll, bro."

Rosanna placed the phone on her dressing table and checked herself in the mirror. An elderly, highly wrinkled grandma stared back at her. The acclaimed Woman of a Thousand Faces smiled as she thought, *looking good*!

On the way to pick up *Actress, Biceps* filled in *Mr. C* on their good fortune.

CHAPTER TWENTY-SEVEN

The team's van was parked across the street from Smitty's place. The photos of Jo-Jo and Ray-Ray were judiciously studied in advance. They were now on the look-out. *Actress* was changing in the back of the van. A curtain behind the rear seats hid a mini dressing table and mirror. A large satchel held the many faces she could morph into.

She had given an academy award performance at Antonio's. Antonio had been watching from his window and saw an old lady struggling slowly to his door leaning desperately on her cane. He had the door open before she could knock.

"Did you bring the money?"

"Oh Yes," her voiced squeaked out as she reached into her tattered purse and removed an equally tattered change purse. She then painstakingly counted the bills. They were as wrinkled as she was. "Here's the money," as she painfully extended her now withered hand that was clutching the bills. "And may God bless you my son, please tell me where I can find him, I want him to know I love him and I desperately want to help him."

He wrote Smitty's address on a sticky note and handed it to her. She then clasped his hand and kissed it as tears formed in her eyes. Antonio was so moved by this performance that as she limped away, he called out, "Wait a minute."

She paused and quizzically inquired, "Yes?"

"Here grandma, you can have a hundred back, it looks like you might need it."

She took it and slowly secured it back into the worn change purse. "Bless you again, my child," she said. When the door closed, she could not help releasing a quiet laugh.

It had taken ten minutes to get to Smitty's, and *Biceps* resolutely held the Voyager 3-3A Night Vision Binoculars which *Eyes* had supplied them with.

Abs asked, "Do you think they are inside?"

"I'm not sure, but these binoculars are lighting things pretty clearly, even through his window, and I haven't seen any movement inside."

Abs then yelled to the back to *Actress*, "Do you think Antonio is pulling a fast one on us?"

"I don't think so, he seemed to really care about poor granny."

"Wait," *Biceps* exclaimed, "two guys just got out of a pick-up and are walking up Smitty's stairs. Shit, both are bald." He then adjusted the digital controls to zoom in on the faces. He had memorized the faces from the pictures

Mr. C had provided. He carefully studied the faces through the night vision apparatus and then barked, "Mother-fuck. It's them!" Remembering that *Actress* was there, he added, "Sorry about the language."

"I've heard worse." She grunted.

Smitty's door then opened and Jo-Jo and Ray-Ray entered. Minutes later, a lamp was turned on inside.

"Okay, they're getting started," *Biceps* said as he motioned to *Abs*. "*Abs*, time to go for it, I'll call *Surgeon*."

"I'm on my way."

With the dome light removed, *Abs* silently exited and approached the pick-up truck. He was about to break in when he saw that the passenger door was unlocked. *What stupid assholes these guys are*, he thought.

Abs quickly opened the door and jumped in, killing the illumination of the inside light. He planted the radio frequency device under the dashboard. *Ears* had provided it. It was similar to the one stuck underneath the BB's desk. *Abs* then reached into his jacket and pulled out an unusual looking can with a switch. He set the switch and attached it under the front seat. The can's powerful adhesive kept it firmly in place. He had stayed in touch with many of the lifers he met in *Special Forces*. The can was one of their gifts to him. He quietly exited and returned to the van.

"We'll keep you posted, but it looks like tonight's the night, you need to be ready *Surgeon*," were *Biceps'* closing remarks on the Go phone as *Abs* re-entered the van. "How did it go?"

"We'll know soon enough once they get in the van," Abs replied while he slipped on the listening earpiece that would confirm his answer.

"Is *Surgeon* ready?"

"Yes, he is at home now and not due at the hospital until 3:00 p.m. tomorrow. So if it is a go tonight, he'll be ready."

"Time to alert *Mr. C*," Biceps said as he hit the speed dial. "*Mr. C. Biceps* here."

"How's it going?"

"It looks like these are our guys, but as you requested, we'll wait for a confirmation," explaining the listening device that *Abs* had planted. "*Surgeon* is ready to perform the minute we get confirmation."

"Good, I agree that we strike tonight once confirmation is secured. The update I'm getting on the detectives is that they are very good at what they do."

"We'll just have to be better, won't we," *Biceps* chuckled.

Another chuckle echoed from the other end, "We will."

CHAPTER TWENTY-EIGHT

"Say cheese," Smitty ordered as his digital camera flashed. He checked out the photos and agreed that they would work very well with the new ID's.

Jo-Jo inquired, "What now?"

"Now I go to my backroom lab and create works of art. It'll take a while, so sit tight and watch some TV," he added while handing the remote to the big screen to Jo-Jo. "If you want something to drink, there is beer in the fridge, but it's not free. Ten bucks a can."

"We paid you the five hundred already," Ray-Ray groused.

"Well think about it like this is Wrigley Field, the five hundred got you good seats but you still have to pay for the beer!"

Smitty smugly left the room as Ray-Ray silently fumed. "That fucker," he hissed to Jo-Jo.

Jo-Jo laughed and said, "We need the bastard, and the fucker sure knows the value of supply and demand. Hell Ray-Ray, we probably would charge twenty."

Ray-Ray smiled at that comment and said, "Fucking-A, we would." They grabbed a beer and plopped on the couch.

Actress pulled the curtain back and cooed, "Looking for a good time boys?"

Abs and *Biceps* turned and were stunned.

"I'm in," *Biceps* bellowed as they gazed at the gorgeous and sultry vampish vixen that *Actress* had transformed into.

"Remember, I may be easy but I am definitely not cheap. The going rate is five hundred an hour."

"Book me for a month," *Biceps* said with a drooling grin.

She blushed ever so slightly at his comment and said, "So I guess that means I look good for the next act, huh?"

"Oh yeah, one look at you and they will be putty in your hands," *Biceps* pronounced.

"Ok, let's get the plan straight again and be ready," Abs interrupted. The silly banter stopped immediately. "Here is how it is going down," *Abs* said, revisiting the plan. When he finished, he asked, "Any questions?" Silence prevailed. "Okay then, let's do it."

They were watching the end of the movie *Scarface* as Smitty entered the room. "This is yours, Pasqual, and this is yours, Frederico," handing over the fake ID's embossed with equally fake names.

They stared at their new names and photos as they carefully inspected the impeccably forged ID's.

"I'm impressed," Jo-Jo said, "especially with the edges, it makes the ID's look like they have been around awhile and not brand new."

Ray-Ray equally impressed asked, "Yeah, how did you do that?"

Smitty smiled and replied, "If I told, then anyone could do it, and that's not going to happen."

Ray-Ray fist bumped him and said, "I understand."

"OK, time to go," Jo-Jo said as he slugged down the last of his beer. He tossed a fifty on the table and said, "That's for the beer." They headed for the front door.

CHAPTER TWENTY-NINE

Actress leaned on a lamppost about twenty feet from Jo-Jo and Ray-Ray's parked truck. She chewed loudly on some gum as she brazenly flaunted her leg, a very long naked leg. The streetlight would glowingly entice them to her like the ancient sirens did to the sailors.

They approached the truck and were about to get in when Ray-Ray exclaimed, "Holy shit, check her out."

Actress smiled demurely at them.

"Hell, we got a room and time tonight, might as well have us some pussy," was Jo-Jo's response.

They quickly approached her.

"Hey baby, looking for some fun?"

Actress slowly assessed them and huskily replied, "You don't look like you can afford me."

"Would this change your mind," Jo-Jo smirked as he produced a wad of one hundred dollar bills from his jean pocket.

"That would make a difference," she cooed. "Your place or mine, I don't do trucks," she said pointing to their ride.

Falling for the bait, Ray-Ray quickly said, "We got us a real nice room at a motel, so we got all night to party."

"What motel is it?"

"The Paradise Inn."

Smiling, she said, "I know it well, very well."

They hooted at her comment, and gestured for her to get in the truck.

"Sorry, my pimp drives me to the motel locations. He is a control freak," she complained.

They nodded as they knew how the pimps operated.

"I'll meet you there. What's the room number?"

"164."

"Oh, just a reminder. I get five hundred upfront before we start to play or it is a no go."

"Not a prob. We'll pay you the moment you knock on the door."

She blew them a kiss and in a panting voice said, "I'm already getting hot to party. See you soon."

As the truck pulled away, she rushed to the van.

"They're at the *Paradise Inn*. I know where it is, do you?"

Biceps pulled away smiling. "I may have had some bootie there. Yep, I know where it is, and I even know a short cut."

Abs cut in with, "Okay, now we listen, everybody quiet." He then carefully placed the listening device in his ear. "Good news," he whispered, "I'm hearing them loud and clear."

"Man, I can't wait to get my pipes cleaned," Jo-Jo said.

"Hell I'm hard already just thinking about that fine ass," Ray-Ray replied, then adding, "her ass is even better looking than Nina's was."

"Her ass may be better, but I wonder if she gives head as good as Nina did on me. Hey, maybe her father has a butcher store like Petras's *Baltic Nirvana*. If she does, then we can really *pork* her. Get it, get it, *pork* her," Jo-Jo cracked up over his play on words.

"I get it, and it ain't that fucking funny," Ray-Ray said as Jo-Jo laughed hysterically.

"All I want is a good fuck, maybe a blow-job or two, then get the hell out of Chicago and head to the beaches down Mexico way," Ray-Ray said.

When Jo-Jo's laughter finally ended he said, "Yeah, baby, the beaches of Mexico, some drinks and some fine women. With the money we got from *Baltic Nirvana*, we can party there for a long, long time."

Then Ray-Ray tried his hand at humor with, "Yeah, we can really *ham it up*, get it, get it?"

Jo-Jo did.

The next thing *Abs* heard was raucous laughter.

"It's a confirmation. Call *Mr. C*."

CHAPTER THIRTY

"*Surgeon*, it's a confirmation. Are you ready?"

"All packed and ready to go, *Mr. C*. When can I expect the van to pick me up?"

"It'll be there be there in thirty minutes."

"I'll be ready," *Surgeon* assured him.

Mr. C's next call was to *The Don*. "It's a confirmation for tonight."

"Good, the garage will be open and all the doors are unlocked for you."

"Remember, it is best if you stay out of sight for the team's benefit."

"I'm old, but not senile. Consider it done."

"Thank you."

"Believe me, no thanks are necessary."

Biceps' shortcut got them to the *Paradise Inn* ten minutes before Ray-Ray and Jo-Jo. The van was nestled nicely out of sight in the shadows.

Biceps said to *Abs*, "Be ready to hit the button the moment their engine is turned off."

"Already palming it."

"I hope this is as good as our Armed Forces chum promised."

"I guarantee it is. Mikey really knows this shit," *Abs* said. They would soon find out if Mikey really did know his shit.

It took a while to get back to the motel as they made sure they kept under the speed limit. A speeding ticket would not be a good thing. Ray-Ray then cautiously dowsed the lights as he entered the parking lot. He parked in front of room 164. "Ok, it's party time,'' he excitedly exclaimed. He then turned the engine off. At that precise moment, they heard a popping noise under the seat and soon were engulfed by an unpleasant odor. Moments later they blacked out.

As the van pulled next to the truck, *Abs* and *Biceps* donned gas masks and peeked inside the truck.

"It looks like Mikey does know his shit. Thank you Mikey," *Abs* smiled.

They hustled Jo-Jo and Ray-Ray into the back of the van. "First we get *Surgeon* then we head to *The Don*," *Biceps* commented.

"Ten-four, bro," *Abs* said as they pulled away.

As he entered the van, *Surgeon* asked, "How long can they be expected to be out?"

"My buddy says for at least an hour," *Abs* replied.

"That should give us about 20 minutes once we get to *The Don's*," Surgeon said. "Just in case, I'll move back there with them. I have some needles loaded that will keep them out a hell of a lot longer."

Biceps added, "You 'da man, *Surgeon*."

CHAPTER THIRTY-ONE

They turned on Thatcher in River Forest with the van's lights on dim and turned left into a driveway completely camouflaged by massive shrubberies on both sides, completely concealing their approach.

They quickly moved their cargo to the massive surgical room enhanced basement. *Surgeon, Abs* and *Biceps* dressed up in their surgical gear. *Actress* stayed in the van, changing clothes and identity once again.

"Are you ready?"

"You bet, and we are very experienced in assisting. *Abs* and I did a lot of assisting the medical docs in the field where conditions are not as quite as nice as this."

"The total procedure will take less than an hour. The shots they were given should keep them out for about four hours. Let's get to it." And they did.

Two hours later, the van parked next to the truck at the *Paradise Inn*. *Actress* had taken the room key from Jo-Jo. She cautiously wore rubber gloves when she had rummaged through Jo-Jo's pockets. She opened the door to the room keeping the lights off. The dome light of the van was also disabled.

Surgeon then discreetly drove the van away saying, "I'll be back in fifteen minutes to pick you up." It had been decided that it would be more prudent not to keep the van parked there for any length of time.

They then firmly duct taped Jo-Jo and Ray-Ray to the two chairs in the room. They appeared to be sitting erect. *Actress* reached into an oversized purse and removed the prearranged signs and handed them to *Biceps*. She then went to the pick-up truck and removed the canister and listening device. The windows had been left open so the windy night erased any trace of Mikey's gift.

Abs and *Biceps* then carefully taped the signs to Ray-Ray and Jo-Jo in the appropriate places. The last sign was placed at their feet. *Biceps* summed up their efforts with a "justice is fucking served."

They completed the task four minutes before Surgeon would return. It was then *Abs* noticed a bulging duffel bag whose end was exposed in a futile attempt to place it under the bed. He opened it and Petras's hard earned money introduced itself.

Smirking, *Abs* said "I have an idea." He used his non-writing hand to disguise its author and penned a note which he then attached to the bag placing it under the cocktail table. He asked his brother, "What do you think?"

"Great idea."

The van came and they left.

CHAPTER THIRTY-TWO

Bill groggily answered the phone.

"Bill, this Bob. Get dressed quick. 9-1-1 just got an anonymous tip that we can find Jo-Jo and Ray-Ray in room 164 at the *Paradise Inn*."

"Who called it in?"

"Don't know, it came from a pay phone and the caller did not leave a name. But 9-1-1 said it sounded like a really old lady."

"I'm on my way, better call some back-up." *Actress's* transformational abilities also applied to her voice as well.

The front desk clerk's eyes were already bloodshot from the bottle of Jack Daniels under the counter as Bob walked in. Showing his ID he demanded, "I need the key to room 164, now!"

Stumbling to the wall where the extra room keys hung, he removed the key and handed it to Bob.

"Don't leave the lobby," Bob said. "Stay put. Understand?"

"No fucking way I'm going out there," he slurred, after noticing the revolver Bob had pulled from his holster. "Good."

"Here is the plan," Bill said to Bob and the back-ups. "We don't give them any time to react, so we do not knock on the door. I'll quietly insert the key and Bob and you have your pistols ready. The clerk said this place is so old that chains were never placed on the inside room doors, so once the key is in we move quickly. Any questions?" They all shook their heads no.

"Let's do it."

The key was quietly inserted and Bill whispered, "On three." He then signaled with his fingers: *one, two, three*. He pushed the door open and they all barreled in. Bill was the first to enter with Bob and the two back-ups close behind.

Shocked by the scenario, Bill shouted, "What the fuck is this?"

The two unconscious bodies had small signs taped to various parts of their bodies. There also was a large sign at their feet. The small ones were taped to their ears, mouths, eyelids, and crotch. These signs respectively proclaimed:

HEAR NO EVIL
SEE NO EVIL
SPEAK NO EVIL
DO NO EVIL

With their guns drawn, Bill and Bob slowly approached Jo-Jo and Ray-Ray.

"Randy, check out the closet and bathroom," Bob said to Officer Albright, one of the back-ups.

Randy quickly moved forward and after a thorough look over, reported, "all clear."

"Don't touch a fucking thing, I want our lab to go over this room with a fine tooth comb," Bill stated.

On closer examination, Bob noticed some blood had trickled down the sides of the suspects' necks. The source was the ear canal.

"Do you think this has something to do with that *HEAR NO EVIL* sign?"

"It sure looks like it," Bill said to his partner.

"Pass me a pencil."

Bill pulled one from his shirt pocket and handed it to Bob. Bill carefully used the eraser side and lifted one of the eyelids.

"Holy shit, looks what's missing," he said as a gaping hole greeted him where an eye once rested. He then used the same procedure to open Ray-Ray's mouth.

As the lips opened, Ray-Ray was not about to give him a tongue-lashing since he no longer had one to lash out with. "Mother-fucker, how much do you want to bet these guys are now eunuchs," Bob said pointing to the signs resting on their crotches that proclaimed, *DO NO EVIL*. There were no takers. "I'm calling this in now," Bill said reaching for his phone. "Hi Beverly, Bill here, we need lab techs here ASAP. Send them to the *Paradise Motel* on Cermak, room 164. Also send an ambulance here pronto. We have the two suspects from the *Baltic Nirvana* caper in custody. Make sure they bring restraining straps for the gurneys. They are unconscious now, but when they wake I expect some major gyrations from them."

Bill then read the sign propped at their feet. It read:

MAY THIS BE A WARNING TO THE BAD GUYS.

GET OUT OF JAIL FREE CARDS WILL NO LONGER BE ACCEPTED.

IT IS NOW TIME TO REALIZE
I WILL BE DISPENSING THE APPROPRIATE CONSEQUENCES.

I AM EVERYWHERE AND I WILL BE LOOKING–

SO BE AFRAID—BE VERY AFRAID.

TRUST ME—YOU DO NOT WANT TO BE NEXT IN LINE—

I WILL MAKE THE BAD GUYS PAY.

– MR. CONSEQUENCE

"Looks like we got us another Charles Bronson," Bob said, referring to the vigilante movie, *Death Wish.*

"In spades," was Bill's reply.

"How much do want to bet that the lab techs find squat in trace?" Once again Bob had no takers.

The police ambulance was there five minutes later. As they removed the bodies, one of the backups noticed the duffel bag bulging with the cash from *Baltic Nirvana's* Easter receipts. The attached note on the bag read:

POLICEMEN,

THIS BELONGS TO PETRAS.

PLEASE GIVE IT BACK TO HIM

"Bill said, "Well, it's obvious that this guy isn't in it for the money.

Bob said, "Bill, if I weren't a cop and sworn to uphold the law, I might like this *Consequence* guy."

He got no response, but did get a few smiling faces nodding affirmatively at his remark.

"We need to fill the captain in on this," Bob said to the back-ups. "Why don't you two follow the ambulance to make sure everything goes smoothly at the prison hospital?" That was where the medics suggested the two be taken. "Make sure you remind the docs there that restraints are highly recommended. When that's done you guys can head home."

"Will do, Bob," said Randy.

"We would go with you, it is pretty obvious we need to clue Captain Krol on this one as soon as we can. My guess he will be shitting bricks when he hears about this baby. Anyone want to bet on that one?"

Once again, Bob had no takers.

Mr. C never knew who was responsible for his sister's death. But if he had, he would have been very, very pleased with his first mission for true justice. Ray-Ray's full proper name was Ramon Cortez Jr. Ramon Sr. was killed in a drive-by shooting over a gang turf war when Junior was two months old. His father belonged to a gang named *Satan's Dudes*. His best friends in the gang were Aldo and Luis.

Yes, had he known Mar-Beth's attackers, *Mr. C* would have been very pleased.

CHAPTER THIRTY-THREE

"Man, even though I've got ten years in, that was definitely a fucking first for me," Sid said to his partner Randy as they left the prison hospital after making sure that Ra-Ray and Jo-Jo were secured properly.

"You got that right, I don't think this is going to be a *One and Done*," Randy said remembering the warning to the *BAD GUYS*.

"So you think this is just the beginning?"

"That, my friend, is one I would bet on," Randy chuckled remembering Bob's no taker betting offers that evening. Randy then fell silent as he excitingly had a thought. The squad pulled into its assigned space at the precinct. "See you tomorrow afternoon Sid."

"Thanks for the warning," Sid kidded back.

Randy smiled at the retort and the smile grew wider as he anxiously headed home.

Entering the front door he shouted for his wife, "Honey, wake up. You're gonna love me for this one." His *honey* happened to be Abigail Albright.

She recently was promoted to a reporter for the Chicago Sun-Times. She drowsily walked down the stairs. "What the hell's all the ruckus about?"

"Remember how excited you were two weeks ago when you got the promotion. I got a feeling your next promotion is right around the corner."

"What are you talking about?"

"Only one of the biggest stories to hit Chicago—ever. And, you're in line for the scoop."

Her eyes immediately shed the dust that the sleep fairy had left behind.

"Okay, you have my attention, what's cooking?"

The next twenty minutes he filled her in on the night's escapades.

"My God, this is huge. I'll be right back." She rushed to grab the phone from the family room and speed-dialed her editor. "Steve, I'm sure you haven't heard or even responded to a request like this in a long time. Steve, stop the presses. Do I ever have a story for you!"

As Steve listened, his greed and voracious appetite for a great story were being satiated. "Abigail, if this is legit, it is definitely a stop the presses story. How soon can you write it up and e-mail it to me."

"Would thirty minutes do it?"

"Yes, it would. Get to work."

She headed for the upstairs computer room. Halfway up the stairs she turned and said, "I'll be writing this up and be sending it to Steve. Why don't you take a quick shower and I'll meet you in bed. I have it on good authority that you are going to get very, very, lucky tonight." She provocatively tongued her lips then proceeded to rush to the computer room.

Abby's comment produced another large smile on Randy's face. Seconds later, he rushed toward the shower undressing on route. Under the hot spray of the shower, his thoughts wandered to the anticipated use that Abby had for her tongue and his body.

CHAPTER THIRTY-FOUR

"Holy shit, did you hear what the BB's brought in early morning today to the prison hospital?"

"No I didn't, Diane, what's so holy shit about it," Mitch said as he handed her a cup of coffee and an éclair.

They took turns bringing the java and pastries in as their daily shifts began.

"Mmm, you bought the good stuff today," she said as she savored the first bite of the éclair. She then took the coffee out of the bag Mitch had passed over. "Yes, you got the good stuff on the *joe* too," noticing the Starbucks logo on the large cup of coffee. "Okay, here's what went down this morning."

Mitch listened mesmerized as Diane described in vivid detail the arrests of Jo-Jo and Ray-Ray.

"Man that is definitely a holy shit situation," Mitch said as Diane finished. "What's your take on it, Diane?"

"Well, if you recall, I was asked to interview the daughter, Nina. So I may not be partial on this one. After Nina told me what happened, my first thought was that those assholes got what they deserved. But the cop in me says we can't have citizens going around playing judge and jury. So while I really don't feel sorry about what happened to them, I have a feeling this is a beginning and not an end. It could turn to chaos quickly, very quickly."

As Mitch nodded, Captain Krol walked up to their desks with a Sun-Times tucked in his arm.

"Mrozek, Ryan, in my office now." He turned towards his office, walking rapidly before either of them could respond.

"I don't think that sounds like a good thing, partner," Mitch whispered to Diane as they followed him to his office. They each grabbed a cup of the good stuff coffee from the Captain's always present carafe before grabbing a seat in front of his desk.

The captain slammed the Sun-Times down with the command, "Read this." Abigail's report was directly under the headline, ***NEW CONSEQUENCES FOR BAD GUYS***.

"We heard about it earlier," said Diane as she handed the paper back.

"We cannot tolerate citizens enforcing their interpretation of the law."

"No we can't, Captain," they chorused.

"Glad to hear that those are your sentiments too." Krol then paused before continuing.

"I want this menace caught ASAP. You two are in charge. Use any resource we have available."

"When do want us to start on this, we are in the middle of the double vagrancy homicide."

"That case has already been reassigned. This one must have your full attention, understood?"

They nodded affirmatively.

"That will be all. Get started today and have a daily report on my desk every morning until we catch this Consequence guy. Dismissed."

Silence reigned between them as they returned to their desks.

"So what's the plan," Diane asked.

Mitch pondered this, then replied, "Let's make an appointment with Sammy and see if she can shed some light on what we should be looking for."

"Good idea, I'll ring her office now."

Samantha Silverstein was the department's profiler. She had spent seven years in Chicago's FBI office. She and her family loved Chicago and when she received the notice for an impending transfer to D.C., she respectfully declined and applied at Superintendent Kowalski's office. Stash had worked with the FBI and Sammy on a couple of cases and he knew she was the real deal. She was hired immediately.

"Sammy here, how can I help you?"

"Hi Sammy, this is Diane Ryan, have you read the Sun-Times this morning?"

"Yes I did. Is this about Mr. Consequence?"

"You nailed it. Mitch and I were assigned the case this morning."

"Lucky you, how can I help?"

"We'd like your take on what kind of character we might be looking for."

"When would you want to meet?"

"As soon as possible, hopefully today."

"I have a full schedule, but I can break away for lunch at 11:00am. I have to be back at the office at 1:00 p.m. How about we meet at Manny's?"

"Sounds great, a hot corned beef on Jewish rye, here I come."

"I'm partial to the pastrami, but I fully understand your enthusiasm," she chuckled while adding, "the kosher pickle on the side ain't too shabby either." Diane laughingly agreed and hung up.

"We meet at 11:00 a.m. at Manny's for lunch."

Mitch smiled at the news and said, "A really good choice. You bring your notepad and I'll bring an appetite." He graciously accepted the resulting punch on the arm.

CHAPTER THIRTY-FIVE

"Yes *Mr. C*, I have written the access codes down. When it downloads what do you want us to do with them?" asked *Eyes.*

Mr. C described in detail the task he wished *Eyes* to do.

"I like that very much. Based on the publicity Jo-Jo and Ray-Ray's plight has garnered, I believe it will be quite the deterrent," agreed *Eyes.*

"I guess we'll see, but I do believe it has its merits."

"My bro and I will hop right on it."

"You mean you and *Ears*," discreetly reminding him to always use code-names when on the phone.

"Right, *Ears* and I."

The access codes that were provided to them provided current names and addresses of rapists and pedophiles that were not currently incarcerated. The tainted excuses that allowed them to roam the streets varied: women fearful to testify; women too embarrassed to testify; children too shocked to testify; mistrials, etc. The brothers were dumbfounded when the number passed one hundred.

"Damn, this is a freaking epidemic," *Ears* remarked.

"One that we hopefully have the cure for," *Eyes* wryly noted. Once the list was complete, they went to work.

After a few hours, they completed the task. It took a little longer because of the rubber gloves they used to hide all trace.

"They're all nicely tucked in," said *Eyes.*

"I'll make a quick run to the post office for some stamps," *Ears* offered.

Eyes suggested, "Don't buy them at the counter, use the machine in the outer lobby and make sure you wear the gloves and no one is nearby."

"That was my plan. In fact, I have a stack of new bills from the bank and I removed the ones in the middle to use in the machine. And yes, bro, I used the gloves when I removed them. You can never be too careful."

Ears returned within the hour and they proceeded to stamp each of the prepared envelopes. Each contained the same message:

I AM SURE YOU HAVE SEEN THE NEWS
OR READ THE SUN-TIMES RECENTLY
REGARDING YOUR FELLOW RAPISTS JO-JO AND RAY-RAY.

I WILL BE WATCHING YOU VERY CLOSELY.

I WILL ONLY BE TOO HAPPY
TO RENDER YOU INCAPABLE OF EVER RAPING AGAIN
SHOULD YOU BE STUPID ENOUGH TO DO IT AGAIN.

IF YOU DO NOT UNDERSTAND WHAT I MEAN—
GET A DICTIONARY AND LOOK UP THE WORD *EUNUCH.*

—MR. CONSEQUENCE

The brothers split up the envelopes and headed out in separate cars. Each headed to ten different mailboxes. Some were in the suburbs, so it took over three hours to accomplish. But that was OK, because you can never be too careful.

Unbelievably, five of the recipients brought the letters to the local police stations and demanded protection. All were told in different words but the words all carried the same message: "It's simple, don't rape anyone in the future and our protection will not be needed."

A similar letter was sent to Abigail Albright. *Mr. C* asked her to use the front page of the Sun-Times to make sure future rapists that had not yet made his hit list also were forewarned. Abigail happily obliged. In case these future rapists did not read the Sun-Times, over the next few days both television and radio used it as their lead story.

The next month Abigail's research revealed a 93% drop in reported rapes. She eagerly noted in her now familiar place on page one, "I don't think it's a coincidence. I guess a big thank you should go out to Mr. Consequence."

Sitting at his kitchen table sipping a hot coffee, a certain individual placed the Times down after reading her column.

"You're very welcome Abigail," the smiling man mused.

CHAPTER THIRTY-SIX

Max and Mike missed mom's fried chicken. They discovered a decent replacement at a restaurant near Loyola appropriately named, *Just Like Grandma's.* Jonas Higby, a long-time friend of the family, also missed Bertha's wonderful Sunday chicken dinners. He had been a guest at Bertha's succulent dinners a few Sundays each month. Dennis fought brain cancer and it won three years ago. Bertha followed him six months later. Her death certificate stated heart attack. Her closest friends claimed it was definitely a heart issue; not a heart attack, but a broken heart.

Jonas had been Tabitha's Sociology teacher at DuSable. It was his influence that fueled her interest in social work. After her tragic death he made a point of visiting with Dennis and Bertha to offer comfort. His initial sympathetic concerns soon transformed to a rock solid friendship. He was a widower as well as being childless.

Bertha would insist that he join them often for a good home-cooked meal. Jonas, whose kitchen skills were null and void, thankfully accepted. Often the dinner conversations would recall moments in Tabitha's short life. Both tears and laughter joined the conversations at these moments. Everyone wanted to remember Tabitha, so no memory of her seemed awkward to discuss, none at all.

With Dennis and Bertha gone, Max and Mike started meeting with Jonas at *Grandma's* monthly. They all shared an equal love of mashed potatoes, fried chicken, and conversation. Lunch usually lasted three hours. Their lunch order never wavered from their beloved meal. Each ordered fried chicken, mashed potatoes, and extra gravy. It wasn't as good as Bertha's but it was close enough to spawn fond memories of those Sunday dinners.

"We lost three more to those bastards this month, and the damn count keeps growing," Jonas angrily declared.

"What bastards, Jonas?" Max asked.

"The damn dope peddlers. You name it, they sell it, pot, meth, crack, and more types of pills that you can count," Jonas said with disgust.

Max intently asked, "What do you mean by you lost three more?"

"These three students were on the honor roll last year. Now they are flunking everything and can barely remember their own names. The drugs have fried their brains big time. What once were bright futures have turned to shit—excuse my French."

Mike carefully asked, "Have the police been looking into it?"

"Ha! You two know the routine. In our neighborhood the police could give a rat's ass. They figure it is part of the culture there to do drugs. Plus, when a pusher gets arrested, he is back on the streets in a few days. The courts really don't care and the drug kingpins and their pushers know it, so there is nothing that can be done to stop this massacre of young minds."

Max shot his brother a knowing look and said, "Who knows, Jonas, hopefully something can be done someday, who knows."

Mike immediately caught the intent behind Max's look. The twins had the simultaneous thought, "Maybe *Mr. C* could help."

"I sure hope so, hope being the key word," Jonas replied.

The brothers then changed the topic to the Bulls chances this year. Jonas was sure that this would be Da Bulls' year to go all the way. The twins heartily agreed.

As the bill was placed on the table, Max was quick to nab it. Jonas and Mike left a generous tip. There was a reason the three waitresses at *Grandma's* always rushed to wait on them each month. The tips always justified the three hour sessions.

Each brother gave Jonas the customary bear hug as they said their goodbyes. "See you guys next month," Jonas said as he ambled away.

"Not if we see you first." All three smiled at the *au revoir* response that was now their customary good-bye.

Once Jonas turned the corner, Max whipped out his Go-Phone. "*Mr. C*, *Biceps* here."

"What's up?"

"*Abs* and I have come up with an idea we need to discuss with the entire group."

"Okay, but why don't I stop by your office in Lincoln Park and we talk about it first."

"When?"

"Would two hours from now work for you guys?"

"That works, see you there."

Two hours and fifteen minutes later *Mr. C* offered, "A very, very good idea. I have always been the proactive type rather than a reactive one. I will set up a meeting for tomorrow night at the same warehouse we met last time. I'll get back to you on the time."

As *Mr. C* walked out the door, Mike chuckled, "I have a feeling the having something done soon that Jonas was hoping for may happen very soon."

Max's laconic reply of "Fucking A," summed it up nicely.

CHAPTER THIRTY-SEVEN

She washed down the last bite of hot pastrami with a frosty mug of Berghoff root beer before nodding to the two detectives. "Thanks for the invite guys. I love this joint, but I just don't make the time to eat here as often as I would like."

Sammy then laughingly added, "Maybe I should be grateful, if I came here as often as I would like, I have a feeling not a thread in my closet would fit me."

Diane added, "Yeah, guys got it made, they just throw their beer guts over their belts when clothes get tight. We girls have to spend the big bucks on new outfits. It's not fair."

Sammy smiled and said, "Yeah Diane, but on the bright side it means that we get to go shopping more often."

Diane responded with a fist bump, "Yeah, baby!"

"Okay, time for the serious stuff," Sammy declared as she spread the notes from her briefcase on the table.

"About time, one more word about shopping and I was gonna gag," said Mitch.

"Mitch, just shut up and listen."

"Yes ma'am."

"Is he always that obedient?"

"I trained him well," Diane smirked.

Sammy started, "First off, my guess is we are dealing with someone whose anger stems from a childhood memory."

"Why," asked Mitch.

"The use of the words: *IT IS TIME TO MAKE THE BAD GUYS PAY* in his warning. A more adult comment would be a word like criminals. *Bad Guys* is definitely a child's synonym for criminal. If he has a hard time letting go of that childlike rendering, it must have been quite a traumatic event for him to emphatically use this form of verbalization."

"So our suspect probably had some tragedy that occurred when he was young," Diane asked.

Sammie nodded affirmatively. Diane quickly jotted it down.

"Any other observations," Mitch asked.

"Yes, a couple more. This guy's home is probably as neat as a pin. The intricacies of what was done to those punks, I mean victims—"

Diane interrupted as her fist banged the table, "You were right the first time. After what they did to that family, punks would be too good a word for them."

"Yeah, I read the report too, Jo-Jo and Ray-Ray were definitely not model citizens."

"Hell, they weren't model animals," Mitch sneered.

"Anyway, as I was saying this *Mr. C* guy has impeccable planning skills. He wants everything in its place, he is very organized. His home would reflect a very neat person."

Sammy paused so Diane could write this down. "Next, we have a real enigma here. In his note he refers to himself in the singular. If he accomplished all what was done by himself, the only thing that could harm him would be kryptonite. The circumstances indicate a group, not a person. By using the singular pronoun, he wants no attention directed to the members of his group, yet he still desires publicity. Either he or others are extremely skilled surgeons. From the reports back from the prison hospital, the procedures that were done were not only effective but expertly done. In my professional opinion, this is definitely a team effort."

Sammie paused for a moment as Diane continued to scribble in her notepad. She continued, "Then, there is the matter of the *Monkey* references in the notes he left behind. Not only did he pinpoint the victims, but their criminal history was known. This would indicate he is quite influential with a solid networking channel, or is very good with a computer. Finding the punks and knowing their MO's indicates he has access to vast information, either through contacts or is highly skilled at hacking." Diane's pen continued its rapid pace. "Then, there is an indication that someone is very, very strong."

Diane looked up from her notepad, "why do you say that?"

"First the abduction and then moving them back in the motel. It is not easy carrying around that dead-weight. If only one person was involved, his strength is incredible. That's another reason I am leaning towards this being a team effort."

Both nodded solemnly as Diane continued to write.

Mitch asked, "Are we dealing with some criminal or an evil psychopath?"

"I would say no. The *Get Out Of Jail Free* decree in his warning indicates someone that is anti-crime. However, his treatment of Ray-Ray and Jo-Jo and the *Monkey* notes stuck on them show he is determined to make sure the *Bad Guys* will not be doing any repeat performances. He is definitely going to be thorough in his actions. My guess is that a logical consequence will probably reflect the crime. Anger definitely exists, but I don't believe executions will become any future consequence. This guy wants the *Bad Guys* to be very afraid and the living hell that is facing Jo-Jo and Ray-Ray is much more frightening than a blip in the obituaries."

"That's the best I can offer right now. As more consequences develop, and I would definitely bet there will be, I would be able to offer some additional perspectives."

“Thanks, this should help our efforts,” Diane said offering her hand to Sammy.

“Remember I am fallible, not infallible,” Sammy said as she squeezed the offered hand.

“You’ve done well, what you offered is logical. I always liked logical,” said Mitch as he too offered his hand.

“Thanks, don’t hesitate to call me as the case progresses.”

The “will do, Sammy” was said in such unison that Mitch softly punched Diane’s arm and said, “*check a Coke.*”

Mitch’s playful use of that decades’ old custom when two people say the same words simultaneously, the one receiving the punch buys the puncher a Coke, set off chuckles all around and signaled the end to the lunch.

Heading back to the office Diane asked, “So, what is your take on Sammy’s conclusions?”

“Like I said, sounds logical, but, this isn’t Sheriff Taylor’s Mayberry. Since we don’t have *Mr. C’s* address, that means that out of the nine million people that inhabit the Chicago area, if Sammy is right, then we should be able to narrow it down to about two million.”

“We need more info, huh Mitch?”

“Ya think?”

“Okay, Diane, now we get to earn our pay. When we get back to the precinct let’s put an Action Chart and an Info Chart together. Then we can try to turn over some stones.”

“How?”

“An Action chart will give us places to go and people to see, hopefully the Info Chart will expand from there.”

She groaned, “Sounds like a long day ahead. Pull over by Starbucks and I’ll spring for some large coffees.”

“That would be a good start.” Mitch stopped by the entrance and Diane rushed in to grab the coffees. Mitch smiled and thought, “It’s much better to be the driver than the gopher; much better.”

CHAPTER THIRTY-EIGHT

The abandoned warehouse on South Pulaski once again welcomed the black van. *Mr. C's* team members exited the van and took their seats. In front, the main table held a podium. Behind the podium was the ski-masked *Mr. C.*

"Welcome. Tonight I would like to share some thoughts on our next mission. *Abs* and *Biceps* have come up with a plan that has merit. Would you please share your ideas with the team?"

Abs stood first and explained, "Rather than wait around while sifting through news for the next target, *Biceps* and I felt we could better accomplish our agenda by being proactive. Let me explain how." He described in detail the luncheon they had with Jonas. Heads nodded affirmatively as he suggested zeroing in on the drug pushers that were poisoning the minds of Jonas's students.

Actress asked, "What do we do with them after we grab them?"

Smiling wickedly, *Abs* answered, "They mess up minds, so will we." He then shared details.

When he finished, *Surgeon* sighed, "Looks like some long nights for me."

Biceps walked up to him and asked, "Can you handle it?"

"In the words of *Biceps*, Fucking—A!"

Laughter quickly replaced serious.

"Based on this plan the op will require *Actress*, *Surgeon*, *The Don's* house, me and *Biceps,*" *Abs* declared as he opened a notepad.

"Here are the final details; the how, when and where of target number one."

"Looks good," *Surgeon* said. The others nodded their approval.

"At least three dealers will be future targets," *Mr. C* added. He explained why a minimum of three was necessary. You now have the first target. The good news is that he works alone."

A smile quickly formed on *Abs's* face as he added, "To make things easier for the future, did I mention that the item we used last time to knock out the punks was not the only one my buddy Mikey sent me?"

Actress chimed, "how many did he send?"

"Three freaking dozen."

The team swarmed him as hugs and high fives erupted over the news.

Mr. C held up a hand, "Today is Tuesday, can those needed for the operation be good to go by this Friday?"

A euphony of voices responded with a resounding "Yes."

"All right then, the first snatch is a go. We will need to determine the dates for the others. *Eyes* and *Ears* will be providing us with the names. I feel we can complete them all within a two week span. *Abs* will be the team leader on this one since he already has this pusher ID'd."

"Yes I do *Mr. C.*"

Forty-five minutes later the van left the parking lot. Five minutes after that, while removing his ski-mask, the driver in a dark sedan left, again with the Stones' *Satisfaction* playing on the CD. He commented to the CD player, "Maybe you can't get any Mick, but I sure the hell am starting to get some."

CHAPTER THIRTY-NINE

At 8:00 a.m., Diane walked in just as Mitch was finishing up the Action Chart. She grabbed a cup of coffee from the bag on Mitch's desk. It was his turn today. Peeking in the bag she asked, "Where are the rolls?"

"Sorry, I got here early and got hungry."

"You pig. For that you can bring the coffee and rolls tomorrow as well."

"Fine, fine."

She grabbed the Action Chart and asked, "So, see anything we need to run down today?"

"Actually I do. I ran down the names of Alekas's family members. They all have very good incomes, therefore they would have the resources to mete out revenge for the family."

"Yeah, but good enough to have tracked them down and carve them up?"

"Well, like Sammy said, either great resources or computer whizzes. The Alekas family has both within its ranks. I feel it's a place to start unless you have some better ideas."

"No, I guess not. Where should we start?"

Mitch pointed to two names circled on the list, Zak Alekas and Yolanda Micuinis. "Zak is Petras's uncle and Yolanda is Petras's niece. Zak owns a chain of heating and air conditioning stores. He does very well. Yolanda is a professor at Loyola. She has a doctorate in computer programming."

"I see why you picked these two. Both have the characteristics Sammy mentioned."

"Bingo. Like I said, it's a place to start." Mitch handed over the targets' business and home addresses as he grabbed the squad car keys. "Let's go, I'll drive," he said.

"I've already checked out where they'll be. Zak is at the main office of the Cool Breeze and Hot Furnace franchises. It's near Belmont and Western.

"It's the second address next to his name," he said. "Yolanda has a planning period from 11:00 a.m. - 1:00 p.m. I made an appointment with her secretary for 11:30am."

Impressed, Diane said, "Wow, you have been busy this morning. I almost feel like forgiving you for eating all the rolls."

"Does that mean you're buying tomorrow," Mitch hopefully asked.

"No, remember I said I could almost forgive you, the key word being almost."

"Damn, you can really be a tease."

"Yep, it comes with years of practice."

After the chuckles that followed, they plotted out the questions they would ask.

*   *   *   *   *

Zak's secretary escorted them to a back office. Heavy and strong oak furniture mirrored the man. He had an aura that proclaimed, *you don't want to mess with me.*

"Good morning Mr. Alekas, I'm Detective Mrozek and this is my partner Detective Ryan."

After a handshake that had Mitch hoping his knuckles were intact, Zak pointed to two chairs and barked, "Have a seat."

"Thank you," they said as Diane had her pad and pen at the ready.

"I assume you are here because of what happened to the criminals that attacked Petras and Nina."

"That is correct," Mitch paused then continued, "Mr. Alekas, where were you this past Wednesday night."

"You get right to the point, don't you? You think I could be this Mr. Consequence guy." He then hit Mitch with a below zero icy stare. "I was with a crew working on the furnace system for Hinsdale High. We were there until midnight. I have the invoices if you want to see them." He then matched his icy stare with an equally cold voice, "Let me tell you something else, Detective. I understand that this was not the first time those scum robbed and hurt people, yet they still were out on the streets instead of being locked in a cage like the animals they are. Because of Mr. Consequence, it sure looks like it's going to be the last time they hurt anyone." His stare never wavered as he continued, "Detective Mrozek, if I could have done what that Consequence guy did to them, I would have—in a heartbeat. But I couldn't, so I didn't."

"Sir, do you have any idea who might have done it?"

"Just so we are clear on this, *NO*, but if you do find this guy, would you please do me two favors?"

"What are the favors?"

"First, tell him he has the Alekas family's profound thanks. Second, if you do arrest him, let him go."

Zak abruptly stood and announced, "I have work to do, so this interview is officially over. Good day."

Diane politely said, "I understand your attitude, thank you for your time."

"You're welcome, but if you are waiting for me to say good luck in your investigation, you have a very long wait." Zak walked them to the door, ignoring the hand offered by Mitch. He then purposefully closed the door.

"Well, you handled that well," Diane sarcastically noted.

"Let's see how you do. Yolanda will be all yours, big shot."

They headed for Loyola. Their hopes were not high.

CHAPTER FORTY

Max to the Mike was closed for the night, but it was not empty. Huddled in the back office were the principals in *Mr. C's* next caper.

"I'm starting to think that you have some ulterior motive in casting me as a hooker again."

Abs grinned as he held up his hand and mimicked the Boy Scout pledge. "Honest Injun, there is no ulterior motive, seeing that sexy you is the best way to get these guys."

Biceps chimed in, "And you sure ain't hard to look at when you dress up like a painted lady."

Actress fluttered her eyelashes and said, "My, my, I don't know if I can take all these compliments."

The *Surgeon* admonished, "Can we please focus? I'm due back at the hospital in two hours."

Abs nodded, "Sorry doc, here is the set-up." He laid out a poster board with the details.

Forty-five minutes later their roles had been discussed and accepted.

Actress exclaimed, "Wow, *Mr. C* really wants to stop the bad guys cold!"

"You say it like that's a bad thing," *Abs* kiddingly goaded her.

"No, I say it with enthusiastic thanks!"

She offered him a fist bump, and all four of them participated followed by hugs all around.

Biceps closed the meeting with, "Since I will be the driver, I'll be picking each of you up. Try to be ready to roll at least fifteen minutes prior to your pick-up time. We don't want any delays. Precision timing will be the key. Agreed?"

Multiple voices merged into a single "AGREED."

Three drug pushers were about to further promote the mantra of *Mr. C:*

Bad guys, be afraid, be very afraid.

CHAPTER FORTY-ONE

"Loyola is about a twenty minute drive from here, so we will get there about fifteen minutes before our scheduled interview. Any ideas on what you are going to ask her?" Mitch asked.

Diane opened her notebook. "I've jotted down some ideas."

"Breeze them by me."

"First I feel some hacking questions are needed."

"Why?"

"Well, like Sammy said, either Mr. Consequence has one hell of an inside network or is able to use cyberspace really well to extract information. Yolanda is an expert in computers, so that makes for a possibly link."

"Very logical."

"Thank you."

"How do you plan to phrase the questioning? Are you going with the attack mode or educational mode?"

"After meeting Zak, I'm guessing this Mr. Consequence has won over the Alekas clan, big time. So I plan on the educational mode."

"Good choice, then what?"

"Then the usual questions as to her activities that night and others in the family. My next questions will be determined in large part depending on the answers we get."

Mitch pulled into Loyola's short term North-end lot, and sighed, "Good luck partner."

"I'll take all I can get."

The secretary led them into a modest office where computers and books hogged the majority of the square footage.

"Thank you for seeing us, Dr. Micuinis. This is detective Mrozek, and I am detective Ryan."

"May I see some ID," a frosty voice asked. Both showed their badges and Yolanda brought out two folding chairs. She sat behind her desk and asked, "What is the purpose of this visit?"

"We are investigating the subsequent attack that took place on Wednesday against the two suspects in the robbery and attack on your uncle and cousin."

"Suspects, suspects," she fumed. "My cousin gave the police the name of that snake and they had the money they stole in their possession. They're guilty slime, not suspects. In fact, you did such a great job, that after they committed numerous crimes, they were allowed to freely roam the streets again, like a pair of jackals."

Diane countered, "I fully understand your frustration, but I'm sure you realize that this Mr. Consequence who claims credit for the attack, is breaking the law."

"Let me ask you a question, Detective Ryan. Do you believe that all blacks should be arrested and sold as slaves?"

"Of course not."

"Well at one time it was legal, but, was it just?"

Blushing slightly at this rebuttal, Diane answered, "No, it was not."

"Do you believe that since the attack on the United States by Al Qaeda, all Arabs should be rounded up and placed in concentration camps?"

"That would be ridiculous."

"Ask the Japanese-Americans how ridiculous it is since it was the law during World War II. Ask the Native-American Indians how ridiculous it was, as they were herded onto reservations. That was the law then, but was it just?"

A soft spoken "no" was the reply.

"What about the seizing of property and valuables and exterminating an entire race simply because we hate them?"

"That would be absurd."

"Ask the Jews in Europe during World War II how absurd that is. To Germans it was legal, but was it just? Maybe what this Mr. Consequence did isn't legal, but it sure the hell was justice!!"

Diane firmly responded, "All of that was in the past, hopefully we learned from our mistakes." "I wish that the police would learn something from their mistake of releasing these poisonous snakes from prison so that they can continue to terrorize innocent people," Dr. Micuinis angrily replied.

"It's not that simple, but please, I need to ask you a professional question."

"Fine, go ahead."

"We are investigating how this Mr. Consequence might have gotten information on Jo-Jo and Ray-Ray. Is it possible that he may have hacked into Police Records?"

A smile formed on Dr. Micuinis's lips. "Ah, now I see the reason you're here. For someone like me it would be child's play. Had I known he would need this information to corner these rats, I would have been honored to be of assistance. But, no, Detective Ryan, he never asked me, and no, I was not involved in any way, much to my regret." Diane knew that it would be fruitless to continue, so she stood, extended her hand, and thanked Dr. Micuinis for her time.

"Well, this turned out to be wasted day."

"Not really, at least we can remove possible suspects in the Alekis clan from the Action Chart."

He paused then added, "She certainly had logic on her side. That is one smart dame."

"Regardless, we still need to catch this guy. Any ideas?"

"Yeah I do. It's lunch time. Superdawg is a few minutes away, let's grab something to eat there and then head back to the station and redo the Action Chart."

Her stomach rumbled approvingly at the prospect of a Chicago dog. "Sounds like a plan. Actually a good one."

CHAPTER FORTY-TWO

Biceps drove the now loaded van to the planned destination, High-Top's drug dispensary location. Based on information *Eyes* had pilfered from police records, High-Top had been arrested five times and the drug lord's high priced lawyers had him back on the streets within days. He catered to the high school drug scene at DuSable. He was one of the bastards Jonas had complained about to *Biceps* and *Abs* over chicken dinner at *Just Like Grandma's*. Not only was he a known dealer, but he was always willing and eager to exchange dope for sexual favors. Hence, *Actress's* role as a hooker again.

"Here's the hypodermic you will need," Surgeon said as he handed the sharp instrument over to Abs. "There is enough Seconal there to act immediately. I'll shoot him up with more anesthetics and he will be out for about eight hours afterward."

Abs asked, "Will that give you enough time to perform your magic on him at *The Don's*?"

"It should, but I also packed additional anesthetics, just in case."

Biceps clapped *Surgeon* on the shoulder. "You are a good man, Gunga Din. Say, it's about twenty more minutes before he closes shop for the night. Is everyone ready?" The team all gave an affirmative yes to *Bicep's* question.

* * * * *

The van was now two blocks from High Top's services near 46th and Wabash. *Biceps* said, "I'll drop Surgeon and Abs off at the Burger King down the street. You two grab some coffee there and wait for me to return. Be close to a window overlooking the parking lot. I should be back within 15 minutes if all goes as planned." He then laughed as he added, "And *Surgeon*, you needn't be concerned about the clientele that frequents this burger joint, just stay real close to my muscle-bound brother!" After quiet chuckles from all, *Biceps* seriously said, "Time to roll." A chilling quiet ensued.

After the quick drop off at Burger King, *Biceps* parked half a block from their target. Actress exited the van, and sauntered towards High-Top, hips and breasts doing seductive sways. *Biceps* hid under a blanket on the floor of the back seat after he put the dome light out of commission. He gripped the Seconal tightly and carefully had it poised to strike.

"Hi, handsome," *Actress* cooed while expertly doing facial twitches indicating an addict needing a fix. High-Top turned around at the salutation and smiled immediately as his eyes took in *Actress's* gorgeous curves.

"Well, hello, hello, what can I do for you, doll?"

Batting her eyes and moving her tongue invitingly over her lips, "Got any rocks of crack?"

"Got plenty. You got money?"

"That's the problem, no I don't. I was told we could negotiate." Her tongue lashed out seductively.

"Yes we can. How about a couple of rocks for a blow-job? Kind of like some blow for a blow."

She laughed. "It's a deal. I get your rocks off, and I get my rocks on." She grabbed his hand and pulled hard. "That's my van. We'll do it in there," she pointed. She moved rapidly. Her hand and her pace forced High-Top to jog.

"Whoa, you must really need a fix. Or, you really love to give head."

"Both."

The answer made him hard.

High-Top sat in the passenger seat. *Actress* inched close to him from the driver's seat. She provocatively encouraged, "Whip it out, big boy, I want all of you."

While he hastily struggled to release his prick, a different kind of prick reared its head. *Biceps* silently plunged the needle in High-Top's neck while the drug dealer was preoccupied.

His head slumped forward.

"Let's go. You can drive. I'm going in the back to change."

"Ten-Four, I'm off to Burger King." *Surgeon* and *Abs* briskly entered the van as Biceps drove away.

A short time later, the van entered the now familiar driveway on Thatcher Ave. *The Don* heard its entry into his garage. He was watching his favorite DVD: *Godfather II.* He heard them hurrying to the basement hospital.

He smiled, lifted his glass of grappa for a toast. "Salute *Mr. C*." He downed the glass of grappa and poured a generous replacement. He sunk into the cushioned recliner and reached for the remote. His favorite part was coming up and he didn't want to be distracted. So he simply adjusted the volume higher while he watched Vito Corleone mete justice out to Don Ciccio. A very similar type of justice was being performed below.

"That looks like a damn ice pick," *Abs* commented as *Surgeon* readied his tools for the procedure.

"Funny you say that. Originally an ice pick was used for this operation. Now this instrument has a fancy name. An orbitoclast." Before starting, *Surgeon* looked at *Abs* with concern. "I explained what I am about to do. I need an assistant. Are you sure you can handle it."

"I'm a former Army Ranger, enough said, let's do it." They did it.

*　*　*　*　*

Kirk, DuSable High School's building superintendent, arrived at school at his usual time of 4:00 a.m. High-Top had arrived one hour earlier. He was sitting in the morning shadows of the entryway. The vacant expression on his face said it all. There definitely was nobody at home upstairs. The sign taped to his chest explained the vacancy. Kirk yanked out his cell and called 9-1-1.

Unknown to Kirk, Abigail Albright was also en-route with a Sun Times photographer riding shotgun. She had received an anonymous call on her cell. A strange voice informed her of Mr. Consequence's latest caper. She was told where she could find the end result, aka High-Top. The digital voice changer did an excellent job of disguising *Ear's* voice. The Go phone could not be traced as it no longer existed.

Cary, the Sun Times photographer just finished taking pictures when Tom Jackson and Mike Krimski, two cops out on patrol, arrived minutes later.

Tom recognized Abigail. "What the hell are you doing here?"

"My job."

She told Tom about the call.

"Did you touch anything?"

"No way. Cary used a long distance lens, we know the proper procedures on cases like this."

"So I guess that means this will be in the papers soon."

"No guess; it's a fact. Bye."

She waved at Tom and Mike as she and Cary hustled to her car.

"It looks like that Mr. Consequence guy has struck again," Tom said, pointing to the sign Cary had been taking pictures of. The words on the sign were:

SOME OF THE WORST BAD GUYS ARE DRUG DEALERS.

THEY GET KIDS TO FRY THEIR BRAINS OUT
SO THAT THEY NO LONGER ARE HUMAN.

THIS PUSHER IS NOW AN EXAMPLE OF HOW BADLY FRIED BRAINS CAN AFFECT YOU—

BE SMART—

REMEMBER RANDALL McMURPHY
FROM THE MOVIE—*ONE FLEW OVER THE CUCKOO'S NEST?—*

HIGH-TOP IS NOW A McMURPHY

YOU OTHER DRUG PUSHERS OUT THERE—

BE WARNED—

IF YOU DON'T STOP, YOU WILL SUFFER THE CONSEQUENCES—

I AM WATCHING VERY CLOSELY—SO DRUG PUSHERS—

BE AFRAID, BE VERY AFRAID.

AS OF NOW I PROMISE—THERE WILL BE CONSEQUENCES—

ASK HIGH-TOP WHAT THEY ARE—

JUST DON'T EXPECT HIM TO ANSWER—

YOU HAVE BEEN **WARNED**

—MR.CONSEQUENCE

"I saw that movie. Jack Nicholson played McMurphy. He ended up getting a lobotomy. Better call this in to Captain Krol. Superintendant Kowalski put him in charge of the Consequence guy's investigation."

"Thanks a lot, Tom. I get to be the lucky guy to wake the Captain up in the middle of the night." Mike groused, but he made the call.

The Captain groggily took the call. He immediately dialed another number. He related the reported activities and gruffly ended the call saying, "You and your partner get down there on the double."

Mitch sighed and headed for the shower while he speed-dialed Diane.

CHAPTER FORTY-THREE

"*Mr. C's* getting us these access codes makes this a piece of cake," *Eyes* commented to his brother.

"I'll take easy over hard any day," said *Ears*.

"What have you got so far that's making you so cheerful?"

"I have two excellent candidates from Chicago's drug trade. Just like High-Top. Numerous arrests, very little jail time, and they like to do business with kids."

"Print out what you got on them and let's do what we do best," *Ears* suggested.

Eye's laughed at his brother's words and said, "Let's."

"So, what is the location of the first one on the list?"

"North, near Lane Tech," *Ears* answered.

Mr. C had his reasons for varying the locations. He wanted the drug dealers throughout the city to be very fearful. He wanted all dealers to know that they might experience High-Top's fate, regardless of their location. A rather creative campaign was to follow. He hoped to create major dents to the drug vehicles throughout the city. At least that was the hoped for expectation.

"Where does the other one set up shop?"

"Chicago Lawn." *Ears* then pulled out his Go phone and called *Biceps*.

"*Biceps*, *Ears* here, we have two targets ready to go. We were able to get a complete picture of their operation. Times and addresses are all there. Both targets work alone."

"Fax them over and *Abs* and I will do the recon. We'll see how they arrive at their distribution center. For these two, I suggest we make use of those toys my friend Mikey sent us."

"I agree, it would definitely simplify things."

"*Abs* and I are ready to roll as soon as we get the faxes."

"Then I'll hang up now. You will have them in a few minutes."

The recon paid off. *Biceps* and *Abs* had used observation and street connections to perfection. Four days later, all needed information had been gathered. Looks like Mikey's toys would do just fine. The pushers, Ty-boy and Julio, both drove their cars to work alone and they were always parked in the same location until it was quitting time. That was midnight for Ty-boy and 1:00 a.m. for Julio.

"*Surgeon*, *Biceps* here. Are you ready for some late night work again?" He gave Surgeon the details. "My brother and I are more flexible than you, what two nights work best for you."

"I'm off day after tomorrow, so tomorrow night would be good. I'm off again next Tuesday, so Monday night would be best."

"I'll be in touch with you on pick-up places and times. On these two, I don't see a need for anyone but you, me and *Abs*."

"Someday, I just have to tell Mikey how we used these babies," *Abs* said as he and *Biceps* removed their gas masks after loading Ty-boy in the van.

"Let's wait until we are really old. I don't think *Mr. C* would be pleased," *Biceps* said.

"Yeah, but I guarantee you, Mikey would be," *Abs* smirked.

Biceps then hit the speed dial on his Go-phone. "*Surgeon*, we are on our way to pick you up. We have the package."

"I'm ready to go, how soon?"

"Fifteen minutes should do it."

"I'll be there."

"What the fuck," were the last cohesive words uttered by Ty-boy.

Hours later, when Ty-boy woke up, sitting under a massive maple tree in secluded LaBagh Woods, coherent words were no longer part of his vocabulary.

CHAPTER FORTY-FOUR

"Cary, wake up quick." An excited Abigail exclaimed. "I just got a call on my cell again from *Mr. Consequence*."

"What is it this time?"

"He does not like drug pushers at all."

"Another High-Top?"

"It sounds like it."

"Where should we meet?"

"It's on the north-side. Not far from your apartment. Wait for me outside and I'll pick you up."

Once again the police arrived while Cary was finishing his photo session with Ty-boy. There was no need to say *cheese.* Ty-boy's smiles would not be showing up any time soon. All that remained were a pair of vacuous eyes that didn't blink at all as the Nikon D3X 24.5MP FX CMOS flashed away.

"Freaking Steve will now stop bitching about the cost of this baby." Cary said as he affectionately patted his camera. "These pictures are going to be Dy-no-mite!"

"OK, JJ," Abigail blurted, as Cary mimicked the catch phrase of Jimmie Walker's character, JJ, made famous in the sitcom *Good Times*.

Officer Alan Wozniak from the 19th District approached the scene. "Is that you Abigail?"

"In the flesh", she smiled. Alan liked Abigail and she liked him. He had worked the child abuse case on Carrie Settles last year. He had provided Abigail with some details on the viciousness of daddy's attacks on Carrie. Those reported facts had given her recent promotion a sizable boost. She was grateful. The public outcry after the details had been published in her article had helped put Mr. Settles in jail for a long time. He was grateful.

"Adam, meet Abigail Albright," Alan said to Adam Leahy, his new partner. "She's one of the good reporters, and better yet, she's a cop's wife," he added.

Abigail smiled at the comment. She extended her hand, "Nice to meet you Adam."

"So, how did you get here so quick?"

"Just like last time," Answered Abigail. "An anonymous call."

"Same here," Alan said. "Ours came through 9-1-1."

"Is it another Mr. Consequence situation?" Adam asked.

She nodded as she pointed to the recently photographed sign attached to Ty-boy's chest.

"I know this guy. He's a bad one. In fact, Adam and I just arrested him last month."

"Well, he sure didn't stay in jail very long."

"No, but it looks like he is going to be in another type of prison for a long, long, time. Definitely looks like a life sentence," Alan said as he paused to read the sign:

MY, MY, IT LOOKS LIKE DRUG DEALERS REALLY ARE STUPID.

I WARNED YOU I WOULD BE WATCHING.

NOW ANOTHER BRAIN HAS SAID GOOD-BYE TO PLANET EARTH.

TO THE REST OF THE DRUG DEALERS—

LISTEN VERY CAREFULLY—

I WILL CONTINUE MY VIGILENCE AND WILL BE WATCHING.

I LEAVE YOU WITH ONE SIMPLE QUESTION:
DO YOU REALLY WANT TO BE NEXT?

YOU HAVE BEEN WARNED—
DO NOT BE STUPID—
STOP DEALING NOW.

—MR. CONSEQUENCE

"He sure looks like another High-Top situation," Alan commented, noticing the similar scars.

"Good riddance," Adam stated.

"That sounds like you might like this Mr. Consequence guy," Abigail chimed with a smirk.

"Abigail, you better not include that comment in your write-up. The mayor will hang our asses out to dry if you do."

"I wouldn't do that to you, Alan."

"Thanks."

"But I will tell you this. After the last article I did on Mr. Consequence, an avalanche of calls and e-mails were all pro-Mr. Consequence. The public really likes this guy."

"Yeah, I know. Most of the cops I know wouldn't lose much sleep if the two detectives assigned to arrest him took a long, long time to catch this Mr. Consequence."

"Do Mrozek and Ryan have any leads yet?"

"How do you know the names of the detectives?"

"They paid me a visit the other day."

"Why?"

"They wanted to try and trace the calls to me from Mr. Consequence."

"They have any luck?"

"They did not say."

"If he keeps calling you, be prepared to have your phone tapped."

"A reporter's phone tapped? That is not going to happen. My sources are supposed to be my confidential sources."

"Yeah, well, don't be surprised if your editor gets a call from the mayor."

"I'm not worried. I'm sure you are aware of Illinois's *Two-Party Consent Law*. The Sun Times endorsed the other candidate last election. The editor and mayor really don't like each other. There's no way my boss is going to give his consent."

"Good luck on that one."

"Bye for now. Cary and I need to get back and write this up."

"Take care, Abigail."

Alan then called it in.

After the report was called in, he said, "Don't touch anything, Adam. The techies are on their way. The desk said they would contact Mrozek and Ryan. They will probably be joining us tonight."

"Do you think the techies will find some trace?"

"Can't say for sure, but word is that the ones who worked the previous crime scenes came up with zilch."

"This guy is really slick. My guess is they will come up with more zilch."

Alan pulled out a pack of Marlboros and offered one to Adam. "Let's sit on the bench over there and have a smoke. I don't think Ty-boy will miss us much," he laughed. "Hell, he won't even know we left," Adam added with a smile. The cigarette smoke framed in moonlight left an appropriate eeriness to the scene.

CHAPTER FORTY-FIVE

The snatch on Julio went down a few days later. It went down as smooth as Ty-boy's. They dropped him off at 2:00 a.m. at the doorway of the Curie Park Fieldhouse, located on Chicago's Southwest-side.

Once again, Abigail and Cary arrived three minutes before the police. This time Cary received the call. Since both lived on the north-side, they saved time by driving separately to the scene. They were just seconds apart as they bolted from their cars and headed to the crime scene. A squad car screeched to a stop next to Abigail's car. Exiting the car were Officer Sean Miller and his partner Lindsay Schmidt from the 8th district, the Chicago Lawn district.

Even though they had never met her before, they recognized Abigail immediately. That happens when your picture is prominently displayed frequently on the front page. The *Mr. Consequence* articles had placed her countenance there on a daily basis.

"Good evening, Miss Albright," Sean offered.

"Good evening, officer." Abigail extended her hand.

"Why am I not surprised to see you here?"

"You must be reading the Sun-Times a lot lately," Abigail cracked.

"Lots of people are. This Consequence guy is definitely a news grabber," said Sean.

"That's an understatement."

Lindsay interrupted, "I'm sure you know the routine by now, do not disturb the crime scene."

"We haven't been close to it, no need to. Cary has his super camera with him. He can take close-up shots from twenty yards away."

"Good. So what have we got here," asked Lindsay.

"If I were a drug pusher in Chicago, I would seriously be looking for another profession," Abigail said.

"Just like the last two?" Sean inquired.

"Yep, take a look," Cary said as he showed Sean the digital images he had captured on the Nikon.

"I know him. Bad hombre. Name's Julio. Hell, those pictures are amazing. They're unreal for being night pictures."

"Thank you, but the D3X 24.5MP deserves most of the credit," Cary said while he lovingly gave his camera a quick kiss.

"How much does a camera like that cost?"

"About seven thousand, and another couple of thousand for the accessories."

"Never mind, that is way out of my league," Sean said with a noticeable sigh.

Cary and Abigail said their good-byes, and sped away. “Let’s get a closer look.”

“Okay, Lindsay, let’s look.”

Slumped by the recessed back door was Julio. His eyes were wide open, but it was obvious that he wasn’t awake.

Sean shivered as he said, “This son of a bitch plays rough. Looks like Julio will be a permanent visitor to La-La land.”

Propped next to Julio was the now familiar warning sign:

STUPID-STUPID-STUPID.
I WARNED YOU PUSHERS I WOULD BE WATCHING.
THESE WILL CONTINUE TO BE THE CONSEQUENCES FOR SELLING DRUGS. THE KEY WORDS BEING *WILL CONTINUE*.
DO ANY OF YOU PUSHERS REALLY WANT TO BE NEXT IN LINE?
KEEP SELLING AND THE ODDS ARE VERY HIGH YOU WILL BE.
THIS I PROMISE YOU—AND I ALWAYS KEEP MY PROMISES.

—MR. CONSEQUENCE

“I better call this in now,” Lindsay said grabbing her phone from her jacket. She finished the call and said, “A team will be here in a few minutes.

Sean offered, “I better call our captain on this one. I’ll let him call Captain Krol. I’m sure Krol wants his detectives here ASAP.”

“Good idea, Krol’s guys are the lead detectives on the Consequence investigation.”

*   *   *   *   *

The next few weeks showed a marked decline for the drug trade. Once that information hit the news, the public’s respect for Mr. Consequence grew.

His next plan against the pushers might cause a further decline.

It just might.

CHAPTER FORTY-SIX

"The Mayor would like to see you in his office today at 10:45 a.m.," Stella said.

The Superintendent placed his coffee on his desk and replied, "Well, that gives me three hours to solve this Mr. Consequence problem."

Stella laughed heartily at his sarcasm. "The way it's been going, Superintendent, it may be three years, not three hours."

He took a sip of the steaming coffee, and answered, "I hope not. Please get either Mrozek or Ryan on the phone. I want my ducks in a row before I meet with Kelly."

"I'll get right on it."

Diane spent the next thirty minutes giving Superintendent Kowalski the details of their investigation so far. Unfortunately, they were the same details Captain Krol had given him the day before, no new information.

"Ryan, I know you and your partner are available 24/7 on this one. However, in addition to the long hours, I also need some results." Diane was about to answer with a "Yes, sir" when a loud click ended the call. She let out a long sigh of frustration.

She called Mitch.

"Good morning Eleanor."

"Good morning Superintendent. He's ready for you. I'll let him know you're here."

Seconds later, a buzzer summoned him into the mayor's office.

"Stash, thank you for coming, please, sit down."

The mayor pointed to an empty chair. The chair next to it was occupied.

"Good to see you again, Stan," said Nathan Bizick, the mayor's press secretary.

"Hopefully you will feel that way after I report the progress on this Mr. Consequence guy."

"We have progress?" Kelly asked hopefully.

"I'll let you decide, Mr. Mayor."

"Stash, you know that behind closed doors, my name is Joe. Ditch the formalities and let me know what's happening," the mayor said with a smile.

Superintendent Kowalski did.

Kelly's smile disappeared.

"Stash, any chance you can wire-tap Albright's phone at the Sun-Times? It seems likely this Mr. Consequence will continue to use her as a source of publicity."

"We've already tried. Goldman, the Sun-Times' CEO, immediately refused, citing the *Illinois Two Party Consent Law*. He said under no circumstances would he compromise any sources related to news reporting."

"What about tracing past calls?"

"We've done that too. The calls to Albright have all been made from untraceable sources. My guess would be prepaid phones. The phones were probably destroyed after the calls were placed."

"And the techies have been unable to find any trace at all in these cases?"

"Nada."

"So we are dealing with someone who is very clever and cautious."

"Not just someone. Our profiler believes a team is involved. Ryan and Mrozek concur. There are too many areas of expertise exhibited in these cases for one person to have. And as you know, none of the victims have been able to offer any clues."

"No shit, Stash."

"If I may interrupt Mr. Mayor," Nathan asked.

"Go right ahead, Nate."

"There has been intense pressure to have a press conference soon on Mr. Consequence. Both newspapers and the local stations are inquiring daily."

"That's understandable. What's your point?"

"Next year's mayoral race is my point."

Stan offered not a word as he always tried to maintain a healthy distance from politics.

The Mayor asked, "Why are you bringing that up now?"

"The public's opinion, that's why. They also happen to be voters. There's been a maelstrom of support for this guy. The public loves him."

"But he is a criminal."

"So were Robin Hood and his Merry Men. The Sheriff of Nottingham lost his job after arresting him. Right now he is Chicago's Robin Hood. If there are others, they are his Merry Men."

Joe nodded and asked, "Any suggestions?"

Nate reached into his briefcase and withdrew a folder. "Here are copies for you," he said handing sheets to the mayor and superintendent. He then took a sip of water and continued. "Suggestion number one is to call a news conference, the sooner, the better. We are going to need the media on our side. Delaying the conference much longer will just tick them off. Suggestion number two would be to be a bit sympathetic regarding the pursuit and capture of Mr. Consequence."

"Just how am I to do that?"

Pointing to the passed out papers, Nate said, "It is detailed on the next three pages."

Nate waited while they silently read.

Mayor Kelly chuckled slightly and placed the papers down. "Nate, when you really want to spin something you have no rival. This is good, very good."

"Thank you Mr. Mayor, I try. That's why you pay me the big bucks!" Stan joined with Joe as they laughed along with Nate at his comment.

Mayor Kelly abruptly stopped laughing and asked, "How soon can write me up a speech?"

"I can have it by this afternoon."

"Great. Set up a noon news conference for the day after tomorrow. Stash, I want you there with me. Meet me here tomorrow at 9:00 a.m. We can look over Nate's speech and prepare ourselves for the news onslaught. Agreed?"

"Agreed, Mr. Mayor, oops, I mean Joe."

They parted with a handshake and a chuckle.

CHAPTER FORTY-SEVEN

"That's the last of them," said *Ears* as he printed out a list of cell phone numbers.

Eyes scanned the list and said, "*Mr. C's* access codes work very well, indeed."

"They sure have. Let's get the Go-phones and get started."

They texted the carefully worded message and entered the cell numbers the message would be sent to. They held off on hitting send.

"How about going to Billy Goat's for lunch at Navy Pier?"

"Good idea. Have a great cheezborger, send the message out, and then send the phones to swim with the fishes," *Eyes* replied as they headed out.

It had taken months of effort for the Drug Squad to gather the cell numbers. The owners of these numbers were dealers operating in Chicago and nearby suburbs. It was a painstaking process to accumulate the forty-plus numbers. It was painless for *Ears*. *Mr. C* had impressive contact abilities which had led to the access code acquisitions. Instead of months, it only took minutes to gather the information. It would now be put to use as a courtesy call from *Mr. Consequence.*

"Cheezborger, Cheezborger, no fries, chips, no Coke, Pepsi," the familiar banter greeted the two brothers as they placed their order.

"You got to hand it to Chicago," said *Eyes*, chomping down on the imitable cheezborger. "It has the best choice of eats in the world."

Ears simply nodded as borger juice cascaded down his cheek from the healthy bite he had taken.

Eyes continued, "The only thing missing on the menu are crispy fresh-cut fries from Big Al's."

Ears nodded again as he proceeded to devour his cheezborger.

"There's a nice secluded spot near the lake," *Ears* pointed out as they left Billy Goat's.

"Looks good to me too," *Eyes* replied. "Let's get it done."

They each sat next to the rails near the water. They carefully checked the message again before hitting send to their intended recipients.

It was in capital letters:

MY-MY, DID YOU REALLY THINK I WAS FINISHED DOLING OUT MY PUNISHMENT TO DOPE DEALERS.

I TOLD YOU I WOULD BE WATCHING.

IF YOU ARE ANXIOUS TO JOIN HIGH-TOP, TY-BOY, AND JULIO IN NEVERLAND, CONSIDER THIS A GUARANTEED INVITATION.

KEEP DEALING AND YOU WILL BE NEXT.

CONSIDER THIS BOTH A THREAT AND A PROMISE.

I WILL BE WATCHING.

THE CHOICE IS YOURS.

—MR. CONSEQUENCE

They hit the send button on the Go-Phones repeatedly and afterward quietly dropped them into the welcoming water of Lake Michigan.

As they walked back to the car, *Ears* commented, "I would love to see the expressions on their faces when they read the message.

"Oh yeah, I wouldn't be surprised if they shit their pants," laughed *Eyes*.

Ears then called *Mr. C*. "Messages sent, *Mr. C*. Do you think it will work?"

"Well, it certainly won't hurt."

* * * * *

Over the next few weeks, the Drug Squad was perplexed over the mass disappearance of drug dealers in their patrolled areas.

At the same time, the leaders of the Cartels were not just perplexed, they were pissed.

Carlo, one of the top guns in the drug trade summed up their thoughts best. "We really need to kill this fucker."

Mr. C heard the reports through his contacts. He smiled and thought, *I guess it might have worked after all.*

CHAPTER FORTY-EIGHT

"Good afternoon, ladies and gentlemen."

"Good afternoon, Mr. Mayor," the crowd chorused from the packed media room of the Mayor's office.

"Before Superintendent Kowalski shares our progress in locating Mr. Consequence, I would like to share my thoughts regarding aspects of this case." A dramatic pause followed. "I do not consider Mr. Consequence to be an enemy. Many honest, hard-working Chicagoans are frustrated over the insane and all too frequent misdeeds that criminals commit in our great city. I echo their frustration. I understand Mr. Consequence is being lauded as a modern day Robin Hood. Heck, I even confess to have briefly shared this sentiment. However, I am bound by the duties of my office. My oath of office requires that I perform my duties to uphold the law regardless of mine or others' sentiments. I will not shirk that responsibility. The citizens of Chicago expect me to follow that mandate. I will not, and cannot let them down. If you are watching this now Mr. Consequence, I will make you a promise. I guarantee upon your surrender or arrest, you will be treated with respect. I promise you will have a fair trial allowing you to voice the reasons for your actions. I believe you are a person of high morals and that you believe you are doing the right thing. However, it has been proven that vigilante law is not the right answer in administering justice. Unfortunately, it can lead to mass chaos. I implore you to surrender. You may call my office directly and I will personally meet with you to assure a safe arrest. Do yourself this favor, make the right decision." He paused briefly and concluded his speech. "Thank you for your attendance here today. I will now have Superintendent Kowalski give you an update. Please hold all questions until he is finished."

There was a hearty applause from the audience that surprised and gratified the mayor immensely. He was also gratified by Nathan's wide grin and *thumbs-up* signal from the back of the room.

Superintendent Kowalski proceeded to recap the efforts made in finding Mr. Consequence. He shared Sammy's theory that it was not one man acting alone.

When he finished, Mayor Kelly announced, "We will now take your questions." A flurry of raised hands and shouts erupted.

"What is your question, Chris?" Mayor Kelly said to Chris Allie, the crime reporter from Channel 5 news.

"Mr. Mayor and Commissioner, the individuals that have been targeted by Mr. Consequence all have previously been incarcerated numerous times, yet they were set free and obviously committed more crimes. What is being done to protect the citizens of Chicago from these hardened repeat offenders?"

"I'll take that question," Superintendent Kowalski said as Mayor Kelly made room for him at the podium. "You bring up a very good question Chris. Our job as police officers is to hopefully prevent crime. However, when a crime occurs, our role is to find and arrest the perpetrators. Once they are arrested, the courts take over. Bonds as well as future trial dates are all determined by the courts in cooperation with the prosecutors.

"The mayor and I have no further input at that point. I can assure you that many an officer has been frustrated when their collar is freed soon after the arrest. Unfortunately, the overcrowded jails and courts plus a limited number of prosecutors have influenced the early release of these criminals. The mayor and my task force are currently working with the city planning commission hoping to come up with solutions to these problems. As you know, it takes time and money. Next question."

"Mr. Mayor, is it true that over 70% of violent crimes are committed by these repeat offenders," asked the Tribune's Vic Frontiere.

"Yes Vic, it is true. That is exactly why the Commissioner and I are moving forward with the task force he mentioned."

After more questions on the city's inability to stem the repeat offender issues, Mayor Kelly did a political dance using responses that Nate had suggested.

"Ladies and gentlemen, unfortunately I must now address the duties of my office. This meeting is adjourned."

As the crowd headed towards the exit, a reporter said, "Maybe this Mr. Consequence can speed things up for that task force."

Many that overheard the comment grinned and nodded affirmatively. Even a couple of *Amens* were uttered.

Nate heard the comment and the responses. He fervently hoped Mr. Consequence would simply go away. As he headed to Mayor Kelly's office, he knew that was a giant case of wishful thinking.

CHAPTER FORTY-NINE

"Guess who is thinking very seriously about next year's mayoral race?"

"Hmmm, could it be Mayor Kelly," said Diane as she hit the off button on the TV remote.

"Ya think?"

"Hell, it sounded like this Mr. Consequence guy was his long lost brother," Diane snorted.

"He sure was trying to be bedfellows with public opinion, that's for sure," Mitch added.

"So what's today's agenda," Diane asked while taking a bite of her breakfast éclair.

"Well, so far he has targeted robbers, rapists and drug dealers. It's definitely a random pattern." Mitch paused as he slugged down the last of his coffee.

"What I really would like to do today is to spend some time with Natalie. I haven't seen her for over two weeks."

"Are you missing your love life?"

"More like lack of one. Mr. Consequence owes me big time."

"But Mitch, you should know by now there is no rest for the wicked."

Mitch nodded glumly then said, "Let's go see if Sammy has some ideas as to where this thing is going."

"Good idea, I'll call her now." Diane said as she grabbed the phone.

"Sammy here."

"Hi Sammy, it's Diane Ryan. Can you spare some time for Mitch and me today?"

"You must be joking. How can a measly indentured servant like me turn down a visit from two big-time celebrities?"

"What is that supposed to mean?"

"I got the word yesterday that if anyone needs to visit me regarding Mr. Consequence, I am to drop and reschedule anything else."

"Ah, so that means, yes, you can," Diane joked.

"Yep. I am at your command."

"When can we see you?"

"Right now if you like, I'll just go ahead and cancel and reschedule what's on my calendar this morning," she deadpanned. As Mitch reached for the last éclair from the bag, Diane snatched it away. "Thanks Sammy, have coffee ready and I'll bring over a Hendrickx éclair. Mitch said he was too full to eat the last one."

"I love when celebrities come and visit bearing gifts. I'll make a fresh pot now. Bye."

"You are full of something, but it ain't éclairs," Mitch grumbled.

Diane just smiled and said, "Touchy-touchy. Let's get going. Sammy can see us now."

Sammy had a tray with a carafe and coffee supplies on her desk. "Help yourselves," she said pointing to the tray. "But first, hand over the éclair. I have a gut feeling that Mitch may not be as full as you said."

"Now why would you say that," Diane laughed.

"Hey, I am a profiler, what can I say."

"A damn good one," Mitch said as he longingly stared at the pastry bag Diane handed to Sammy.

"Hmm, this is heaven," she said biting into the éclair. "Let me finish this first, then, we'll get started."

Noting the look on Mitch's face she added, "And no, Mitch, sharing this is not an option." Seconds later, the éclair disappeared. Licking her lips, she said, "Okay, what can I help you with today."

"Finding this Mr. Consequence guy for us would great!"

"Sorry Mitch, I used up all my miracles for the month. Give me your observations on the drug dealers he took down."

They gave her the blow by blow of the incidents.

"Wow, like you mentioned after Jo-Jo and Ray-Ray, Mr. Consequence is making sure these *Bad Guys* are permanently out of commission."

"A lobotomy will do that to a guy," Diane added. They then handed Sammy the investigative tech reports that were submitted on all the pushers. Sammy read them intently.

She placed the reports aside and said, "He, or one of his team members, is one very skilled surgeon. The person doing the cutting is definitely no amateur. I also believe he used money, sex or force in each of the assaults."

"Why?" was asked in unison.

"With their criminal past, I can't visualize any of them walking silent into the night with Mr. Consequence. I feel he either baited them with money or sex, or took them forcefully, or some combination of these three. I can almost guarantee that some sort of knock-out drug or device was used."

"But the blood tests taken afterwards only identified normal anesthetics used in surgery," Diane posed.

"Those require either the patients' cooperation or they are already unconscious. In my opinion, it's the latter. Whatever was used to initially knock them out must dissipate quickly, becoming untraceable."

Mitch said, "If you're right on this, then that would make it easier for Mr. Consequence to haul them off for surgery."

"Exactly, however it is still not easy to haul dead weight. I still believe we have some major muscle working here."

"Let's have some coffee, and then see if you can summarize what we are looking for and where we can find it," Diane said pensively.

Mitch reached for the carafe and said, "Good idea, I'll pour."

Sammy took a sip of the brew, and said, "Here is my summary. This guy, and I am certain it is a male, definitely has past issues that were unresolved. I believe the issues revert back to his childhood. Perhaps he was abused or was the victim of crime as a child. I also believe he not only has a group of people assisting in the missions, but they are extremely dedicated. The dedication is directed either to him or due to similar issues they have encountered in their personal lives. At this point I believe it is a little bit of both. I believe it is quite obvious that one of them is a surgeon. Here is an enigma. Not only is the surgeon quite proficient, but there must be a very well equipped operating room available to him. You just can't operate on a kitchen table using silverware."

"Why is that an enigma?"

"Well I just can't fathom him wheeling his targets in on a gurney through hospital doors without being noticed."

"Good point," Diane jotted down.

Mitch commented, "So, it probably is some sort of private facility."

Sammy nodded, and continued. "I also believe there are some well-muscled men involved as well as a woman involved who is a sexual lure for the victims. The random occurrences do have one common thread. All the victims had multiple arrests on their records. I believe he and his entire team are extremely upset that the legal system allows them to repeatedly go free to commit mayhem again and again. My hunch is that there will be future missions. All will be designed to strike fear in the so called *Bad Guys* in the city. His selection process will probably focus on those criminals that have committed offences numerous times in the past, but still are on the streets. The multiple attacks on drug dealers may be a clue to tracking him down."

Mitch asked, "Why do you say that?"

"He definitely wants to get *Bad Guys* in all aspects of crime to understand that none of them will be safe. Therefore selecting more than one individual that has committed specific crimes repeatedly reinforces his threat that *He Is Watching* all of them."

"Thanks, Sammy. This helps with narrowing our search quite a bit. Diane and I will look at records of drug dealers that have numerous arrests and get the word out to the street cops so they can keep their eyes and ears peeled."

"That would be a place to start, but I feel he doesn't discriminate against different crimes. The thread that links them would be multiple arrests."

"If that is true, we will only have hundreds of thousands of repeat offenders to check out," Mitch groaned.

"I didn't say it would be easy."

"Your reasoning for a team effort makes a lot of sense. We'll go the extra mile on any suspects that match your description of the team's skills," Diane noted.

"I'll be happy to conduct in-depth interviews with any gorgeous women we come across," Mitch solemnly offered.

They all laughed and Mitch and Diane left to arrange their next action list.

CHAPTER FIFTY

"That's enough of this shit. We aren't going to let them walk all over our asses. It is time for a lesson." Jamal Stone announced.

Jamal is the leader of a Black Disciple (aka BD) gang set in Englewood. The Gangster Disciples (aka GD) had made a major score on cocaine and marijuana and were selling off the excess in Jamal's *BD* turf.

"You all got your guns ready?"

The six members Jamal assigned to the revenge squad answered "Yeah!" Laughter and braggadocios comments soon followed.

"Those GD mother-fuckers are going down!"

"Their fucking ass is grass and I'm the fucking lawnmower!"

Jamal held up his hand for silence. The shouts soon subsided. "Good hunting," he said as he saluted them with the BD honored *trey* sign (thumb over little finger with remaining fingers extended). Six hands flew up returning the salute.

"Let's roll,' said the assigned driver, Hakeem. The group piled into the van and headed for 102nd and Perry Avenue. This was BD's turf. The group was a highly decorated crew. They had 27 felony arrests among them.

As a van approached, a GD lookout shouted to three GD's who were setting up shop in a recessed entrance of an abandoned building. "Heads-up, this might be trouble."

It was. The van accelerated and screeched to a halt at the curb of the abandoned residence. The door of the van pushed open as six automatic weapons fired at the GD's. The brief warning had been enough for the GD's to pull their guns and rapidly returned gunfire at the assailants. Hakeem yelled, "Close the door, we're out of here." The van sped away.

The GD lookout was dead; his body oozing blood. One other GD had blood gushing from his arm. The BD's were luckier. Only one leg wound.

Oh, there were two other injuries. Tanya, age eleven, and Gabrielle, age ten, who had unfortunately chosen to play hopscotch near the shootout. They didn't hop out of the line of fire fast enough. Their wounded bodies and blood obscuring the carefully chalked hopscotch sketch they had created.

When the police arrived, all that was left of the gun battle was a dead man and two seriously injured girls.

Officer Nolan barked into his phone. "Get an ambulance here as fast as you can. Two little girls have been shot. They are still alive." After giving 9-1-1 the address, he turned to his partner. "Goddamn it, if these gangbangers want to off each other, good riddance. But leave these babies alone."

Nolan then administered to the girls trying to staunch the bleeding the best he could until the ambulance arrived.

Officer Parks, Nolan's partner grimly said," these murdering sons of bitches will simply consider these young girls to be collateral damage. They look at it as the price of doing business. God damn them." He then bent down to assist Nolan.

There is someone who may not believe that this price of doing business is right.

Mr. C just might think the consequences should be forthcoming.

CHAPTER FIFTY-ONE

"Man, that was one freaking long day," Mitch thought as he approached his East Erie condo. He and Diane began the day isolating private surgical facilities that matched Sammy's suspicions. They did background checks on the owners that ferreted a few dozen possibilities. These owners had filed criminal charges on various offences that were never resolved by any convictions. The charges ranged from common thefts to various forms of assault.

This led to a full day of tracking down and questioning the subjects. No real lead had developed. Now Mitch was bone tired and starving. Hence, the enticing aromas emanating from the bag of late-night Chinatown take-out that he had nestled on his front passenger seat.

Sam was waiting as Mitch entered the valet area. With a wry smile he said, "I believe there is a surprise for you in the lobby, Mr. Mrozek."

"Sam, after the day I had, I hope it's a good one."

"I believe it will be very satisfactory."

He grabbed the Chinese take-out and headed towards the door. Paul greeted him with the usual, "Good evening Mr. Mrozek."

"Evening, Paul." He noticed a similar wry grin on Paul's face.

"Oh, goodie, you brought Chinese," Natalie exclaimed as she recognized the Won-Kow Restaurant label on the bag.

"Sam was right, this surprise is very satisfactory," Mitch said while he embraced her and they kissed. When the kiss ended, Paul chuckled as he watched them gleefully walk to the elevator.

As the door of the elevator closed, they devoured each other. Once the elevator reached the penthouse floor, they wasted no time in getting to Mitch's condo. The two then undressed each other.

"God, I have missed you so much," Mitch huskily whispered.

Natalie countered with her now familiar line, "back atcha, handsome. I'm off tomorrow so I decided to wait you out tonight."

"How long were you waiting?"

"Since 7:00 p.m."

"Well, I'll just have to make sure the wait was worth your while."

She joked, "but aren't you afraid the food will get cold?"

"I have a microwave."

"I like your priorities," her voice cried as she playfully planted hickeys over his bare chest while he removed the last remaining stitch of clothing between them.

Afterwards they showered and slipped into soft cushy robes, then they contently lounged in bed while eating nuked plates of egg rolls and sweet and sour pork.

"We could really have some fun if you take the day off tomorrow," Natalie salaciously moved her tongue while posing the suggestion.

"Honey, I know we would. But there is no way I can until this guy is caught."

"This week would have been three weeks in a row we haven't gotten together if I hadn't shown up. That's not good for any relationship," she pouted.

"I know it isn't. My partner and I will just have to try harder," he sighed.

Knowing the long hours Mitch had logged in the investigation, she now felt guilty. "I'm sorry for being bitchy. Let's just enjoy the times we do get together," she said as she moved the now empty plates to the floor.

She then pulled him close and opened his robe.

The next morning, after quietly showering and dressing, he gently kissed the sleeping Natalie and left a note on her pillow. The note read, "Thank you for camping out in the lobby last night. It was a fabulous surprise!"

With thoughts of last night's activities diminishing, his focus soon turned to work, with his mind soon being populated with ideas for that day's Activity Chart. He knew the start of the morning would be a good one. It was Diane's turn to bring the rolls and coffee.

CHAPTER FIFTY-TWO

Max spooned some brown sugar over his oatmeal and splashed some cream over it. He was seated in the small kitchenette just off their main office. Max detested coffee, while Mike needed its caffeine punch every morning. He just did not like having to make any.

Mike took turns obtaining his morning java fix from the three nearby outlets that he believed served damn good coffee: McDonalds, Dunkin Donuts, and 7-11. Today he had a large cup from 7-11 in one hand and a newspaper in the other.

He took a satisfying sip and unfolded the Tribune. When he turned to page three, he loudly declared, "God damn it!"

The unexpected remark so surprised Max he dropped his spoon in his bowl. It was quickly submerged in oatmeal quicksand. "What the hell caused that?"

"This picture," he pointed to a smiling picture of a beautiful young girl, Gabrielle Wilson. "Those fucking gangs had a shoot-out yesterday and she's in serious condition at Roseland Hospital because a stray bullet hit her in the back."

"Bro, this is Chicago. Unfortunately, this stuff happens every day. Why did this one set you off?"

He took a long pull from his coffee before he answered. "Do you remember that cute girl I had a crush on that lived down the hall from us when we were kids?"

"I sure do. You were totally smitten by her. Her name was Nadine, right?"

"Yes, that's the one. I lost track of her when we joined the army. About two years ago I found her on Facebook. I have been staying in touch with her. She married our classmate Russ Wilson right out of high school. They have three kids. He drives for the CTA. She is a stay at home mom. She recently posted some pictures of her kids. This was one of them," he said while pointing again to the paper. "She posted it on Facebook a few months back. It had the heading, My Little Angel Gabrielle."

Max digested the information and a pensive look resulted. "Mike, this may be something that *Mr. C* might like to pursue a little further."

"Great idea Max, or should I say, great idea, *Biceps*!"

"It certainly is, *Abs*."

The brothers burst out laughing.

The laughter passed quickly as the brothers then plotted different scenarios. If they were to get *Mr. C's* blessing, they knew a practical plan would be a requirement.

There were three issues to consider. One, what should the consequences be. Two and three, who would they be grabbing and how was it to be accomplished. Within an hour they had the makings for a solidly planned mission.

Abs glanced at the notes they had jotted down. “To make this one work, it looks like we will need you and me, *Surgeon*, *Mr. C*, and probably *Eyes* and *Ears*, depending on what *Mr. C’s* resources turn up.”

“I agree, let’s set up a meet with *Mr. C*,” *Biceps* said reaching for his Go Phone. “*Mr. C*, this is *Biceps*. *Abs* and I have an interesting proposition to pose to you. Can you make it to our office soon?”

“Thursday would be the soonest I can get over to your place. I can stop by around 11:00 p.m. Does that work for you?”

“It does.”

“Good, I’ll see you then.”

“He will be here around 11:00 p.m. on Thursday.”

“Great. Let’s discuss the consequences for these bastards some more. I just thought of a good one that would definitely be the proper consequence for these fuckers with their itchy trigger fingers.” *Abs* shared the consequence with his brother. When he was done, *Biceps* simply smiled.

A very wide smile.

CHAPTER FIFTY-THREE

After her usual strenuous early morning workout, Rosanna was relishing the fruit smoothie that Max had concocted as they relaxed in his office. As her straw made slurping sounds signaling a now empty glass, she exclaimed, "That was really good. Someday you will make someone an excellent husband."

"I'm glad I'm black, or you'd be looking at my blushing face."

Friendly chuckles followed the remark.

Rosanna's hand suddenly reached across the table and grasped his hand. "I have a question to ask you."

"Shoot'"

"When you said I looked really sexy when I dressed up as a lady of the evening, were you serious or just bullshitting me?"

"No, I was dead serious."

"How about when I just dress normal, do you find me attractive then?"

"Sweetheart, you would look sexy dressed in a potato sack."

She paused for what seemed like an eternity. "If you feel that way, why haven't you asked me for a date in the three years we have known each other?"

"Why do I feel that is a loaded question where I am in trouble no matter what I say?"

"Just tell me the truth. I promise I will not be mad at you."

Taking a deep breath he said, "Rosanna, the first time I saw you in the gym, my heart went pitty-pat. That old expression immediately came to mind. I think I'm in love! When I got to know you better, I realized you were the total dream package for any guy. Then I had a reality check. I thought: why would a glamorous movie star want to go out with a gym rat like me. So I settled for the next best thing: your friendship."

Both her hands now enveloped his as she said, "You foolish man. I came from the same tough neighborhoods as you did. I would never date someone who wanted me just because I am some glamorous movie star, as you called it. I want to be with someone who likes the real me, not some fantasy person that *People* magazine creates."

She squeezed his hands tighter, looked him straight in the eyes and offered a profound comment, "In fact, I believe it is very important that lovers also be friends."

"Are you saying if I asked you out, there is a possible chance I would hear a 'yes'?"

"Yes."

He eased off his chair, walked over to her and cupped her face in his hands. "Before I ask you for a date, how about we first find out if we have some chemistry going for us."

"That is one fine suggestion," she said as her lips moved to his. The initial tentative kiss rapidly became passionate, leaving them both a bit breathless as the kiss ended.

"I guess we passed the chemistry test."

She smiled back and said, "Hell, we didn't just pass, we aced it!"

"How about joining me for dinner and a movie?"

"Sure."

"I did not mention a day yet."

"It doesn't matter. Sure is still my answer."

He cupped her face once again as a gentle, yet ardent kiss ended the discussion.

CHAPTER FIFTY-FOUR

Mitch was smiling and whistling the theme song from *Bridge over the River Kwai* as he approached the office he and Diane were sharing. Diane was setting out the rolls and coffee as he approached.

"My, my, someone sure is in a good mood today."

"I'm simply rested, that's all."

"Oh, for a minute there, I thought you might have fingered Mr. Consequence."

"No such luck"

"The only other reason for that smile would be you got laid."

Crimson soon covered his face.

Seeing the blush, Diane snorted, "Bingo, I hit the nail on the head."

"A gentleman is always discreet. All I will say is that I may have had a friendly visitor stop by to say hello."

"That visitor wasn't named Natalie, was she?"

"That name rings a bell," Mitch offered. He then abruptly said, "Let's get to work."

The playful ribbing stopped as they reached to grab their favorite roll and a cup of coffee.

Diane started, "I've been giving some thought to our conversation with Sammy. I believe our best bet is to continue to follow up with possible surgical locations. To help us with some clues, I made two appointments for us today. The first one is 11:00 a.m. at Rush with Dr. Reynolds and the next one is at 1:30 p.m. Northwestern with Dr. Cooke."

"And why would we be visiting them?"

"Reynolds is an expert on anesthesia and Cooke heads up one of the surgery departments at Mercy. Both have been around a long time and are highly respected. Maybe Reynolds can give us some information to help us discover what Mr. Consequence is using to subdue his victims. If we know the what, then maybe we can isolate the where."

"That makes sense, what about Cooke?" She reached into her briefcase and took out a folder. She opened it and up close pictures of the victims' surgical scars were laid out. "I thought if we show him these pictures he might shed some light on who can do these or where these surgeries could be done—or both."

Mitch reached for the Action Chart, placed it on the table and said as he wrote her suggestions on it, "Partner, you done good. Let's do it."

She smiled at the compliment. "Not bad for a blond cop, huh?"

Mitch wisely played it safe with his answer. “Hell, they would be great ideas for any cop!”

That earned him a quick hug and a “Thanks, I needed that.”

CHAPTER FIFTY-FIVE

Nurse Cindy Walters was eating her usual Chef's salad in the hospital cafeteria when Susan Burdwell, her friend and co-worker slammed her tray on Cindy's table. Susan's hot dog jumped out of its bun blanket while her cup of jello danced.

Cindy cautiously inquired, "Having a bad day?" Susan took a deep breath and growled, "That rotten son of a bitch."

"Who got you so riled up?"

"Clifford Packowski."

Cindy knew the name. "Please don't tell me Patty was in the emergency room again."

"Yep. This time she said she tripped on a curb as she was getting out of her car."

"How bad is she?"

"She had contusions on both sides of her face and a bloody nose. Fortunately, it wasn't broken, this time."

"How many *accidents* has she had this year?"

"This was her fifth visit to the emergency room so far. She asked for privacy when she was told to put the gown on. I peeked through the curtain. She had bruises running up and down her ribs and chest."

Cindy, now as upset as Susan, said, "That fucking Clifford. When will Patty see the light and leave that bastard."

"Hell, I tried to get her to file charges every time she has been in. But she gets this deer-in-the-headlights look in her eyes and says 'no, no, it isn't Clifford. I'm just a clumsy person'."

"I know what you mean. The last time I treated her, I tried like hell to convince her to check into a shelter house. I got the same response."

"God damn him!"

"I wish."

No longer hungry, Cindy pushed her salad aside. Susan took one bite of her hot dog and did the same. "Susan, we can get mad, but there is nothing to stop Clifford's attacks unless Patty presses charges."

"I know, but jerks like him really piss me off."

They grabbed their trays, dumped the remains of their lunches in the trash, and headed back to the ER.

Jack Baxter had been sitting nearby with his back facing the two nurses. He quietly chewed on his sub sandwich. He had overheard the entire conversation. *Maybe, just maybe, it's time that someone reminded Clifford there should be consequences for his vicious forays.*

With a faint smile and a twinkle in his eyes, he mused, *and I just may know that someone.* Satisfied with this thought, he took a healthy bite of his sub.

CHAPTER FIFTY-SIX

"Please come in," Dr. Reynolds offered. "Would either of you like some coffee?"

"Yes, thank you Dr. Reynolds," said Diane while Mitch simply nodded.

"Help yourself." He pointed to a side table where the Bunn coffee machine and condiments were stationed. The coffee table offered large porcelain cups with the Rush Hospital insignia prominently displayed.

They took their coffee and set them on the coasters Dr. Reynolds had placed on his desk. They sat down on the two chairs that fronted the desk.

"So how may I assist you today, detectives?"

"As I mentioned on the phone, we are the lead detectives on the Mr. Consequence case, and we believe your expertise might assist us."

Diane then explained Sammy's theory that Mr. Consequence must have used some quickly administered knockout drug in order to incapacitate his victims. Dr. Reynolds jotted notes as Diane explained the reasoning behind this conclusion.

When Diane was finished, Dr. Reynolds placed his notes in front of him. He glanced down and said, "In order to shed some light on what might have been used, it is imperative to understand how anesthesia can be administered. It must be done by injection, inhaled gas vapors, an IV, or a combination of these. To render someone unconscious without detection by sneaking up close would most probably be an injection. Inhalation could also be a possibility. For the victims to be unaware, some pretty impressive diversion tactics would be necessary."

Mitch nodded as he reiterated Sammy's thoughts on the probability of a team effort. "Sammy also said either money, sex, or force would be likely in any diversion tactics."

"She sounds like a real smart lady. I would say that I would have to agree with her logic."

Dr. Reynolds continued. "As for detecting the source of the anesthesia, what was done, and when it was done are critical elements."

A confused Mitch asked, "Please clarify."

"An example should help you understand. Let's assume Seconal or a similar drug was injected. If a blood test were taken it might not discover any Seconal as it usually is undetectable in this type of test between 1-2 days. However if a hair follicle test were conducted, it would be traceable for almost 90 days."

"Looks like we need to visit the victims and give them a haircut. But I'm not familiar with hair follicle testing. How does it work," Diane asked.

"Well, you should clip the hair as close to the scalp as possible. One and a half inches would be about the length. A standard screen requires 40+ milligrams of hair or approximately 90 to 120 strands in order to trace a substance. The different thicknesses of head hair, thick, coarse versus thinning fine, is the reason for this variation."

"Thanks, that definitely gives us something to check out"

As Dr. Reynolds reached for his coffee, he stopped suddenly. "I just thought of something," he said.

"We're all ears doc, fire away." Diane hoisted her pen, ready to write.

"There is one way that might really catch a person off guard, but, as far as I know, it is not available to the public."

"If it isn't available, then who has it?"

"The military." Dr. Reynolds answered Mitch's query. "Special Forces would have access, and by now I would guess the CIA might also have access."

"Access to what," asked a puzzled Diane.

"I attended an anesthesiology seminar at Walter Reed Military Hospital about five years ago. We were having cocktails after a long day, when one of the Walter Reed scientists told us that they had perfected a tiny device that is remotely controlled. When it is set off, a gas substance is released that when breathed in immediately renders anyone unconscious. The residue aftermath dissipates in the air within minutes. The interesting part is there is no trace of the gas in the victim's body only four hours later. It was developed to assist clandestine military operations."

"Who might I call at Walter Reed," Diane asked, ready to jot down a name.

"Unfortunately, nobody is there anymore."

"Why?"

"It closed down in July of 2011, I believe. Any contacts I may have had would not be at the new facility. The old Walter Reed General Hospital was merged with the National Naval Medical Center in nearby Bethesda, Maryland. I understand the anesthesiology department was not part of the merger since the number of Naval staff anesthesiologists was quite adequate. So the anesthesiologists from there are spread throughout the rest of the country now. Plus, these seminars are simply a nice diversion from our everyday work. I remember the person's conversation about the device, but I could not recall his name. Our group from Rush mainly stayed together for most of the business sessions and all of the social gatherings. None of us really got to know the other anesthesiologists very well. We have a group meeting later this afternoon. I will ask anyone that was at the seminar if they remember the name of that scientist. Sorry about that."

"No need to apologize, Doctor. We would appreciate if you checked with your associates this afternoon. I'm sure Mitch and I would do pretty much the same at any police seminar."

"Yeah, having a few drinks with friends is a great alternative to work," Mitch added.

"It's nice to know we doctors have something in common with police officers," he said with a grin. "If you wish to follow up on the device, I believe he said it was developed for the Army's Special Forces. You may want to contact them."

"We will doc. I only hope the red tape in the Army is a lot shorter that the Chicago Police bureaucracy."

"If it isn't, Detective Mrozek, then you might want to check with the CIA. I'm sure they would be willing to share their secrets."

Laughing, Mitch and Diane thanked him for his time.

"I think after we meet with Dr. Cooke this afternoon, we should check out the hair follicle thing. What do you think Mitch?"

"Sounds good."

"We have time to grab some lunch. How about we stop for a combo at Al's?" "That sounds even better."

Mitch drove while Diane made notes to add to the Activity Chart.

"Please let this lead to something," she hoped.

CHAPTER FIFTY-SEVEN

"Right on time," *Abs* said as *Mr. C* entered the office.

"It's all that great officer training I got in the army," he smiled.

"Yes sir," *Abs* and *Biceps* mockingly shouted while performing a crisp salute. *Mr. C* returned the salute and sat down by their desk.

"So what is this important mission you would like the team to consider?"

"Have you ever had a major crush on a girl when you were a teenager?"

"More than one," he smiled.

"Well, I had a major one on a girl named Nadine."

"This story has a point, I hope."

"The little girl that was shot the other day is Nadine's daughter."

"I see your point. What do you propose?"

Abs and *Biceps* calmly discussed the multiple scenarios they had planned. *Mr. C* listened intently.

When they finished, he said, "I really like the second plan you mentioned."

"We do too."

"However, I have one caveat to add."

"We're listening."

"I believe it would be safest to target one gang for now. If necessary, we could expand from there."

"Just like we did with the drug pushers?"

He nodded.

Abs commented, "I bet you're thinking about the drastic drop in the drug trade that occurred after the multiple missions."

He nodded again.

They then exchanged ideas on how to best accomplish the operation.

"It looks like we have no choice but to put Mikey's toys to work again," *Biceps* noted.

"That's my thought also."

Abs asked, "Do you think Surgeon can do it all? It will require mucho multi-tasking."

"We'll ask him at our next meeting. Speaking of *Surgeon*, he called me today and he also has an interesting mission in mind." *Mr. C* then shared the story about Clifford and Patty. "In fact, *Surgeon* has a very interesting consequence in mind that would require your talents."

"What does he suggest?"

Mr. C. related *Surgeon's* idea.

"What a fucking great idea," said *Abs* as he high-fived his brother.

"I thought you might like it."

"I have already checked with the others. The meet is scheduled for midnight tomorrow. Does that work for you two?"

The brothers nodded.

He rose from his chair and said, "All right then. I'll see you tomorrow."

They stood, walked around the desk, bear-hugged, and then he left.

CHAPTER-FIFTY-EIGHT

"Good afternoon Dr. Cooke. I'm Detective Ryan and this is my partner Detective Mrozek."

"I understand you would like for me to view some post-operative photos. Today's schedule is a busy one for me. So let's get to it and see what you've got."

Diane removed the envelope from her briefcase. Dr. Cooke shook the photos free and arranged them based on the particular surgical procedure. He produced a magnifying glass from a pocket in his smock and carefully examined each photo. Carefully written notes were taken. He placed the magnifying glass and pen down and reached for the notes he had taken.

"I'm ready for your questions."

Diane took the lead. "What sort of specialist could accomplish operations such as these?"

"Actually, a pretty large range could have done the work on the ones you have listed as Jo-Jo and Ray-Ray. Those two had operations whose goal was to destroy, not cure. That would be a piece of cake for just about any surgeon. The operations on the drug dealers is a completely different story. My guess is these were done by a very skilled brain surgeon."

"Why?"

"Believe it or not Detective Mrozek, a lobotomy was once considered a preferred cure for mental illness. In order to perform this operation a precise knowledge of the brain is necessary. In this procedure a surgeon scrapes away the connections to and from the prefrontal cortex. The cortex is the anterior part of the frontal lobes of the brain." He then removed a Philips screwdriver from his desk drawer. He wave it in front of them and said, "Not only is a precise knowledge of the brain necessary, but a precise tool is needed for the skull since the operation is performed through the eye socket of the patient. The tool resembles this screwdriver."

Diane winced at the thought.

Mitch took over the questioning. "It sounds like you are leaning to a conclusion that a brain surgeon is probably involved."

"Yes, that would be correct."

"Our profiler believes it may be a team behind these Mr. Consequence episodes. Could it be more than one surgeon or is there something about the technique that confirms a solitary surgeon?"

"Since we usually don't carve our initials on a patient after a surgery, it would be most difficult to isolate who did the work. The only part of these pictures that I can isolate would be the lobotomies. I would definitely say a brain surgeon. But as to who, your guess is as good as mine."

Mitch continued with another question. "Where could these operations have taken place?"

"Just about any well-lit and disinfected room would be sufficient."

"So it would not be necessary to be done in a hospital?"

"Not at all."

"Before you leave detectives, I would like to point out additional needs of these operations. In every one of these procedures, an assistant, or nurse if you will, would definitely be a necessity. Someone fully educated in the use of anesthetics would be another. Your profiler is correct in saying this is no individual effort."

They thanked Dr. Cooke, shook hands, and left.

CHAPTER FIFTY-NINE

After the interviews Mitch drove to meet his uncle for a late lunch.

"I'm starving, where are we meeting for lunch?"

"Magda's."

"What the hell is a Magda's?"

"Only the best Polish food in Chicago."

"Well, knowing our similar tastes in food, I guess I'll give it a shot."

"Thanks. I haven't been able to meet with my uncle for lunch or dinner in weeks. I told him we were too busy to meet with him. He used his impeccable persuasion tactics on me."

"What did he say?"

"You and your partner have to eat sometime. Give me the time you will be having lunch and we can meet at Magda's. My treat."

"I like the *my treat* part."

"I think you'll like the food even more."

"That's even better!"

Mitch rolled into the parking lot and Uncle Matt waved to them from one of the window booths. As they approached the table, Uncle Matt embraced Mitch while planting kisses on each cheek in Eastern European fashion.

When he noticed Diane standing quietly behind Mitch he took her hand, kissed it, and exclaimed in a robust voice, "If I could get a partner as lovely as you, I'd be a cop!"

"I warned you about his persuasive tactics."

"No need for tactics when all I do is speak the truth."

"He makes a very good point, Mitch," Diane said as she pecked Uncle Matt on the cheek for the compliment.

He rubbed his cheek and with a soulful look said, "Young lady, you have ruined my day."

"How did I do that?"

"After that kiss, I now have nothing to look forward to the rest of the day." He winked at Diane, they laughed out loud, then snuggled into the booth.

"So, are you familiar with Polish food?"

"You tell me. My last name is Ryan."

"You poor girl, having to eat boiled potatoes and cabbage as your *haute cuisine*. Does she have a good appetite Mitch?"

"When it's good stuff she can eat more than me."

"Wonderful, please allow me the honor of ordering for you."

"Please do, but I have to warn you, I am really hungry."

"That is music to my ears." He then signaled to Helga, his favorite waitress, who stood nearby waiting for his summons.

Steaming bowls of sauerkraut soup arrived first. The soup was splashed over boiled potatoes and topped with thick pieces of chunk bacon. Uncle Matt had ordered his favorite smoked butt dish while Mitch chose the Polish sausage and pierogi platter. Diane's dish was the Magda Sampler. It was an enormous plate of sausage, smoked butt, golabki, pierogi, butter drenched dumplings, and a potato pancake.

Twenty minutes later Diane speared the last remaining morsel, a dumpling, and savored it by chewing slowly.

"My tata would have loved you. You clean your plate very well. So you liked it."

"All I can say is, I'll meet you back here anytime. This was unique and super good."

"Good to hear, how about tomorrow?" That brought chuckles all around.

"Uncle Matt, as much as Diane and I would love to meet you here every day, we just can't. Our case is just taking too much of our time. I promise to get together sooner than it was this time around."

Uncle Matt raised his hands in submission. "I of all people know the meaning of being too busy."

"That's an understatement."

He looked at Diane and asked, "So how is your investigation going?"

Diane sighed. "Not as well as we would like it, but we have been making progress."

"Forgive me for saying, but many Chicagoans hope you never catch the guy, including me."

"Don't we know it. He's become the latest version of Robin Hood. And like Robin, our profiler thinks he has some of his Merry Men along for the adventures."

Diane then shared some of Sammy's insights. "She really thinks it's a team led by this Mr. Consequence. She believes his warning *IT IS TIME TO MAKE THE BAD GUYS PAY* indicates a childhood trauma that was never resolved."

"Why?"

"She said the use of the term, *Bad Guys*, would be a child's response."

Mitch had been trying to get a word in, but Diane was on rapid chatter. Finally, he lightly kicked Diane under the table and interrupted. "Hey guys, I came here to get away from work and relax. I really am tired of talking about Mr. Consequence. Can we please talk about something else?" Diane eyes flashed at Mitch, over the interruption, and the kick.

"Sorry, Uncle Matt. We really haven't been making much headway on the case and talking about it makes me feel even worse about it."

"I understand. I too need to get away from the grind once in a while."

"Thanks for understanding."

The remainder of the lunch visit focused on the Chicago Bears' prospects for success this year.

Helga reappeared and asked, "dessert, anyone?"

"But of course. Bring us a big platter of kruschiki. Sprinkle lots of powdered sugar on them. And a pot of coffee would be nice."

Diane asked, "What is a kroosh-cheeky?"

"Lovely lady, it is a gift from heaven. That's why they are called *angel wings*."

Helga returned and laid the bountiful platter on the table. Diane reached for one and took a bite. "Oh My God!"

"They're good, huh?" Uncle Matt asked with a twinkle in his eye.

"Oh yeah."

The platter was soon relieved of its bounty.

Helga brought the check and Uncle Matt paid and left his usual big tip. Helga scooped up the cash, smiled at Uncle Matt and said, "Thanks honey, I really appreciate it."

"And I appreciate getting great service from a beautiful woman."

Her blush trickled down her face to the back of her neck as she happily pocketed the tip and walked to the register.

"You just made her day."

"That was my intent, Diane. Helga is a widow who works long hours in order to send her two daughters to college so they might have a better life. I respect and admire that."

Mitch stood, signaling an end to the lunch.

"Remember, don't be a stranger."

"I promise I won't."

The two men embraced once again and Uncle Matt got another peck on the cheek from Diane. He touched the kissed cheek and said, "That was even sweeter than the kruschiki."

"You are pretty sweet yourself. Thank you very much for lunch."

"It was my pleasure."

It was a fitting ending to a sumptuous meal.

When he closed his car door and adjusted his seatbelt, a past memory suddenly occurred to Uncle Matt. He considered it for a moment, and then vigorously shook his head and loudly exclaimed, "Nah." He started the engine of his Mercedes-Benz S65 AMG and pulled away.

Diane and Mitch climbed into the sedan and Mitch suggested, "Let's head back to the office and arrange to check out that hair follicle test Dr. Cooke suggested."

"Okay. By the way, your uncle is one really nice guy."

"Tell me something I don't know."

"But you didn't have to butt in and be rude to him, and kicking me under the table wasn't especially appreciated either."

"I'm sorry. Like I said, I'm feeling a lot of pressure on this case and I just didn't want to spend what little free time we have talking shop. Forgive me?"

"Only if you treat me to lunch at Magda's again. In the very near future."

"It's a deal."

Silence then settled in as they were drowsy from the big meal and their minds were preoccupied considering their next moves.

CHAPTER SIXTY

It was the midnight hour and the team members were all present and accounted for, except for *The Don*, of course. *Mr. C* addressed the team wearing his usual fashion accessory: a ski mask.

"Thank you all for being prompt. Tonight we are going to discuss the possibility of two missions. *Abs* and *Biceps* have suggested a target. The *Surgeon* also has one. Before they fill us in, *Eyes* and *Ears* have information regarding the progress of the police investigation they would like to share with us. Go ahead guys."

Ears stood. "My brother and I have obtained some interesting developments. The two detectives are now convinced that our work is definitely not being accomplished by a solitary individual. They believe that a team with specific skills is at play. They suspect a very skilled surgeon is involved."

He nodded at *Surgeon*.

Surgeon smiled at that and said, "At least they were kind enough to call me very skilled!" Laughter followed.

"They also suspect some heavy muscle." He nodded to the twins who stood and flexed their biceps while mimicking body builder poses. More laughter ensued.

"They also suspect someone may be luring the victims through sexual promises." He nodded to *Actress* who rose, displayed a coquettish smile and blew kisses to everyone. More laughter followed.

"Lastly, they are curious as to the location of the surgery being performed. They now believe it could be somewhere other than a hospital."

Silence reigned for a moment as they digested this information.

A confused *Surgeon* asked, "How the hell are you guys getting all of this info?"

Eyes then stood, nodded at *Mr. C* and in an exaggerated German accent replied, "Ve have our Vays!" More laughter erupted.

Mr. C then raised his hand signaling for silence. "Thank you, *Eyes* and *Ears*. You certainly are living up to your codenames. This reinforces the imperative need to proceed with impeccable caution. When we are discussing the next two possibilities, let's make sure we focus on tactics that will be trace-free. So far we have been very careful about that, but even so, the detectives have still hit pretty close to home."

Affirmative nods were given by all.

"*Abs* and *Biceps*, please share your thoughts on your suggested mission."

Abs stood. "You all probably read about the drive by shooting the other day where a gang member was killed and others were injured. Two of the injuries were two young girls playing nearby. One of the little girl's name is Gabrielle.

When I was a teenager, I was in love with her mother. So you can understand when I say these drive bys are really pissing me off. Here is what my brother and I propose." He then described the plan that they had developed.

"With Mikey's toys I believe we can pull this off without a trace. However, it will depend on whether or not *Surgeon* can accomplish his role in a reasonable timeframe."

Surgeon spoke. "What you are proposing would take a maximum of two hours tops as long as you and your brother assist me."

"That timeline would work," *Abs* replied.

Mr. C asked, "All in favor, raise your hands." All arms extended immediately. "Okay, it is a go. *Eyes* and *Ears*, we will wait for your feedback on when and where would be best. How soon could you pinpoint a time and a place?"

"Less than a week should be enough."

"I will wait for your call. *Surgeon*, you now have the floor."

Surgeon then described the scene at the hospital's lunchroom. "Here is what I propose." After he finished, *Actress* yelled, "BRAVO." *Surgeon* smiled at the comment and said, "Knowing your past situation, I thought I would have your approval."

Mr. C cautiously inquired, "The plan has merit, but I am concerned about the possible connection to *Abs* and *Biceps*."

Biceps answered with a smirk, "What he means is they may discover some black guys are involved."

Everyone laughed.

"*Mr. C*, I think that can be remedied very easily," Abs countered.

"How?"

"My bro and I could wear a full length spandex outfit. Wearing gloves and a really scary mask would easily complete the disguise."

Mr. C considered this a while, and then nodded. "That would work." He addressed the group again, "All in favor." Before he could finish, all hands were spiking the air. "*Abs* and *Biceps*, can you do the recon on this Packowski guy?"

"It shouldn't be a problem."

"Great. Meeting is adjourned. I'll be in touch after I get the info from the spotters we discussed this evening. Good night all."

As they exited, *Eyes* poked *Ears* in the ribs and whispered, "Check that out."

He pointed to *Actress* and *Biceps* who were walking to the exit door holding hands. "It seems like some members of the team are bonding nicely," was his retort.

"It looks more like very nicely, that lucky SOB."

"A very lucky SOB"

CHAPTER SIXTY-ONE

They immediately pulled out the Action Chart and Diane added the information the two doctors had given them. They then highlighted the data they felt was most important.

"That Dr. Reynolds sure knows his shit. The hair follicle lab report found Seconal as the culprit, just as he suspected. Nice call on that one Diane."

"Knowing what it is helps. Let's check out where someone can obtain it.

They went to their computers and searched it in Google. "This is interesting. The major supplier of Seconal was Eli Lilly. However they took it off the market."

Diane added as she shut down her computer, "And it looks like U.S. doctors no longer prescribe it."

"So where does that leave us?"

"Looks like tracking its purchase is an episode from Mission Impossible."

Mitch agreed, and asked, "Where do we go from here?"

"Let's get the Action Chart out and brain storm some more."

After a lengthy discussion, Diane placed a check-mark next to one of the highlighted sections. "I feel our next best step should be to follow up on this one." She pointed to the highlighted line; operations required a very skilled surgeon.

"Okay, how do you want to do it?"

"Dr. Cooke said it is most probably a brain surgeon. Let's start calling the heads of brain surgery from every hospital."

"What would we tell them?"

"We explain what we learned and ask if they have noticed any strange behavior recently from any surgeons in their department. We also ask if someone has been asking for an abrupt change in hours recently. If we get some hits, we list them and arrange for personal interviews."

Mitch reached for the two yellow-page phone books he kept in his bottom drawer and handed one to Diane.

"What do I need this for?"

"I like to be thorough. I'll start with the A's and go down. You start with the Z's and go up. That way we make sure we don't miss any of the hospitals."

"By having two of these, I assume you have used this technique in the past."

"Larry and I spent many an hour telephone surfing with these babies. It even worked a couple of times," he grinned.

She opened the phone book to the list of hospitals. “I guess we better get started.”

“Let’s.” Mitch opened his book and they started the phone marathon.

CHAPTER SIXTY-TWO

Natalie was running late. She was hustling over to the Italian Village Restaurant to meet with her sister Judy. Her Monday morning taped interview had been with Glenn Bablarski, the Board of Trade's latest poster child. Amassing twenty million in profits over a two week span definitely qualifies one for poster child status.

She was impressed by his obvious skills and the humility that accompanied them. It didn't hurt that he was a sweet piece of eye-candy. The fact that he was single was an added attraction.

He was in no hurry to leave once the interview was a wrap. For over an hour they chatted about where they came from and where they would like to go.

Natalie was flattered by his attention. However, she was both excited and uncomfortable when it became apparent their future plans were definitely compatible.

Her relationship with Mitch was the cause of her discomfort. Her mixed feelings received another jolt when he left saying, "I'll give you a call sometime soon."

Then she remembered. "Oh shit, Judy's waiting for me."

She was fifteen minutes late as she rushed to Judy who standing by a booth signaling her. "I was hungry, so I started without you."

Natalie glanced down and saw a last lonely bit of calamari on a platter.

The waiter appeared before Natalie could get a hello in. "Good afternoon, miss. May I get you a beverage?"

"Yes, a glass of Pinot Grigio would be nice."

"Coming right up." He placed the menu next to her and went to get her wine.

"Sorry I'm late, Jude. There were some issues at the station I needed to fix before I left." She was too embarrassed to share the real reason.

"That's fine. I'm just glad you were able to meet with me today."

The waiter returned and placed the wine down and asked, "Are you ready to order ladies?"

"Go ahead Jude, I'm still deciding."

"I'll have the house salad, with blue cheese dressing, and have them sprinkle extra blue cheese on it, a bowl of the minestrone, eggplant parmesan, and the death by chocolate for dessert."

Natalie was wide-eyed when she heard Judy's food order litany. She simply said, "I'll have the seafood salad with lite Italian dressing."

The waiter noted the orders and headed to the kitchen.

"I thought you were ordering for the four people at that table." The table she referred to seated four very portly ladies. "Plus, what's with all the veggies for lunch? You always said that the grilled Italian sausage was your favorite dish here."

"Well it is, but I thought veggies would be better for the baby."

"What baby? Oh my God, you're pregnant," she shouted.

Judy meekly nodded.

Natalie bolted over to Judy's side of the booth and wrapped her arms around her. She noticed the customers staring at her over the commotion as she returned to her seat.

Facing the stares she said, "Everything is okay. In fact, it is very okay. My sister is going to have her first baby."

The stares transformed to smiles and erupted in applause from everyone.

"You're embarrassing me."

"That's what big sisters are for. Now tell me all the wonderful details."

Between mouthfuls, Judy shared how she had been trying to conceive for the last three months and how thrilled they were. "Plus, Teddy has always loved the country life over the city life since he was raised on a ranch in Wyoming. He now has an opportunity to follow his dream. His widowed aunt Amy wants us to join her in Montana. She owns an enormous Bison ranch and offered a partnership to Ted if we would work the spread with her. Getting pregnant was the clincher. No way do we want to raise our child in a big city. It's the right move for us, especially with a baby in the oven."

Just then, their food order arrived. They dug in heartily after the good news was announced.

"I am so jealous," Natalie exclaimed after finishing her salad.

"Yeah, right, Miss TV personality jealous of a future farm girl."

"A farm girl that is going to have one beautiful baby!"

"There is that, I guess. Will you be the godmother?"

That opened the faucets. Wiping her tears with her sleeve, Natalie said, "If you didn't ask me, I would never speak to you again!" They squeezed hands and laughed.

Judy spooned the last remnants of the death by chocolate dessert. "God, that was good."

"If you keep eating like this, you'll be looking like a hippo soon."

"But I'll be a happy hippo." They laughed again.

Natalie called for the check. The waiter approached empty handed and explained, "The owner overheard the earlier outburst and insisted your lunch be *au gratis*. That's French for no charge!"

"Congratulations," he offered to Judy.

"Tell your boss that we appreciate his generosity, and this is for you." Judy gave him a twenty.

He graciously thanked them as they exited the restaurant.

"Teddy and I will be celebrating on Friday. Will you join us for dinner?"

"I'd love to."

"Feel free to bring a date, Teddy is treating!"

She figured Mitch would be working on the Consequence case but answered, "I'll try my best."

After hugs and kisses they went their separate ways.

A melancholy mood snuck up on her as she walked back to the station. She somberly thought, *Judy is five years younger and already is living the American girl's dream. A country home with a white picket fence, a man who loves her, and, she is going to be a mommy.*

She reflected on the earlier private conversation with Glenn

By the time she reached her desk she had concluded, "I've got to make a choice."

CHAPTER SIXTY-THREE

"*Mr. C, Ears* here, we have a confirmation and a location for a pick-up on the Black Disciple gang."

"That was quick, how did you do it."

"Well, Orkin is a frequent visitor to the homes in that part of town. *Eyes* and I dressed up as Orkin guys and were able to plant our peek-a-boo toys. Once we got the info we needed the toys were removed. That way, no trace."

"Good work. What is the plan?"

"The gang is heading out on Friday at 10:00 p.m. for a drug score."

"That is three days from now. I will contact *Abs* and *Biceps* about setting up Mikey's gadget. I will also confirm the mission with *Surgeon*. He is the one that has to be available."

"Roger that. Over and out." *Ears* shut down the Go-phone.

Mr. C then speed-dialed *Biceps*.

"*Surgeon* is available. Can you and *Abs* rig their van with Mikey's canister?"

"It should be easy *Mr. C, Abs* and I blend in well with that neighborhood."

"Good. The mission is a go. I will contact *The Don* and let him know that we will be visiting on Friday. How is that surveillance on the Packowski guy going?"

"Very well. Every Friday he hits the same bar after work. He parks in the back lot. He gets there early so he usually is the only car parking back there. The takedown should not be a problem."

"It looks like Friday is one lucky day."

"Maybe for us, but it sure the hell isn't going to be for the Bad Guys." *Mr. C* smiled at the remark as he hung up.

*　　　*　　　*　　　*　　　*

Abs asked his brother, "Where did you put it?"

"Underneath the driver's seat."

Abs gave his brother a fist bump after hearing his answer.

It was 11:00 p.m. on Thursday.

On Friday evening, *Abs*, *Biceps*, and the *Surgeon* waited in their van which was positioned behind a large truck about thirty yards from the Black Disciple van. It was 9:30 p.m.

Abs instructed, "The moment they start the engine, I'll trigger the device. You pull up next to the van and I will climb in and drive it to *The Don's*. You and *Surgeon* will follow me there. Are we all clear on that?"

Both of them responded. “All clear.”

“Okay, let’s get ready,” *Abs* said as he carefully got his gas mask in place.

At 9:45 p.m. the gang left the house and entered the van. There were six of them.

“Looks like all the members are accounted for,” *Biceps* said as he counted them. “Just the way we like it.”

The engine started. *Abs* pushed the button. They quickly drove to the gang’s van. *Abs* got out and opened the driver’s door. A cloud of Mikey’s Magic escaped from the van. Abs placed the sleeping driver over a comatose passenger and pulled away. *Biceps* followed.

Thirty minutes later, both vehicles were driving up the now familiar driveway of *The Don*.

The Don was seated in his usual chair sipping the ever present glass of grappa when he heard the garage door opening. He lifted the glass and toasted, “To another successful evening.” He drained the grappa and poured another.

Making sure the gang would remain unconscious, *Surgeon* administered the needed anesthetics. The visual that *Eyes* had observed with the toys they had left behind in the Orkin run, indicated all members of the gang were right-handed. This was important in order for a successful mission.

“Scalpel,” *Surgeon* announced and *Biceps* placed it in his hand. The mission began.

One hour and forty-five minutes later, it was done.

“Let’s get them back in the van. Is the sign in place?”

“Indeed it is bro,” *Biceps* replied.

Surgeon wondered as he lifted a bag with the remnants of the mission, “How can we get rid of this so there are no comebacks?”

“Already taken care of,” *Biceps* smiled. “While you guys were working, I called *The Don*. He said to leave the bag on the table. He has a friend of a friend that owns a mortuary. It will disappear with his next customer who is scheduled for this morning. The ashes are to be scattered in Lake Michigan this afternoon. So the answer my friend, will be blowing in the wind.”

“Sounds good, Bob Dylan,” *Surgeon* said as he high-fived *Biceps*.

Biceps added, “Don’t forget. *Mr C* said to make sure we set aside one of them.”

Abs produced a sandwich bag and wiggled it. “I did not forget, let’s move.”

The gang was secured in the van and *Biceps* drove to the agreed upon drop-off point: an alley behind abandoned houses on the South Side. They all agreed it was an appropriate location to get rid of trash.

As they left the alley, *Abs* called *Ears*. "*Mr. C* wants you to call our friend Abigail when the sun comes up. That will work just fine because Surgeon's knock-out drops will keep them sleeping until mid-morning. Plus, no one goes in that abandoned alley." He made the call. Ten minutes after the call to Abigail, he called 9-1-1.

Tom Jackson and Mike Krinski were the responders once again. Cary was already clicking away as *Abs* was kind enough to leave the side door of the van open just for this purpose. The door faced a dilapidated garage, so the opened door went unseen by any possible passer-byes. Tom recognized Cary immediately.

"Where's Abigail?"

"Over here, Officer Jackson," she said as she walked out from behind the van. "And no, Cary and I have not disturbed the crime scene, so don't even ask."

Mike looked inside and his eyes focused on the latest message from Mr. Consequence which was scrawled on a large poster board:

NO MORE DRIVE-BY SHOOTINGS FOR THIS GANG.

SEVERED TENDONS HAVE A TENDENCY TO STOP THAT.

MISSING TRIGGER FINGERS CAN ALSO BE A MAJOR DETERRENT.

HELL—THEY WILL NOW BE HARD-PRESSED
TO WIPE THEIR BUTTS.

THIS IS JUST THE BEGINNING—YOU BAD GUYS OUT THERE—
KEEP SHOOTING AND YOU WILL BE NEXT.

—MR. CONSEQUENCE

"Yes, indeedy, I do believe I have a front page picture here," Cary gushed as he showed Abigail the picture: a close up of a stitched wrist with the hand missing a trigger finger.

"And I have the perfect headline for my story: Mr. Consequence's Version of Gun Control."

Cary patted her on the back enthusiastically as they raced back to their car.

Abigail shouted to the officers, "Bye guys."

After checking out the scene, Mike held up his palms and said, "I know, I know. I need to call Captain Krol right now."

Tom simply nodded.

CHAPTER SIXTY-FOUR

"Let's look at what we've got," Mitch said after they had manned the phones for the last three hours. "I have four possibilities, how about you?"

"Five," Diane said as she held up her notepad. She then asked Mitch, "What are yours?"

Mitch, glancing at his notepad, said, "Two of the brain surgeons have been asking for a number of days off the past month. Two others have a reputation for being extreme Right Wingers. The last one is a surgeon from Pakistan whose department head said he acts very strangely."

"They sound pretty much like mine, except for your Pakistani."

"It's well past the lunch hour," Mitch said as he checked his watch. "How about we put together a plan of action over corned beefs at Manny's?"

"That works for me." Then the phone rang.

"Detective Mrozek here."

"Hi Mitch, this is Natalie."

"What's cooking?"

With a somber voice she said, "We need to talk."

Mitch recognized the symptoms her voice portrayed. He had been there, done that.

"So talk."

"Not over the phone, I'm downstairs in the waiting room. Can you spare me a few minutes. I promise not to take too much of your time."

"Okay, I'll be right down."

She was alone in the waiting room so Mitch took her in his arms and reached in for a kiss. All he made contact with was her cheek.

She got right to the point. "Mitch, something happened at lunch today that put me in a tizzy."

"What happened?"

She recounted the lunch with Judy.

Mitch knew where this was headed.

"I suddenly realized my biological clock is ticking. My God, Judy is five years younger than me. Five years!" She paused as she pulled a tissue from her purse, dabbed her eyes, and blew her nose. "The time you and I spent together was really great, but today I realized I want more. I want what my sister has, a husband, a home, and yes, a baby. I know we agreed to no strings attached, but I need to ask you, are my wants in our future?"

Knowing words would not be sufficient, Mitch shook his head no.

"I met someone on my show today. I can't be sure, but I think he could possibly turn out to be what I am looking for."

Mitch gathered her in his arms, kissed her forehead and said, "Natalie, I will always treasure the times we shared. I only want you to be happy. If breaking up frees you to follow your dreams, then I understand it is something you have to do."

More tears trickled down her cheeks.

"But understand this," he continued. If this new guy doesn't treat you right, tell him you have a friend who is a very mean and tough cop."

"Oh Mitch, thank you so much for understanding." She followed that up with one last lingering kiss. Mitch then did his best Bogie impersonation and said, "Remember this, kid, we'll always have Paris." She laughed, smiled, and left.

Mitch trudged slowly back to his desk.

"Bad news?" Diane asked when he returned.

"Only for one of us. Let's go eat."

Sensing his mood, Diane attempted to cheer him up. "My treat today."

Mitch looked up and a smile slowly formed. "You really don't have to, but I accept." That earned him a punch on the arm as they headed to Manny's.

They were almost out the door when Captain Krol returned from his now daily morning meetings with the mayor. He entered the squad room and barked, "Mrozek, Ryan, in my office now."

"There goes the corned beef sandwich I was fantasizing about."

"Just hold on to that fantasy. Maybe later, still my treat."

Captain Krol was standing by his door when they approached. The fact that he slammed it shut after they entered was not lost on either of them. Mitch's thought as the door loudly exclaimed its agony was, *Looks like that corned beef sandwich may remain a fantasy for a long, long, time.*

Krol muttered as Mitch and Diane took a seat, "Mr. Consequence has struck again. Look at this." He passed over the Sun-Times. Cary's prized photo was prominently displayed over half of the page. Abigail's headline for her story was THE headline: ***Mr. Consequence's Version of Gun Control.***

"The mayor is having fits. The phone's been ringing off the hook at City Hall. It seems the public wants the mayor to hire this guy, not arrest him." Mitch silently read Abigail's details of the event and passed it to Diane when he finished. "Captain, I assure you we are following all possible pertinent information. Not having any physical evidence is slowing the process down."

"I understand that, Mrozek. Are you sure the forensics team has done due diligence?"

"Sir, they have gone over every nook and cranny with a fine tooth comb, and NADA."

"Captain, because of this lack of physical evidence," Diane said, "Mitch and I have been pursuing possible hows and whos. In fact, we spent most of the morning assembling possible suspects regarding the surgical techniques that are being used. We were about to leave and do that when you summoned us." She wisely did not mention the corned beef sandwiches at Manny's.

"Tell me about the whos on your suspect list."

Diane pointed out Dr. Cooke's assessment that a very skilled brain surgeon is a high probability. She explained the phone surfing hunt she and Mitch had conducted this morning.

Mitch passed him the list of suspects and explained why they might be of interest.

"This is good creative thinking. Sorry about my gruffness but the Superintendent and the Mayor are expecting immediate results. I explained to them that the lack of trace has made our investigation difficult."

"Did they understand that?"

"You have to understand Ryan, the longer our superiors are away from fieldwork, the easier investigations seem to them. So they are pushing hard for results, not excuses."

"Well, time's a wasting sir. Diane and I better get a move on."

"You're right, Mrozek." The captain stood and shook their hands while adding, "Good Luck and Good Hunting. Let me know your results ASAP. I'm sure the mayor will be checking with me all afternoon," he sighed.

Better you than us, Diane thought but did not verbalize.

"Are we still stopping for that corned beef sandwich first?"

"I always thought our bodies and minds functioned best when properly fueled," Diane said with a smile.

"I like the way you think. I also like the fact you are buying!" The comment earned Mitch another friendly jab.

"Make sure you bring the list, we'll plan the interviews over lunch."

Mitch replied, "Already ahead of you on that one. I even wrote down the phone numbers for each suspect so we can call them on our cells for appointments."

"Good boy. You are very thorough."

"No, very logical." That got him another jab as they head out for the hunt.

CHAPTER SIXTY-FIVE

"*Mr. C, Biceps* here."

"What have you got for me?"

"*The Don* has it set up for Friday. Another friend of a friend took care of it. Man, I sure am glad he is our friend!"

"What about the takedown?"

"The plan is to take this Packowski guy down with chloroform. *Surgeon* has prepared a concoction that will put him out for an hour. The fun begins when he wakes up."

"What's the plan once you are finished with him?"

"More chloroform to keep him under wraps for a while then we drop him off with his sign by the trash dumps behind one of the battered women's shelter homes. Then *Ears* makes his calls to Abigail and 9-1-1."

"Which shelter house?"

"Not sure yet. There are a few on the near north-side. *Abs* and I plan on scoping out one that would allow an easy drop-off without being seen."

"Sounds like you have your ducks in a row—now get quacking!"

They both laughed as they hit the end call buttons on their Go-phones.

"Come on bro, get a move on. I want to finish the recon on the shelter houses before 6:00 p.m."

"What's the hurry?"

"Got a dinner and movie date with a pretty girl."

"*Actress*?"

"My, my, you sure are a nosy one."

"Maybe, but I am accurate, ain't I?"

"Yeah, it's with Rosanna."

"What fancy place are you taking her to?"

"She hates eating out because she is always swamped by fans and she doesn't want to do her disguise thing, so she is cooking at her place plus she has Netflix and a big screen TV. She says she makes a world class Steak Adobo."

"I love Steak Adobo. What time does she want us to be there?"

"She wants ME there at 7:00 p.m. You, maybe never!"

After exchanging brotherly punches, they climbed in the car and headed to recon the shelter houses.

Mr. C then called *Ears*. "Is everything in place ready to send?"

"My brother and I uploaded the phones with your message and Cary's front page picture this morning. We were waiting on your call. The access codes you provided were as good as gold. We have all the cell phone numbers."

"I understand you and *Eye*s plan to send and dispose just like you did with the drug dealer messages."

"Yep, when we are done, the phones will be swimming with the fishes."

"Afterwards, we plan another stop at Billy Goat's."

"Enjoy your cheezborgers!"

"We surely will." *Ears* closed the phone and he and *Eyes* walked to their familiar secluded rail overlooking the lake.

The messages and accompanying picture were sent to key members of major gangs throughout the city. It was a simple message:

HELLO. IN CASE YOU FORGOT, I AM WATCHING—

I THOUGHT THIS SUN-TIMES PHOTO OF
THE NOW TRIGGER-FINGERLESS BLACK DISCIPLES
MIGHT JOG YOUR MEMORY—
OH—DON'T FORGET THEIR WRISTS ARE NOW TENDONLESS TOO.
I DO NOT TRUST YOU—

IF YOU DO NOT WANT THE SAME CONSEQUENCE
I REQUIRE A SHOW OF GOOD FAITH.
IT'S REALLY VERY SIMPLE.

GATHER YOUR GUNS AND PLACE THEM IN A DUFFEL BAG
OR BAGS IF NEEDED.

AT PRECISELY 7:30 P.M. THIS FRIDAY YOU ARE TO VISIT EITHER
THE CHURCHES OF ST. ELIZABETH OR ST. JEROME.
ENTER THE CHURCH AND PLACE THE BAGS ON THE LAST PEW ON
THE LEFT SIDE. YOU MAY RECOGNIZE RIVAL GANG MEMBERS
DOING THE SAME—DON'T BE ALARMED—

YOU ARE TO IGNORE EACH OTHER OR FACE THE
CONSEQUENCES—THEY VALUE THEIR FINGERS AND WRISTS AS
MUCH AS YOU DO.

IT WOULDN'T HURT TO LIGHT A CANDLE
WHILE YOU ARE THERE.

IF THIS IS NOT DONE—
PREPARE TO FACE THE CONSEQUENCES.

—MR. CONSEQUENCE

When they were done, the phones dove into Lake Michigan to begin their *swim with the fishes*. Afterwards, Billy Goat's cheezborgers hit the spot.

The day before, *Mr. C,* using *Ears's* voice machine had called the pastors of each of these churches. He introduced himself, and explained his plan to them.

They readily agreed to arrange for church doors to be closed except for duffel carrying parishioners. Both were enraged over past gun activity in their congregations and had presided over many funerals of innocents. They were ecstatic to learn someone was willing to make a difference. Father Gunther phrased it best when he closed the conversation with, "Bless you my child. May God protect and keep you."

"I won't turn that down." He ended both calls with a grin.

A call was placed to the local police stations late Friday night by both churches reporting the strange deliveries of duffel bags. The pastors feigned the same surprise as the responding officers did at the contents of the bags. *Mr. C* had instructed each gang member to write a special message. Buried at the bottom of each bag a note read. *Complements of Mr. Consequence.*

"Praise the lord," cried out Father Gunther.

Unexpected "Amens' were mouthed by a few of the officers as they gathered the hardware.

Officer Konecki, whose cousin was wounded the year before by a random gunfight, summed up the feelings of his fellow officers with this thought; "I really, really, am starting to like this guy. Stay Free, Mr. Consequence, stay Free."

CHAPTER SIXTY-SIX

She raced from the kitchen to answer the buzzer. "Who is it?"

"Prince Charming."

"Come on up. Prince."

Max rushed and headed to the elevator. His heart was pounding and palms were sweating as he hit the penthouse button. Rosanna was waiting outside the door as he exited.

As the door closed behind them, the hand he held behind his back sprang forward holding roses and a bakery box.

"Oh, how sweet," she exclaimed as she grabbed them both while sniffing the aromatic scent of the roses.

"What's in the box?"

"I remembered you raving about the flan at Escobar's bakery, so I brought dessert."

She opened the box. Peeking in, she asked, "Is that cup next to the flan what I think it is?"

"If you are thinking authentic Mexican caramel sauce, then you would be accurate."

"YES!" She planted another kiss on his lips, took his hand, and led him into the dining room.

The table was beautifully arranged and an ice bucket with an opened bottle of Cristal nestled in an ice bath. "The champagne is nice and chilled, would you like a glass before dinner?"

Max noticed the Cristal label and said, "Boy, oh boy, would I. But, I am not sure my palate is educated enough to be allowed a taste of this stuff. Did you know that this was voted world's best champagne by the Luxist Awards?"

"Indeed I did. I always serve the best for the best." She reached for the bottle and gently filled their glasses.

Max raised his glass and toasted, "To the most beautiful woman in the world."

"What's her name." she cracked.

He kissed her forehead and religiously whispered, "Rosanna, of course."

"I'll drink to that." They sipped the bubbly nectar, savoring its exotic flavor. However, their eyes lingered on each other, mentally savoring each other as well.

They started the meal with a spinach salad with bacon dressing. The salad soon disappeared from their plates. "Now it's time for my masterpiece." She left for the kitchen and returned with two steaming plates of Steak Adobo, fried plantain slices, and festive looking Mexican rice. All were assembled for a beautiful presentation.

"If this is half as good as it looks, it will be the best meal I have ever had." He toasted the chef and they proceeded to embark on their epicurean journey.

The meal was so overwhelmingly delicious, conversation was at a standstill as they eagerly sought the next mouthful.

As Max swallowed the last bit of steak, he stated, "This was not half as good as it looked."

Surprised by his remark, disappointment quickly clouded Rosanna's face.

He purposely paused, and then said, "It was ten times better than it looked!"

A glowing smile pushed the disappointed look aside. "If you thought this was good, wait until you taste Escobar's dessert."

She again left for the kitchen and returned with two dessert dishes holding mounds of flan that were thoroughly drenched with warm caramel sauce.

After tasting his first bite he said, "I definitely am stopping by Escobar's more often. This is heaven!"

Rosanna simply nodded agreement as her tongue was preoccupied by the sinfully smooth flan.

Netflix never materialized. Instead, the evening was spent with another bottle of Cristal and warm conversation. Both were enthralled by revelations of the lives they had lived.

"You know, you are quite an amazing young woman."

"You are pretty amazing too."

Max placed his arm around her and pulled her close. Hungry kisses and hands that sought to tenderly caress each other desperately reached out.

They were at a fevered pitch when Rosanna gently pushed away. "I'm sorry, but if you are feeling the same emotions I am, then we really need to stop."

"Why?"

"I promised my mama that I would be a virgin on my wedding bed."

Puzzled, he said, "What about those rumors of affairs with your leading men?"

"Silly man, that's why they call them rumors and not facts. The producers spread them to sell the movies."

He sat up straight after hearing her explanation and said, "I can respect your wishes, I can wait until then."

"Thank you—Hey, was that a proposal?"

"Um, probably more like wishful thinking on my part."

"And how do you know it's not my wish also?"

Flabbergasted by her words, he remained silent for a long time as he gazed in her eyes. Finally he said, "I guess I'm about to find out."

He sprang up and moved in front of her and went down on one knee and reached for her hand. "Rosanna, I am madly in love with you and everything that you are. Will you marry me?"

"I need to think about it," she said with a pause. "Okay, I've thought about it. YES!"

The marital promise was sealed with a long kiss. They held each other and giddily made their future plans.

Max said, "I love you."

"I love you too, but a perfect ending to the evening just occurred to me."

"What's that?"

"We share a giant bowl of hot buttered popcorn and watch a romantic movie."

"Sounds great, but I have one request."

"And the request is?"

"It has to be one of your movies. I can't get enough of watching you on screen. I have seen each of your films at least ten times."

She reached in the video cabinet and withdrew an album of DVDs. "Pick one while I make the popcorn."

"While you do that, any champagne left?"

"My dear, I buy Cristal by the case. In fact a bottle is already chilled in the fridge."

Max then unexpectedly pinched himself.

"Why did you do that?"

"I wanted to make sure I was alive. The way this evening has gone, there was the possibility that I had died and gone to heaven."

"How sweet," she yelled, looking over her shoulder as she hurried to the kitchen to make the snack and grab the bubbly.

As the popcorn was consumed and the bottle of Cristal drained, they soon nodded off to sleep. They remained in each other's arms with their faces etched with contented smiles.

CHAPTER SIXTY-SEVEN

Abs walked ahead and opened the door of the abandoned warehouse which was located in a deserted Industrial Park on the near north-side. When he saw the arrangements, he remarked, "Those friends of friends *The Don* has sure do good work."

"Don't forget that the best work they offer is Omerta," *Biceps* added as he mimicked zipping up his mouth.

"You better get dressed for the main event, but I still think we didn't have to involve *Actress* on this caper," *Biceps* said with concern.

"Bro, I know you've been hit by that Love Thunderbolt, but do you really think we could have convinced her not to be a part of this one."

Remembering her grimly voiced comment, "this one is for Renaldo," during last night's planning session, *Biceps* nodded and said, "I guess not."

Biceps then jumped up and said, "I'm going to pick her up now. We will be back with the package about 5:30 p.m. Leave the overhead door unlocked so I can move in quickly."

"Will do, Happy Trails to you and Actress."

"Thanks, Roy Rodgers." They clasped hands in a power handshake and *Biceps* headed out.

On the front passenger seat of the van sat a six-pack cooler containing a heavily laced cloth of chloroform.

The blond waiting on the corner had a body like Rosanna's but with a big difference, a forty-inch bust. Any resemblance to *Actress* was nil, as a new latex face emerged under the wig.

Biceps attempted to kiss her as she slid into the passenger seat, gently placing the cooler on the floor.

"No," she said as she pulled away. "It took me an hour to make this new face. I don't want to mess it up."

"Okay," he said with a dispirited sigh.

"There will be plenty of time for kissing when we finish the job."

That immediately transformed his dejected lips into a neon smile. "Okay!"

They arrived at Packowski's watering hole ten minutes before his anticipated arrival. True to their previous recon activities, the parking lot was empty.

"You ready?"

"I was born ready," she said shouldering a large purse as she exited the van. *Biceps* parked in an adjacent alley next to the lot and carefully put on his rubber gloves and opened the cooler.

She saw the dark blue Camry pull into the lot with the car and license plate matching the details *Biceps* had given her. She started her trek across the lot.

"Damn," she cried out as she faked a stumble falling to the ground while the large purse regurgitated its contents. As expected, Packowski rushed over to help. The fake fall that now positioned a clear vision of the phony forty plus inch tits hastened his approach.

"Let me help you here miss," he said leering at her chest while offering his hand to help her up. As *Actress* held his hand tightly, she purposely struggled to rise, exposing even more of the phony flesh. Using the stealth he had used many times as a Ranger, *Biceps* easily enclosed him in a headlock while covering his nose and mouth with the tainted cloth. He went down like a sack of concrete.

They reached under each shoulder and assisted what looked like a very inebriated drunk into the van. The van slowly ventured out of the alley.

"That went well," she said as she headed to the back of the van to the makeshift dressing table.

"Yes it did. I wonder how many rounds he will last?"

"Before or after he pisses his pants?"

They laughed heartily as *Actress* began the transformation back to herself.

"Wow, it's as good as you said. It looks like a real boxing ring," she said, as they entered the warehouse. *Biceps* carried the indisposed Packowski and dumped him on one of the chairs in the ring.

"It is a real one, *The Don's* friends only provide the best. Even better, once we're done, *The Don* will make a call and everything in here will disappear without a trace."

"Man, I'm sure glad he is on our side."

Biceps chuckled, "I may have heard that before."

Out of the shadows a heavily muscled *Abs* emerged and entered the ring. He was wearing gloves and a spandex suit that covered his entire body. An evil looking Darth Vader mask completed the subterfuge which easily concealed any detection of his black features. He reached into his pocket and pulled out a vial of smelling salts and popped the vial and stuck it in Packowski's nose.

Moments later Packowski released a hacking cough and awoke. When he regained full consciousness, fear was written all over his face as he took in the surroundings and the massive man in the Darth Vader mask. *Actress* had been prophetic. He immediately pissed his pants.

A bell sounded and *Ears,* using the voice alteration machine in the shadows announced, "Welcome to tonight's match. In the challenger's corner sits Clifford Packowski, aka The Patty Beater. Opposite is the champion, aka The Avenger. Let me remind the participants that tonight's bout features no rules. Anything goes. At the bell, come out fighting."

The bell sounded.Clifford did not move. *Abs* walked over and easily brought him to his feet in the center of the ring. He playfully started punching him about the face. The intent was not to inflict pain but to rile Clifford and motivate him to attack.

Clifford fell for it. That's when the real punishment began. Using skilled combat moves, Clifford soon was bleeding externally and internally. A few of the well placed punches and karate chops soon produced the desired result: broken bones. In minutes, Clifford lost consciousness once again.

His battered body was hoisted back on the ring's chair. *Ears* brought a camera and a sign into the ring. He placed the sign up against Clifford'slegs. The camera captured the fight's bloody result very nicely. Especially the right arm that jutted out in different ways proving something was indeed broken. *Ears* returned to the shadows and his voice box after the photo op.

Abs stuffed another smelling salt vial up his nose. He groggily opened his eyes. A voice soon got his attention. "Mr. Packowski, this is a warning. You are never going to hit Patty again. Nod your head if you understand."

He quickly obliged.

"If you are lying, a return bout will be scheduled for another time. I am everywhere and I will be watching you and sweet Patty very closely. There will be hell to pay if Patty shows up at the hospital with one of her so-called accidents. Understand?"

Again, his head quickly bobbed up and down.

"Oh, how rude of me. I did not introduce myself. My name is *Mr. Consequence*."

His eyes bugged out at that revelation.

Biceps easily slipped behind him and placed the chloroform rag over his mouth and nose once again.

The van and its occupants left the warehouse. *Abs* called *The Don*. One hour later the *boxing ring* no longer existed. *Ears* asked, "Where is the drop-off going to be?"

Abs answered, "We thought it would be appropriate to place our friend Clifford in the back alley of the woman's shelter house on Sedgewick."

"Good choice. I have done benefits for that place. The people there do awesome work," *Actress* added.

They did a pass-by and the alley was empty. *Abs* and *Biceps* easily propped Clifford up with the sign on the next pass. *Biceps* drove away and said, "Mission accomplished."

"Not yet," *Ears* said, pulling out his Go-phone and voice machine. "Time to call our good friend Abigail, and then 9-1-1, of course." He proceeded to do so.

Abigail and Cary arrived soon after the call.

Cary immediately started clicking his beloved camera.

"Looks like he lost this fight big time," Abigail said noticing the sign that read:

CLIFFORD WILL NO LONGER BE SPARRING WITH PATTY.
HE NOW HAS A NEW SPARRING PARTNER—ME—
MR. CONSEQUENCE.

I REALLY DO NOT TOLERATE SPOUSE OR CHILDREN BEATERS—
IF YOU ARE ONE OF THEM—BEWARE—
YOU WILL BE MY NEXT OPPONENT—

ASK CLIFFORD WHAT THE CONSEQUENCES ARE—

REMEMBER—I WILL BE WATCHING—
I AM EVERYWHERE

—MR. CONSEQUENCE

The squad car killed the siren as it parked next to Abigail's car. The officers approached the scene.

"Let me guess, you're Randy's wife Abigail."

"The one and only."

"I'm Officer Scott Sier, and this is my partner Jake Ashbury. We know Randy very well. As you can guess, your name's been popping up at the station quite a lot lately."

"Just doing my job Officer Sier."

"So what is it tonight?"

"Take a look," she said as she moved aside.

"Whoa, somebody took a beating."

"I have a hunch that it's better him than Patty," she said, pointing to the sign.

"Any idea who he is?"

"No."

"Hey Jake, carefully check if he has a wallet." Using a kerchief, Jake slid the wallet out of his back pocket. He opened it.

"We have an ID."

"What's his name?"

"Damn it, Abigail. This is a police matter."

"Come on Officer, you know I will eventually find out anyway. Please, just give me a name and we will be on our way."

"Okay, but only because you're Randy's wife. The ID says he is Clifford Packowski. Now go. Jake and I have work to do."

She verified the spelling of Packowski then saluted him as they left with a forceful, “Thank you, Sir!”

Scott called it in, making sure that someone contact Capt. Krol and that an ambulance would be needed. Then they waited for the troops.

“Wife beaters and child abusers are the scum of the earth.”

“I agree, Jake. If this guy was using some Patty as a punching bag, I’m not gonna shed any tears over his misfortune.”

“This Consequence guy is breaking the law, but I have to admit, his methods kind of make sense to me,” Jake said.

“You sure aren’t alone on that one. But, keep that thought to yourself, since we now live in a *Politically Correct* society. Comments like that can get a guy busted.”

“Yeah I know, Scott, but it’s a damn shame that’s how it is.”

“Yes it is.”

A groan interrupted their conversation as Clifford was waking up. The first guest he had when he woke up was pain. Hence, the groan.

As if on cue, the ambulance arrived.

CHAPTER SIXTY-EIGHT

"Son of a bitch, doesn't this guy ever sleep?"

"We're not getting too much of that either, Diane."

It had taken two days of long hours to complete the interviews with the surgeons. During that time, the Sun-Time articles about the gun drop off and Mr. Packowski's well-deserved beating lay across their desks: compliments of Captain Krol.

"Have you turned on the news lately?"

"Not really. Hell, we've been too damn busy. When we are done for the day, the last thing I want to watch is the public telling me how terrible I am for trying to find and arrest Mr. Consequence. Why do you ask?"

"You are right on, Mitch. The public is ready to confer sainthood on this guy after the last two capers."

"I can't say that I blame them too much. The cops recovered a major arsenal from that church thing he did. Those were more guns than the gang squads had confiscated in the last two years. That has got to have some effect on future street shootings."

"Yeah, I must admit, as a member of the fairer sex, I smiled at Clifford's picture in the Times."

"Oh well, regardless, we have a job to do. Let's get started," Mitch said.

Diane pulled out her pad containing the details of the interviews with the surgeons. "Based on the conversations we had with all of them, it appears that each would be capable of the operations that were done."

"I agree, Diane. Were you suspicious about any of them?"

"Dr. Taggert seemed to have a nervous tic as we questioned him and Dr. Akhtar sure seemed like he would much rather be in Pakistan than Chicago and I felt that Dr. Sacto was a little too glib with his answers." Diane paused and added, "And Dr. Feeney seemed like he was a big fan of Mr. Consequence. How should we follow-up on these guys?"

Mitch quietly gathered his thoughts and suggested, "The next logical step would be to gather the suspected approximate times that Mr. Consequence's operations took place. Then we check if these surgeons have alibis for these times."

"That won't be easy, but nobody ever said detective work was."

They then pulled out the Action List and Diane wrote the Medical Departments comments about the suspected times on her pad.

Diane then said, "I also think we should pay a visit to those churches where the guns were dropped off."

"Why?"

"I find it rather odd that no parishioners were present in the church when the drop-offs took place. I would like to talk with both pastors about that. My guess is they might have had some advance knowledge of what was going down that night."

"You make a good point. After we check out the surgeons, we'll visit the churches."

Diane then jumped up and said, "Let's get a move on now before Captain Krol gets back from the mayor's office."

Mitch quickly rose and smirked, "That's even a better point."

Diane grabbed the notepad and off they went.

CHAPTER SIXTY-NINE

It was after 9:00 p.m. as Diane trudged up to her apartment on the second floor of a two-flat in Old Town. She had put in a fourteen hour day. These were common hours after being assigned the Mr. Consequence case. It had been a full day tracking the whereabouts of the suspected surgeons on the evenings of Mr. Consequence's missions. That was a bust. Each had a solid alibi. The interviews with the pastors went nowhere. Afterwards, Diane thought, *when I go to confession, I'm going to their churches. They know how to keep secrets.*

She remembered she was very hungry and thought what was available in her fridge. Nothing came to mind. As she climbed the stairs to her apartment, she discovered a pleasant surprise in front of the door. It was a plate of baked ham, green beans, and au gratin potatoes, tightly covered in Saran Wrap.

Her landlords, Anne and Wally, lived downstairs. They never had children and Diane became their *adopted* daughter. They often placed leftovers by her door for her. She scooped it up greedily, and placed it in the microwave.

She savored every mouthful as the contents of the plate quickly vanished. Her tense muscles craved a hot bath. She splurged with a bubble bath, and very hot water. A chilled glass of Chardonnay was a nice addition.

Refreshed and her hunger satiated, she headed to bed. As she lay in bed alone, she fantasized having a man's body pressing against her.

Damn, it's been over ten months since I have had a lover, she thought. The face of Mitch unexpectedly appeared as she dreamily considered a fantasy lover. A wide smile appeared as she imagined the possibilities.

The smile vanished abruptly as she recalled the conversation she had with him concerning her *dating rules*.

"Shit, why did he have to be a cop?"

CHAPTER SEVENTY

"Are you sure they won't suspect anything?"

"No way, *Eyes*," *Actress* answered. "I visit these houses for abused wives and children every month. I often ask to use their computers to check my e-mail."

"Okay then. Here is the flash drive. Wait until you see that someone has logged in before you ask to use the computer. Go to files and transfer the name and address information of all present and past residents and their family members to the flash drive. You do know how to use a flash drive, right?"

"Please. I am not a dinosaur. I am quite capable of using one."

"Just covering all the bases."

"I understand."

Actress returned late that afternoon with the flash drive chock full of information. *Eyes* and *Ears* spent the evening preparing *Mr. C's* request. Surgical latex gloves encased their hands as *Eyes* printed out the letters while *Ears* stapled the picture he had taken of Clifford in the boxing ring while filling in the blank spaces on the pages.

The letters contained a simple message:

DEAR MR. ABUSER,
YOUR FAMILY'S FORCED VISITS TO THE SHELTER HOUSE HAVE BECOME VERY ANNOYING TO ME. WHEN I GET ANNOYED—THERE ARE CONSEQUENCES-(SEE ATTACHED PHOTO)-THE MAN IN THE PHOTO IS CLIFFORD. HE MADE THE MISTAKE OF ABUSING HIS FAMILY. AS YOU CAN SEE, HE PAID THE CONSEQUENCES. THIS IS A FINAL WARNING. IF YOUR SPOUSE OR GIRLFRIEND OR YOUR CHILDREN TURN UP AT THE SHELTER HOUSE
OR AN EMERGENCY ROOM—YOU WILL BE MY NEXT VICTIM.
REMEMBER THIS. I AM EVERYWHERE
AND I WILL BE WATCHING YOU.

—MR. CONSEQUENCE

Following their previous routine, the next day *Eyes* and *Ears* traveled throughout the city and suburbs using multiple mailboxes to cover the trail of the letters.

"Do you think these will have an impact?"

"Well bro, it sure seemed to work on those rapist assholes that we sent the previous messages to."

Eyes said, “You have a point there. Attempted rapes soon plummeted after they were sent. Plus, as *Mr. C* said, it certainly can’t hurt.”

Over the next few months, *Actress* had a hard time suppressing a grin as her visits to the almost always filled Shelter Houses now had numerous vacancies. The managers of these facilities could not understand why the drop-off occurred. *Actress* understood.

CHAPTER SEVENTY-ONE

The pain had increased, so Dr. Stein ordered additional lab work for Tony. He now had the results. They were not good.

The concerned look on the doctor's face told Tony everything he needed to know. "The news, she ain't so good, right doc?"

Dr. Stein gravely shook his head. "No it's not Tony, the cancer is rapidly progressing. Maybe if we go with some chemotherapy."

"No, I told you once before, no drugs. How long do I have?"

Stein had to clear his throat before answering. "A few weeks at the most." Tony's responding smile surprised Stein. He rested his hand on Tony's shoulder and said, "I'm sorry Tony."

"Don't be. You did all you could. Now I can look forward to seeing my Carmela."

Dr. Stein then grasped Tony's hands. "When you meet up with her, tell her I said hello."

They both chuckled at that and as Tony rose to leave, he said, "Will do, doc, will do."

He got in his prized classic Cadillac Eldorado. Before starting the engine, he reached into the glove compartment. He pulled out the unused GO phone and dialed.

"Hello."

"*Mr. C*. It's *The Don*. My time is up."

"How long do you have?"

"The doc says weeks at the most."

"Then it's time to put our final plan into action. I am very sorry to hear the news. You have been a tremendous asset to the team."

"Hopefully, I have done enough good so that God will forgive my past sins. I really want to meet my Carmela in heaven."

"I'm sure you will."

A moment of forced silence followed the remark.

"Now it's time to get to work. Do you have any questions as to how this needs to be played out?"

"No, I know what to do from here."

"*Don*, it has been an honor to know you. My sincere thanks."

"You are very welcome. The honor was also mine. My thanks to all of you for giving me this opportunity for redemption. It was very much appreciated. Good-bye for now. I am heading home now to make preparations for our final chapter."

Both phones clicked off.

The Don then took out his regular cell phone and speed dialed his attorney as he drove away.

"Gallo and Mancini, Attorneys-at-Law, Elisa speaking, how may we help you?"

"Hi, Lisa Pizza."

"This must be Tony Baloney." They both laughed heartily at the pet nicknames they had coined for each other. Tony considered Elisa the daughter he never had. They had grown very close over the years.

"Yeah, it's me. I need to speak with the head guy."

"Sure Tony, I'll put you right through."

"Donald Gallo speaking."

"Don, it's Tony."

"How goes it with Don De Dago?"

"Not so good. It's time to move ahead with the arrangements we made last month."

"Are you sure Tony, remember if I start this, there is no turning back."

"I know. Just do it."

"How will you live if you give everything away?"

"Living is no longer an issue, Don."

After a slight pause, Don understood the meaning behind those words, "I am very sorry to hear that. There is no hope at all?"

"None."

"I'll get right on it today. I'll bring the final papers to your house tomorrow. I'll need your signature along with a witness."

"Bring Lisa Pizza with you for your witness. It will give me a chance to say good-bye to that lovely girl."

"We're all going to miss you Tony, you were always a man of honor."

"Thank you. Will 1:00 p.m. work for you tomorrow?"

"For you, I will make it work."

"Thanks again Don. You have been a good attorney as well as a good friend to me and Carmela."

"Well, I hope you see her soon in your next life."

"Me too. *Ciao.*"

He smiled all the way home as he anticipated eternity with Carmela at his side.

CHAPTER SEVENTY-TWO

"Damn, I'm at wit's end with this guy. I can't see a single clue here," Diane grumbled as she re-scanned the Action Chart.

"There has got to be a clue here somewhere, we just haven't pinned it down yet," Mitch insisted.

"Where the hell did your optimism spring up from?"

"Years of experience has taught me that no one is perfect, let's analyze this from the beginning again. He had to have messed up somewhere," he said as he grabbed the Action Chart.

"Okay, I guess it wouldn't hurt.

They methodically checked each item on the chart. Mitch then pointed to the interview with Dr. Cooke. "This one really bugs me."

"Why?"

"These incidents were performed somewhere. Obviously not a hospital since it would be impossible to do them incognito. Cooke stated that a well-lit, disinfected room would be a good fit."

"And your point is?"

"Have you ever observed a surgery? The lamps used are extreme. There is a reason for that. They need to be very bright so mistakes are kept to a minimum. The average lighting in a home would not even come close."

"That explains why nurses are always wiping the perspiration from the surgeon's forehead. Intense light means intense heat."

"Exactly."

"So again, what's your point?"

"Let me think about that for a minute. My instinct tells me there is a clue here."

During the silence, Mitch proceeded to wrack his brain, hoping to nudge a clue along. He finally had a Eureka moment. "I've got it." He rushed to his computer.

"What have you got?"

Google was up on the screen as he typed, *where can surgical equipment be purchased in Chicago?*

"Good news, only twenty-nine supply houses in Chicago." He hit print. The names of the businesses and phone numbers printed out on four pages. He handed two to Diane. "We start calling each company. We ask them if any purchases were made by an individual and not a hospital."

"You know, sometimes you can really come up with a good idea. This makes a lot of sense."

"Thank you, my dear. Let's get started."

They reached for their desk phones and began the calls.

An hour later, Mitch had eleven suspects and Diane had nine. As they looked over the names and addresses, Diane stated, "I see a definite common thread here."

"What is it?"

"Money, lots of money. Each address is in a very upscale neighborhood."

"Are you saying we won't find a lot of cops and firemen living in these neighborhoods?"

The gulp of coffee she had just taken was in danger of being sprayed at Mitch as she struggled not to laugh at his comment.

She recovered quickly and said, "Only if they happen to be our Superintendent and the Fire Commissioner. Okay, joke time is over, how do want to do this?" Diane thought for a moment and added, "Let's ask the captain for two assistants. I take my list, you take yours. We each team up with one of the guys and report back here when we are done."

"How should we approach the suspects?"

"Simple. We flash our badges and politely ask for a moment of their time. We ask why the purchase was made and ask to see it."

"If they say no?"

"Simple again. We tell them we will soon be back with a warrant, and will then search the entire house. Nobody wants that hassle."

"Sounds good, Diane. Let's go see the captain."

Captain Krol endorsed the plan and readily provided the requested manpower. He suggested two medical technicians.

"Great idea, Captain. These guys have a good working knowledge of the equipment we'll be looking at."

"That's what I thought. Call me the moment you complete the visits, Mrozek."

"Will do, Captain."

The Captain then called the Medical Technicians. He hung up and said, "They will meet you at your desks in a few minutes. Good luck."

"Hi Mick, hi Jeff."

"What's up Mitch?" Mitch laid out the strategy. "You can go with me Jeff, Mick will go with Diane. Hopefully we can hit them all by the end of the day and meet back here afterwards."

Looking at the distance between addresses, Jeff said, "I hope you guys can drive fast."

"Silly boy," Diane said, "that's why we have flashing lights and sirens."

They quickly dispersed as Captain Krol entered and ordered, "Are you still here? Get going."

Their targets seemed to have other common threads besides money. They were old and sickly. The majority of the home owners did not want to waste time getting to a hospital. They each had a doctor on call in anticipation that their infirmities would require immediate attention. They had equipped their homes with mini-hospital rooms. Money was no object. The medical equipment in their homes reflected that point.

The two teams scoured each location hoping to find a shred of evidence. It was Diane and Mick who got lucky.

It was Mick who first commented on the name. "Do you know who this guy is?" Mick asked as they approached the River Forest home.

"I sure do. It should be fun."

"If he answers the door with a violin case in his hands, I'm outta here."

Diane patted his cheek, "we'll be fine. He's retired."

"You are aware we have no jurisdiction in River Forest."

"So we'll just have to be extra polite, come on."

On the third ring, a now frail looking Tony Dagonatti answered the door. Diane did her polite spiel and wisely made good use of her feminine charms. Thanking Tony profusely while gently holding on to his hand produced an invitation to view the medical room.

It was very similar to the others and they were about to take their leave when Mick noticed a strange looking object in a far corner of the room. Curious, he walked over and was about to pick it up when he abruptly stopped and reached in his pocket for an evidence bag.

He delicately used tweezers and placed it in the bag and walked over to Diane. "Look at this."

Diane's eyes grew wide as she stared at a severed finger of a black male.

"That looks like a trigger finger."

"Yes it does."

"Let's go up and visit some more with Mr. Dagonatti."

"I'm right behind you, and I think that is where I will stay. I'm a technician. You're the cop."

"Follow me, wuss."

"We would like to have a few words with you Mr. Dagonatti."

"Go ahead, but you better be quick, I don't have a lot of time."

"Planning to go somewhere?"

He smiled, thinking about Carmela, "I certainly hope so."

She then produced the plastic bag with the finger. "Do you recognize this?" He coughed weakly without leaving his chair before answering. "It looks like I need to get a new clean-up staff."

She then read him his Miranda Rights. "I am arresting you in connection regarding the crimes of Mr. Consequence."

He surprised them both by laughing. "Crimes? You call them crimes. Has true justice become that jaded?" He shook his head sadly.

She unhooked her handcuffs and said, “We need to take you down to the station.”

He smirked at the cuffs. “There will be no need for those, officer. I will go willingly, but may I suggest Rush Medical Center instead. Oh, and please invite the mayor. I believe he made an offer to be present at Mr. Consequence’s arrest. I want him to keep his word. I will only speak to him. Do this and I promise I will not lawyer-up.”

“Why Rush?”

“My oncologist, Dr. Stein wants me there by tomorrow morning so that I may be comfortable during my last few days.”

“Are you telling me you are dying?”

“Bravo, no wonder you made detective.”

“Keep an eye on him Mick, I need to make a call.”

She speed dialed Mitch.

“Detective Mrozek speaking.”

“Mitch, this is Diane. You will not believe what is going on.”

“What gives?”

“Stop what you and Jeff are doing and meet me at Rush Medical Center as fast as you can.”

“But we aren’t done yet.”

“There is no need, I’m bringing in Mr. Consequence.”

“What did you say?”

“I have Mr. Consequence in custody, but he needs to be at a hospital.”

“Did you use your karate moves on him or what?”

“Look, this is serious. I need you to call Captain Krol and have him call the mayor. It is important that they meet us at Rush. This guy says he will only speak to the mayor.”

“Consider it done. I’m on my way.”

Tony sat in the back seat with Mick as Diane speeded to Rush.

One nervous thought would not leave Mick’s head on the journey: *I hope Diane did not miss any weapons when she frisked him.*

Mitch was already there when Diane pulled up at the entrance.

“I told Jeff he could take the car and head back to the station. You want to go back with him, Mick?”

“Gladly.” Mitch pointed to where Jeff was parked and Mick moved rapidly to the car.

Mitch glanced in the back seat and saw a feeble-looking old man sitting there.

“This is Mr. Consequence?” he incredulously remarked.

“No time to talk now. Help me get him to a room. A Dr. Stein supposedly has one ready for him. I’ll fill you in once we get him situated in a room.”

They helped Tony out of the back seat and walked with him while each of them supported his elbows. Diane flashed her badge and mentioned Dr. Stein's room arrangement. The receptionist clicked her computer and Tony's file appeared.

"He is not due until tomorrow, but it won't be a problem. The room is empty and it's ready to go." Diane glanced at her name tag and said, "Thank you Monica. Which way is the room? We will take him there."

"A nurse will have to go with you, those are the rules."

"Fine, please hurry. By the way, the mayor will be here shortly. Send him to Mr. Dagonatti's room the moment he arrives, okay?"

Monica blurted, "Mayor Kelly is coming here?"

"He's the only mayor Chicago has. Yes, he is coming here."

"I'll make sure he gets to the room promptly."

"Thanks, Monica," Mitch said, as a nurse approached pushing a wheelchair.

When they left, Monica pulled her pocket mirror from her purse and gave her make-up and hair a once over. She excitedly thought, *I'm going to meet the mayor!* Then she rushed to the rest room and did the necessary touch-ups on her face and hair. She hurried back to her desk, her eyes glued on the entryway.

CHAPTER SEVENTY-THREE

Mitch and Diane stood guard outside Tony's room and she gave Mitch the lowdown on her visit to the River Forest home.

"Unbelievable. I can't wait to hear what he wants to say to the mayor."

"It won't be a long wait," Diane said as she saw Mayor Kelly, Superintendant Kowalski, and Captain Krol exit the elevator down the hall.

"Mr. Mayor and Superintendant, these are the two detectives that have captured the alleged Mr. Consequence: Detectives Mitch Mrozek and Diane Ryan." Handshakes were exchanged.

"Before we interview him, tell me how you were able to tie him to the Mr. Consequence crimes."

Diane explained to the mayor the reasoning behind their investigation of Medical Equipment Companies and how that led them to Tony's home.

"He did say he wanted to speak to you personally, Mr. Mayor."

"All right then, let's do it."

"Mr. Mayor."

"Yes."

"Just some friendly advice, he really does not like it when we call his escapades *crimes*."

"Thanks, I'll keep that in mind."

They all entered Tony's room.

"Ah, Mr. Mayor. I see you are a man of honor. You kept your promise to come and arrest me personally. I respect that, especially in a politician."

"I try, but I have some questions for you before any charges are made."

"I will do my best to answer them."

"Before I start, have your rights been read to you?"

"Yes indeed. Detective Ryan did so very efficiently."

"May we record this conversation," Superintendant Kowalski asked. "You may." The recorder clicked on and the questioning commenced.

"Are you the man known as Mr. Consequence that has committed the…." The mayor paused before he almost said the word crimes and he continued, "Attributions for revenge against the suspects in other crimes?"

"They were not suspects. I assure you they were guilty. Yes I am he."

"Why did you do it?"

"I understand that you are a good Catholic boy. Do you believe in God, Mr. Mayor?"

"Of course I do."

"I believe in Him also. I am dying, Mr. Mayor. I was diagnosed eleven months ago. I now have a few days left."

He jabbed his thumb at the Superintendent. "He can tell you that things I have done in my lifetime may have prohibited me from entering the Pearly Gates. The love of my life, my Carmela, made me promise on her death bed that I would change my ways. I decided to help make a better world for the innocents. You all know that present laws and courts allow vicious criminals to go free so that they can continue to do these despicable acts of violence over and over again. I wanted to help stop the injustices. I invented Mr. Consequence. I desperately want to join my Carmela in heaven. I needed to show good faith to God by these good deeds."

"That's the why of it, now we need to know the who? You did not do these things alone. Who helped you?" He solemnly shook his head and uttered the solitary word, "Omerta."

"You may as well tell us, we will find them eventually."

Tony smiled, "Superintendent, you surely know the influence I carry with my former organization. It is nothing for me to summon a task and have it gladly done. I will tell you this. It never was the same person or persons. That was the best way to keep my work from being discovered. They hailed from different states and countries." With a large smile he continued, "Especially from Sicily. I am disappointed they were careless about the finger, but since my end is near, it matters little. I have nothing more to say."

"You should be aware that your victims and their families may be filing civil suits against you seeking compensation."

"Let them. They will gain nothing. Other than my hospital bills being taken care of for my last few days and my funeral expenses fully paid, you are looking at a penniless man."

"You, penniless, that's a laugh," said the Superintendent.

"Every cent has been given away to outstanding charitable causes. You may check with my attorney, Donald Gallo if you doubt me."

"You planned all this very well."

"Thank you, I have always had the reputation of never being careless, I have no intention of starting now."

The recorder clicked off, signaling the end of the questioning. The mayor agreed to post guards outside the room, realizing the hospital room would contain him as well as any prison cell.

He also had a self-serving thought: *My benevolence in allowing him to remain in the hospital could look very good to the voters in Chicago*. He hastily retreated from the room, eager to meet with Nathan. He was sure Nathan could put a very positive spin on the speech he was already planning for the press conference the next morning.

As the brass were about to exit, Tony called them back. "I forgot to mention. I have already appointed my successor." His eyes glinted at their shocked expressions. Satisfied by the reaction, Tony then closed his eyes and went to sleep.

CHAPTER SEVENTY-FOUR

Tony succumbed to the cancer fourteen days after his meeting with the mayor. The press conference speech the mayor delivered the morning after his visit with Tony produced two appreciated results. The mayor appreciated the polls that came out ten days later that showed him with an 82% favorable rating. Nathan appreciated the sizeable raise that accompanied the polling results.

Tony's funeral had to be delayed for two days. Tens of thousands Chicagoans wanted to thank the man who had returned justice to the masses, so the Esposito Funeral Home extended the wake for two days.

Mr. C and his team all came to pay their respects, but they did so individually. There were two reasons for this. The ever cautious *Mr. C* thought it would be unwise to attend as a group. He also wanted to keep his identity a secret from the team members who were still not aware of it.

They knew they would be anonymous bystanders because of the overflowing crowds. They attended the wake because they all knew Tony was a man that liked to be shown respect.

*　　　*　　　*　　　*　　　*

Two days after the funeral, a package arrived at the Sun-Times addressed to Abigail. Enclosed was a cassette with a note attached. It read: *Here is a Good-Bye Gift for You.* It was signed, *Regards from Mr. C.*

She rushed to the staff's break room to retrieve an ancient Boom Box some of the older reporters used when they wanted to listen to some of their classic cassettes.

She lugged it to her desk and plugged the cassette in. Tony's voice greeted her. *"Hello, my good friend Abigail. I appreciated your efforts in publicizing my good works. Here is my last present to you. I thought you might like to know that even though I am no longer of this world, before I died, I appointed a successor. I have died, but Mr. Consequence will live on. I am guessing you might find some room on the front page to report this bit of news to the good citizens of Chicago. Thank you."*

Abigail didn't just find some space for it: it was the next day's headline.

The majority of Chicagoans cheered when they read her story. The Bad Guys cursed.

*　　　*　　　*　　　*　　　*

Happily, the next group gathering of the team would be a celebration. It was a small private ceremony: Max and Rosanna's wedding.

Mr. C sent the newlyweds a case of champagne but had explained that he would not be attending so he could retain his anonymity. The team was disappointed, but they understood.

The wedding celebration was in full swing at Rosanna's condo when the doorbell rang.

Rosanna asked Max, "Who could that be?"

"It's a surprise. I invited someone who is very special to me. I'll get the door." Max briskly crossed the room.

After opening the door, Max and the man standing there embraced.

"Come on in and meet the Missus," Max shouted as he grabbed the man's hand and pulled him towards Rosanna.

When they reached her, Max said, "Do you remember me telling you how much I admired and respected my commanding officer in *DESERT STORM*?"

Rosanna nodded.

Pulling the man forward, Max said, "Rosanna, I would like you to meet my Lieutenant."

The lieutenant warmly pressed her hand in both of his and said, "Congratulations. I am a great admirer of the work that you do."

His remark immediately produced a knowing smile on Max's face.

CHAPTER SEVENTY-FIVE

It was weeks following the wedding, when on a late Saturday night, a solitary outline of a man stood at the foot of a grave marker in Resurrection Cemetery. He solemnly placed his hand on the stone.

As his eyes moistened, he whispered to the person buried there. "I kept my promise to you, Mar-Beth. I wanted to honor your name. I made Bad Guys pay for causing pain to other unprotected victims and their loved ones. They will not be inflicting pain anymore. I wish I could have been able to save you from your unspeakable horror, but I hope you share my sincere happiness that possible future victims have been saved by the actions of Mr. Consequence."

He reverently knelt and kissed the stone. "My love forever, Mar-Beth." He rose and slowly walked away from the marker that proclaimed:

HERE LIES A LOVING DAUGHTER AND A LOVING SISTER
YOU WILL ALWAYS BE IN OUR HEARTS
MAY YOU REST IN PEACE

Her name was etched under these words.

MARY ELIZABETH MROZEK.

Mitch was about to enter his Chevy when he heard, "Good evening, Mitch."

He nervously turned and saw his Uncle Matt approaching. "Or should I say, good evening, Mr. Consequence."

"What are you talking about?"

"Mitch, Mitch, you never were a good liar."

He sat down on the nearest bench and patted the space near to him, "Come, sit with me and I will explain how I know these things. You told me you would be visiting Mary Elizabeth this evening. I waited to approach you until you finished visiting with her."

Mitch warily sat down.

"At your sister's wake, I was standing right behind you when I heard your determined promise, *SOMEDAY I WILL MAKE THE BAD GUYS PAY*. I have never forgotten that moment. When we lunched at Magda's and Diane brought up that comment about Bad Guys, I initially was suspicious of the coincidence between your promise and the fact you were the one pursuing Mr. Consequence. But it seemed too far-fetched, so I dismissed it."

"Why have you changed your mind?"

"I went to visit a good friend in the hospital."

"Who was that?"

"Tony Dagonatti."

Mitch took a while to gather his senses. "I didn't know you had friends in the Outfit."

"How naïve are you? Do you really think that any successful construction company in Chicago doesn't have some ties with the Outfit?"

"How did Tony fit in?"

"The Outfit has many friends and family members that seek honest work. What is the point of wielding all that power if you can't provide jobs for them? Tony possessed enormous power. He approached me. He was impressed with the successes I had accomplished. He had a number of General Contractors whom he favored. Fortunately, Tony was very trustworthy when it came to our business dealings. I made it clear I only used quality products and people. He respected that. He was smart enough to realize quality was the cornerstone of my success. He made it clear to the contractors that he referred to me that they were to comply with my insistence of quality products and work. Tony held much influence over them. It was not healthy for them to disobey him."

"So how does all this relate to your Mr. Consequence deduction?"

"The business arrangements we made evolved into a friendship. I would visit him occasionally and share a glass of grappa with him. When he was in the hospital arrested for confessing to be Mr. Consequence, I paid him a visit."

"How did you get to see him? He was being guarded with no visitors allowed."

Uncle Matt gravely shook his head. "Mitch, you really are naïve. Money talks, bullshit walks. I have lots of money. Guess who's been a major contributor to the mayor's campaign fund as well as the Police Charities?"

"So an exception to see Tony would not have been a problem for you."

"Not at all."

"I can't believe he told you I was Mr. Consequence."

"He did and he didn't."

"Okay, you have my attention. What transpired between you two?"

"Tony was smart, but I had a difficult time believing he orchestrated the doings of Mr. Consequence while his health was fading so rapidly. Also, I felt the discarded finger that nailed him was a little too convenient, especially since you and Diane mentioned that there was no trace left behind in his encounters with the Bad Guys. So I baited him."

"How?"

"I told him I knew he was not Mr. Consequence. I told him that I knew who the real Mr. Consequence was. I looked him in the eye and told him about a young boy who had lost his sister due to a gang rape. I told him that this young boy promised someday to make the Bad Guys Pay. Tony's eyes got really wide and he started to say, 'How did you know about....' He then stopped talking and simply looked at me and said the single word, "Omerta."

Mitch, wary of his uncle's intentions, said nothing. Uncle Matt continued. "At that point, I clasped his hands and said, 'do not worry my friend, it is my Omerta also.' His concerned look vanished. He smiled at me and said, 'I always respected you as a man of honor. I will miss you, my friend.' I told him best wishes in his next life and I left."

Mitch anxiously awaited his uncle's next words.

He did not have to wait long. "You may choose to confide in me or you may remain silent. I just want you to know that I am very proud of you. Justice is not easy to obtain in this crazy world of ours. The work of Mr. Consequence was a blessing to society. Now, do you wish to say anything to me?"

Trusting his uncle, he replied, "You guessed correctly. I am Mr. Consequence."

"Why did you choose this path?"

"I conceived this plan while I was in the army fighting in *DESERT STORM.* Say what you will about Islam, but I learned they take their form of justice seriously. I am sure you have heard the stories about thieves having their arms cut off and criminals that are sentenced to death are executed the next day. I may not have agreed with their laws, but I saw the possibilities for true justice if consequences were forthcoming. When I left the army, I thought I would try the so-called legal way of fighting the Bad Guys, so I became a cop."

"And you became an exceptional one."

"Thank you. But I soon realized my efforts trying to rid the streets of Bad Guys was not working. Not when the laws allow these vermin back on the streets in the blink of an eye. That report about over 70% of violent crimes being committed by repeat offenders is totally true." He paused for a moment, then continued. "I then thought back to the plan I conceived in Iraq and decided it was time to put it in action. I recruited a team to assist me. I will not tell you who they are, but I will tell you all of them had Mary-Beth-like incidents in their lives that provided them with ample incentive to join me. My experience as a detective helped us escape detection by leaving no trace behind."

"And you being the detective chasing Mr. Consequence didn't hurt," Uncle Matt laughed.

"That was an unexpected surprise, but a good one. It sure made it convenient for us."

"Thank you for trusting me with this information. It makes this easier to hand over." He removed an envelope from his pocket and gave it to Mitch.

Mitch gasped when he saw the contents. "Uncle Matt, this is the code for an overseas account containing over twenty million dollars!"

"It is now yours to use."

"I can't accept this."

"Maybe not, but Mr. Consequence can. Here's the deal. You are my only heir. I do not wish to wait until I am dead to be able to pass my estate to you. This amount represents a fraction of what I am worth. It may seem like a fortune to you, but it is a mere pittance to me. I have some suggestions on how you can put it to good use."

"I'm listening."

"Good. I do not wish to see the wonderful works of Mr. Consequence fade away. I know your hands are tied working as a detective. Why not switch careers and become a private investigator. Your team is still intact. You can continue to help people with the backing of this money, kind of like that guy did years ago on the television show, *The Equalizer*. That is the reason for my gift to you. I will not take it back."

"I have to admit, this is a very tempting proposition. Let me think on it and I will get back to you."

"Fine, just remember, the money is non-refundable. Whatever you decide, it remains yours to use as you wish."

Mitch hugged his uncle fiercely. "I love you Uncle."

Uncle Matt hugged back just as fiercely and said, "Like those young people say, 'back at you'."

They laughed at the comment, parted and headed to their cars.

Mitch sat in his car still dumbfounded at his uncle's shrewdness. He couldn't help thinking, *the saying the team had about The Don sure rings true for Uncle Matt also. I'm sure glad he is on our side*.

His uncle's suggestions whirled through his mind as he was about to turn the ignition key, when he suddenly stopped and a smile stretched across his face.

He reached in his pocket and pulled out his cell phone. He went to his address book, selected a number and speed-dialed it.

"Hello," a sleepy voice answered.

"Hi Diane, this is Mitch. I have an important question to ask you."

"It better be important. I was in cahoots with the sandman when the phone woke me up."

"I assure you it is very important."

"Okay, shoot. What is this important question?"

"What are your rules regarding dating private investigators?" His smile grew wider as her response was favorable, very favorable.

Acknowledgements

I would like to thank my family and friends for their belief and encouragement as I pursued this venture.

I would also like to thank the numerous members of the Chicago Police Department that offered insight in the workings of everyday police work.

Thanks also to Louis Lehman, my pharmacist, who helped me understand the effects various drugs would have on the human body.

Thanks also go out to Mike Whicker, who was a great help in my quest to be a published author.

Last, but not least, sincere thanks to Birdbrain Publishing whose direction and willingness to help make this story the best it could be was invaluable.

Ed Benedyk is a native Chicagoan and graduated from the University of Illinois at Chicago with a degree in English. He spent 34 years as a manager with Prudential Financial Services. After retiring from Prudential, he taught English Literature at F.J. Reitz High School in Evansville, Indiana. He and his wife have three adult children and reside in Evansville. Ed may be contacted at: edbenedyk@aol.com

Other Books available from Bird Brain Publishing

The Miracle of Stalag 8A – Beauty Beyond the Horror
Olivier Messiaen and the Quartet for the End of Time

by

John William McMullen

"On 15 January 1941, in a German prison camp in Silesia, music triumphed over Time, breaking free of rhythm and liberating a quartet of French prisoners and their listeners from the horrors of their time. The Quartet for the End of Time has earned its place in the canon and history of Western music, but, more important, it has earned its place in our hearts. Its musical beauty, at once terrifying and sublime, exalts listeners and performers alike, and the story of its creators stands as a testament to the powers of music and human will to transcend the most terrible of times." **– Rebecca Rischin, Associate Professor, Ohio University School of Music, and author of FOR THE END OF TIME: THE STORY OF THE MESSIAEN QUARTET (Cornell University Press, 2003; 2006).**

"McMullen is a master par excellence when it comes to historical fiction. His latest is worthy of the Shakespearean phrase, 'if music be the food of love, play on, give me excess of it.' ***The Miracle of Stalag 8A*** **is a deeply moving piece reminiscent of the dissonant sounds of the quartet itself, which breaks with temporality in order to touch the endless moment of timelessness. Mingled with undying faith in a time of horrors that induced**

disbelief in many, the music gives us a hope, in the words of the novel, for a 'virginal peace pregnant with possibility'." – Steven C. Scheer, Ph. D., author of *The Heart Ages, But It Doesn't Grow Old*

"World War II engulfed so many and so much in its darkness, and yet its upheaval also called some to create a revelation of faith and hope. As Messiaen's music captures both this desolation and praise, McMullen recreates with simple directness the human situation of Messiaen and his fellow prisoners and their triumphal first performance of this master work of twentieth century music which transcends time." - Rev. Harry Hagan O.S.B., Associate Professor of Scripture, Saint Meinrad Seminary.

"*The Miracle of Stalag VIIIA* points to the way in which the composer's music encapsulated yet transcended its circumstances to speak to people of diverse beliefs, and none." – Dr. Christopher Dingle, *The Life of Messiaen* (Cambridge University Press, 2007).

"The musical world interprets the miracle of Stalag 8A as the perfect performance of the "Quartet for the End of Time" in inhuman conditions by musicians suffering from cold and slow starvation. Most critics will wax rhapsodic as they praise McMullen for building his novel to the crescendo of the premier of the "Quartet," that briefly released both captives and captors from the brutality of their situation and moved them all to silence. However, the miracle that McMullen also subtly chronicles is the coming together as one the four musicians: Messiaen, the faithful-Catholic and mystic composer; Pasquier, the fallen-away Catholic agnostic cellist; le Boulaire, the atheist violinist; and the irrepressible Akoka, warrior Trotskyite Jew and master of the clarinet." – Phillip E. Pierpont, Ph.D., Professor of English and former Academic Dean, Vincennes University, Vincennes, Indiana

The enigmatic Messiaen, avant-garde composer, devout Catholic, and ornithologist, composes the Quartet in Stalag 8A, transforming man's inhumanity to man with hope. Yet to the avant-garde, he was too traditional and too religious; to the traditionalists and religious, he was too avant-garde. As a result he will always stand somewhere outside of Time. – *The Publisher*

Poor Souls is an account of American Catholic parish life, laced with subtle, yet probing satire, as told through the eyes of seminarian Martin Flanagan.

Set in the Diocese of Covert at the Parish of Our Lady of the Poor and Forgotten Souls in Purgatory, Catholics and non-Catholics alike will delight in Hyacinth, the ever-vigilant, long-time parish housekeeper; Pastor Emeritus, Father Boniface; the irascible and irreverent Father Jack Ash; and a host of other dysfunctional souls.

Beyond the sanctuary, Poor Souls reveals a great mix of sin and grace among broken believers.

Praise for *POOR SOULS*

"...The intention of this writer is to highlight the ordinary, and indeed the sinful, as being transformed by grace into something worthy of God. *Poor Souls* is a front-runner of the Catholic novel, though this is not immediately apparent because of its unpretentiousness. So why does it haunt me and why do I want to hail it as an outstanding Catholic novel? Because the writer is an unswervingly honest professional with something pertinent to say, and because he says it with quiet sobriety without ever resorting to 'pious-speak'." – Leo Madigan, Fatima-Ophel Books

“...There is a realism that made me double check the genre to make sure it wasn't nonfiction. You probably know the people in this novel....” – Amanda Killgore, Huntress Reviews

“POOR SOULS gives the reader a rollicking tale of seminarians and priests in their service of the church. McMullen, writing as an insider, masterfully strikes insightful chords of humor without resorting to ridicule.” – Clark Gabriel Field, (The Celibate)

“An unexpected revelation of life in the seminary and parish, McMullen reveals the very human lives of Roman Catholic clergy knowingly yet lovingly. McMullen’s novel is so real it will make you laugh and cry at the same time. Uproariously shrewd and marvelously told.” – Doug Chambers, (The Writer’s Express)

“McMullen’s tale of seminarian Martin Flanagan is a delightful read, especially in these times when many people are concerned about the future of the Catholic priesthood.” – BJ Conner, (Irish Legacy)

“Half of the Catholics who read POOR SOULS will love it; the other half will want to burn the author at the stake.” – Bill Groves, Manager of Corporate Services, Ivy Tech Community College

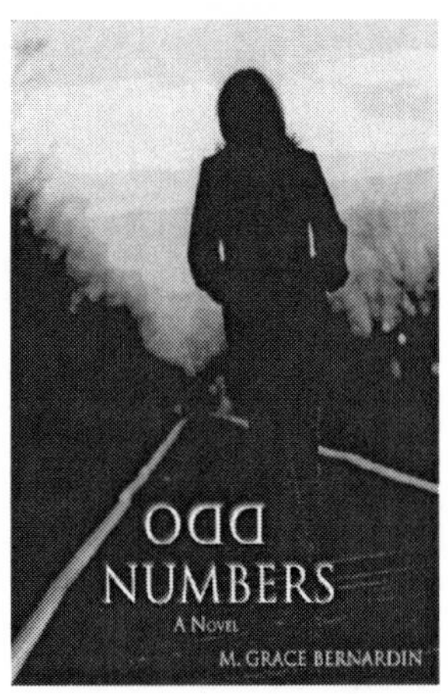

ODD NUMBERS
by
M. Grace Bernardin

Is it possible to find love in the heart of the Midwest between a strip mall and a cornfield? This is the quest of three friends who meet in the 1980s at the Camelot Apartments, located amidst the suburban sprawl of the southern Indiana town of Lamasco.

Frank, who moves from the East coast to Lamasco to start a market research firm, is a well-bred, charming, polished Ivy Leaguer with a penchant for classical music.

Vicky, the noisy downstairs neighbor who is constantly trying to drown out Frank's classical music with rock and roll, is a tough-talking, whisky-guzzling, Harley-riding lady bartender from western Kentucky with a reckless spirit and a haunted past.

Between Frank and Vicky is Allison, an image-conscious, self-improvement junkie who gives up a promising marketing career in Chicago to return to her hometown of Lamasco at the urging of her high school sweetheart and fiancé.

An unlikely friendship forms between Allison and Vicky as they discover that underneath their very different veneers, they have many similarities, one of those being a secret passion for their neighbor, Frank.

ODD NUMBERS spans twenty-plus years and ultimately culminates with the startling collision that reconnects this odd love triangle.

Praise for ODD NUMBERS

"Touching, clever, and at times delightfully off the wall, Odd Numbers is a gulp of fresh air. The best storytellers know that characters are everything, and Bernardin's characters Vicky, Allison, and Frank, are like us-flawed but hopeful. Bernardin's prose reminds me of Willa Cather, her descriptions elegant but not blustery or garish. Those among us who esteem a well-crafted sentence have a new wordsmith to add to our list of favorite writers. Odd Numbers is a finely crafted story of the human heart."

- Mike Whicker, author of the bestseller, *Invitation to Valhalla* and *Blood of the Reich* (Walküre Press)

"An inspiring read, courageously honest and full of hope for all of the flawed.... Deeply thoughtful characters revealing inner virtues and vices, outward strengths and weaknesses, climaxing in a sublime symphony of charity." - Judy Lyden, author of *PORK CHOPS*

Portrait of Woman in Ink – a Tattoo Storybook

By Kelly I. Hitchcock

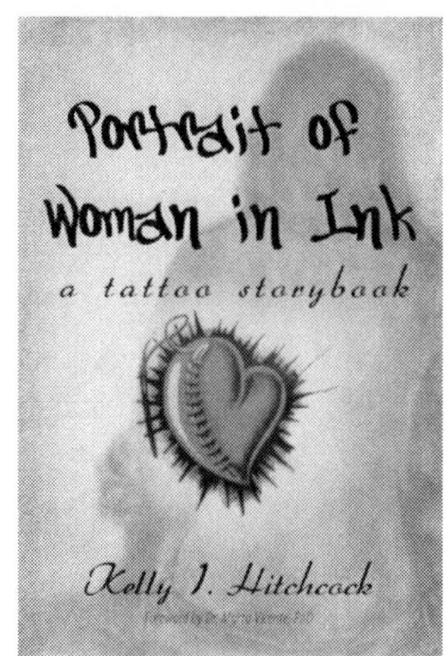

Twelve women, twelve tattoos, and a narrative thread that weaves them all together, Portrait of Woman in Ink: A Tattoo Storybook is a collection of stories that answers that lingering question in the back of your mind when you see an inked woman: what does your tattoo mean (or perhaps – what were you thinking)?

From a parent's suicide to the birth of an unlikely child, the stories behind why women tattoo themselves are literally worn on (and sometimes under) their sleeves, and retold on these pages.

Complete with artwork from the original tattoo artists and a foreword by Dr. Marta Vicente, one of academia's foremost voices in Women's Studies, this series of literary vignettes celebrates real, everyday women and their tattoos that, while they may seem insignificant at the time, are a symbol of the larger struggles and triumphs that make them who they are. These stories explore the idea of tattoos bringing together women from different worlds, and teaching them how these worlds might not be as far apart as they think.

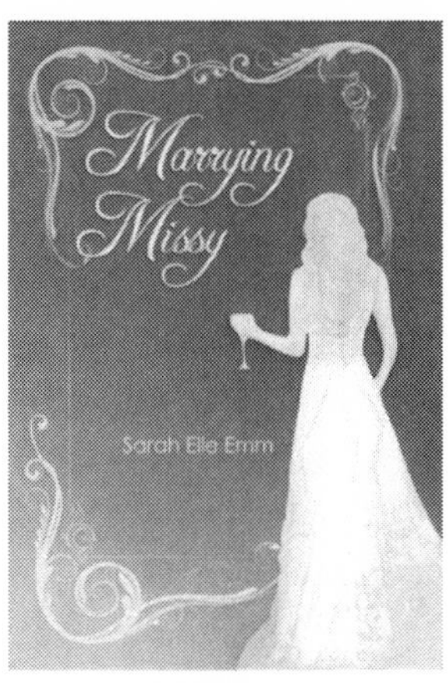

MARRYING MISSY

by

Sarah Elle Emm

Tate Sullivan is in a fix: her best friend, Missy Martin, is getting married.

With constant criticism from Missy Martin, Buckhead heiress and bride-to-be; stress from her intense nursing job; and a short-temper on the rise from her high powered, attorney husband, Georgia-native, Tate Sullivan is engaged in the ultimate balancing act.

Tate has to cope with sleep-deprived night shifts, her closet nicotine habit, her husband's apparent workaholism, her mother's meddlesome behavior, and her ongoing attempt to educate Missy about not making borderline racist remarks about everyone who doesn't have money or look like her.

When a collision with a runaway Golden Retriever lands Tate in the arms of the newcomer to Atlanta, Dr. Jackson Greenfield, Tate begins to think her mother has concocted the ultimate scheme. Wedding planning has never been so nerve-racking...or dangerous.

Marrying Missy reveals the complexity of those who are merely planning a wedding, preparing for a marriage, and those who aren't sure what their marriage is—or has become.

Sarah Elle Emm captures the world of wedding planning for a particular Georgia princess, but sublimely reveals all that is so often forgotten in that process–love and marriage. - The Publisher

**Muhammad and the Birth of Islamic Supremacism:
The War With The Jews 622-628 A.D.
By
David Hayden**

"A clear and comprehensive survey of the foundations of Islam according to Islamic tradition, this book vividly illuminates the links between the teachings of the Qur'an and the actions of Muhammad and the behavior of modern-day jihadists and Islamic supremacists. If this book were read and digested in the Pentagon, American policy toward jihad would be a good deal more coherent and effective than it is."
- Robert Spencer, author of the New York Times bestsellers *The Politically Incorrect Guide to Islam (and the Crusades)* and *The Truth About Muhammad*

"With graceful prose, extensive research, and rigorous argument, David Hayden recovers the historical truth of Mohammad's destruction of the Jews of western Arabia. Sweeping aside the current propaganda that makes Muslims the historical victims of Jewish aggressors, Hayden details the methodically brutal slaughter and plundering of Arabia's long-established Jewish tribes that marked Mohammad's rise to power in the 7th century, and that created the template for Islam's subsequent expansion, including today's Muslim terrorists and anti-Semites. Anyone who wants to understand the true history behind today's conflicts in the Middle East should not miss this indispensible guide to Islam's bloody origins." - *Bruce S. Thornton, Research Fellow at Stanford's Hoover Institution*

"David Hayden set out to piece together the jigsaw puzzle of Muslim chronological history from Muhammad's hegira from Mecca to Medina in 622 to his death in 632 to determine what motivated modern day Islamic jihadists' justification for murder and terrorism. Hayden's research enabled him to create a detailed framework for his masterfully crafted and shocking interpretation which not only destroys myths such as Muslim-Jew cooperative existence during the early medieval period; but also indicates which Muslims (today's 99% majority 'Islam-as-a-religion-of-peace' advocates or the estimated 1% Islamic minority jihadists----still a staggering 10,000,000 individuals) interpret their religion correctly. One can only wonder how much this Islamic disagreement was part of the 2011 'Arab Spring' rebellions, and the present day aftermath."
– James F. Paul, professor emeritus of history and philosophy, Kankakee Community College, IL

"Debunking false history and misinterpretations requires first of all thorough and diligent research. David Hayden has based his book, Muhammad and the Birth of Islamic Supremacism: The War With the Jews 622-628 A.D., upon such careful and complete research. His extensive research is combined with a careful and thoughtful analysis. Mr. Hayden has removed the veil that shrouded the founding of Islam by Muhammad. While acknowledging that the overwhelming majority of modern Muslims are peace loving and believe in religious co-existence, David has laid bare the competitive violent crucible in which Islamic faith was born. This led to brutal struggle with all contemporary faiths, particularly Judaism on the Arabian Peninsula. To suggest otherwise is to deny historical reality. The violence of this struggle led to extensive horrific abuses as well as ethnic cleansing and religious persecution. Only by knowing our past both individually and collectively can we understand the present and progress toward a better future. David Hayden's book is a significant step in this direction. As such it should be welcomed by all."
- Richard L. Wixon, Ph. D., Professor of History, Lakeland College, Sheboygan, Wisconsin

Defector From Hell
by
John McMullen

A fallen angel named Twiptweed defects from hell and writes to an agnostic college professor to let him know what in hell Satan is up to on earth.

Written in the tradition of C.S. Lewis's *Screwtape Letters* which appeared in 1942, McMullen's fallen angel addresses those living in the late twentieth and early twenty-first century.

One can only speculate concerning an actual defection from hell. As for hell and its inhabitants, it seems that the final disintegration into nothingness is preceded by a certain spiritual schizophrenia of being totally alienated from God, neighbor, and even one's very self. Yet if hell is to be described as a place of terrible flames and burning torment, could it be that those who freely choose their way into hell are all "burned up" by the flame of God's love?

"As any Christian boy knows—or used to know—Satan is prowling about looking for souls to devour. Well, this is one fallen angel who is not... Of course, you must never allow His Royal Lowness to see these letters. I have gone to extremes to secure these thoughts beyond his security clearance since it is forbidden to reveal to a human being the plot of Hell...Remember...your enemies are not merely flesh and blood. Watch your step; all of hell is. Believe me...."

—from Twiptweed's first letter to the Professor